Revenge & Forgiveness

A.J. TORRES

Revenge & Forgiveness

Cover Art by Nicole Deal

Content Warning/Trigger

Out of respect for my more sensitive readers, please be advised that this book contains the following: Mild Cursing, Mild Blood/Gore, Violence, and Death that some may find unsuitable/disturbing.

I dedicate this novel to my wonderful husband and son, Marcus and Alistair. It's because of the two of you that I wanted to write this fun story of heroism and hardship that originally was going to be a videogame. I love you both.

OTHER STORIES BY A.J. TORRES

The Call for Finis Series

Pride
Lust
Gluttony (Coming Soon)

CONTENTS

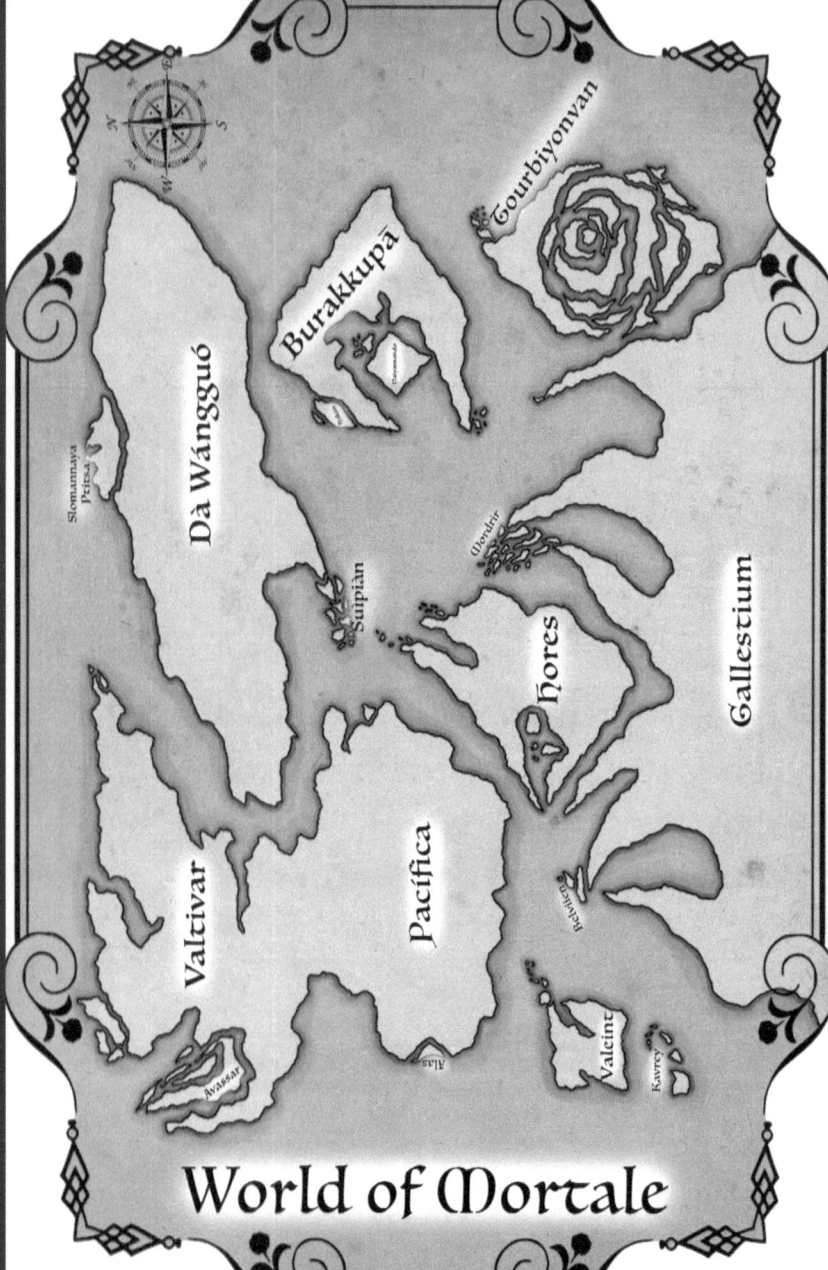

World of Mortale

KAIUS

THE KNIGHT AND THE MAGE

"KAIUS. KAIUS BRAVEHEART? Dónde estás chico?"[1]

"Aquí, señor."[2] Kaius answered, hastily grabbing his azure-plumed silver helm from atop his nightstand and slid it over his head. He stood from his cot and straightened to attention, watching as his superior made his way across the crowded barracks.

The tall man stopped before Kaius, looking him up and down with arms crossed and brows furrowed. "Hmph! Former squire to the King himself and now a knight of the kingsguard at the tender age of sixteen. If that's not the biggest insult to the men and women

---

1   Spanish for *Where are you boy?*
2   Spanish for *Here, sir.*

under my service I can think of, I don't know what is." He spat. "They worked for years to be where *you* are now."

Kaius' brows twitched, feelings of anxiety striving to overtake his excitement as a few of the surrounding soldiers snickered at the exchange.

"What great feat have you accomplished to be honored with such distinction?"

Kaius opened his mouth, ready to answer, but the Captain stopped him with a raised hand.

"Don't answer. Nothing. You've done nothing."

"I am honored to be a knight of the kingsguard." Kaius responded, straightening his posture and puffing out his chest, trying his absolute best to exude confidence. "I promise you, regardless of what privileges I have been afforded, I will work hard to be worthy of this station. I won't disappoint you, Captain."

His superior glared at him for a moment. "We'll see about that." With a scoff he continued, "Anyway, your first task is a simple one. You will be delivering a message from the King to two recipients. The first is the Grand Mage, your brother Vincent. You should find him holed up in his tower. The second is her highness, Princess Alaia Ligera. I was told she is relaxing in one of her gardens overlooking the sea. Both are to meet King Cecilio in the throne room at once. He wishes to speak with them. I trust you know how to get where you need to go." The Captain's eyes narrowed into slits, nearly obscuring them.

Kaius' shoulders briefly slumped in response to the man's ire, but he quickly straightened himself back to attention. "Yes sir. I know where they are, sir."

"Good, now get going." He stepped to the side, allowing Kaius to leave through the entryway and out of the Knights Quarters.

The sun crawled its way into the bright blue sky, its warm rays beaming down against him as the chilly fall winds were weak at best. Sweat dampened his black and azure garb beneath the silver armor while his light azure cape billowed as he hurried toward his destination.

Finding cover beneath the shadow of the Rosado castle, he sighed with relief. Lightly lifting his helm, he attempted to wipe away the sweat gathering on his brow. The metal of his gauntlet stung as its warmth kissed his forehead, smearing the salty liquid across his skin. He made a mental note to buy a handkerchief. At the very least it would make wiping sweat away a bit easier.

Kaius walked through the rouge-colored halls of the castle, passing many open windows and closed doors. He came upon a hall that was unusually darker than the rest, far to the Northwest side of the castle and continued inside. There were no windows within and very few lit braziers. The air was surprisingly cool.

It had been some time since he'd seen Vincent. Six or eight months give or take, and their last visit was quite unpleasant to say the least. Kaius tired of the fighting that had become commonplace between them and said to himself a silent prayer, hoping that today's visit with his brother would be civil.

Kaius' gaze lowered to the white marble floor, his thoughts growing heavy. He recalled the last words his brother said to him: *How could you, Kaius? How could you!? They're using you. Using us both! Why can't you see that!?*

He stopped in the middle of the hall, unsettled. "Why, Vincent? Why would you believe that?"

Kaius looked up and was taken aback as he noticed a white stone statue portraying the Goddess of Life and the Holy Light, Queen of Bregadine the godly realm, the Mother. "Oh," he exclaimed with a whisper, "I forgot You were here, Mother." He walked up to the statue and touched Her outstretched hand with his, taking in Her tall form on the small pedestal.

The Mother's wavy hair fell long to the ground, surrounding Her bare feet poking out from beneath Her elegant robe. A hand rested gently over the crowned heart symbol carved into Her chest. The Mother's face was strong and sharp, Her eyes gazing softly down upon him while Her lips formed a faint smile. He found a light coating of dust and grime covering Her shoulders and head. She looked as though She had been left to the elements for some time.

"That's odd. Has no one been here to clean You?" Kaius stepped back to inspect the Mother's statue further. "It has been a while since I prayed at one of Your temples. Let me make up for that."

He grabbed the fabric of his cape and began wiping away the filth as best he could. It might not make for a suitable substitute for water or cleaning oils, but it would have to do. Kaius meticulously dabbed and wiped the cloth against the stone surface, careful not to cause any offense to Her Holyness.

Kaius worked his way down to clean Her feet and the pedestal. There he found symbols belonging to the other gods the Mother had given birth to either on her own or with another deity, obscured under layers of dirt.

"Let's see, the hourglass is named for Vremya of Time. The crossing scythes are definitely Marwolaeth of Death. The swan . . . that was either Ilinya of Innocence or Primma of Peace. Next is . . . wait, which is this one?" Kaius squinted, trying to focus his eyes to discern the symbol, but struggled.

Wiping away the residual grime, he began to make out the symbol of a nettle. Kaius' eyebrows rose with curiosity. "A nettle?" A strange chill crept up his back suddenly, causing his skin to prickle. A foreboding feeling filled him with unease. "Whose symbol is . . . Maybe it has been too long."

He hastily wiped away the few remaining spots of dust from the Mother's statue and found three small candlesticks tucked behind Her pedestal. "Well, this is lucky."

Kaius grabbed them and checked the wicks. All three, though covered in dust, were in pristine condition. He smiled and turned to the hanging brazier beside him on the wall, touched the wicks to the flame, and returned to the Mother.

The offering plate, now perfectly clear of debris, resided at the Mother's feet. Kaius kneeled down and tilted the candles over the plate, letting a small portion of wax drip down in three pools, then affixed the candles in place.

He clasped his hands over his chest and bowed his head in respect. "Mother, I'm sorry for not visiting You for some time, and for not providing a proper offering. However, please accept these candles to represent not only myself, but also my brother Vincent and Princess Alaia. Keep us forever protected in Your radiant light, and . . ." Kaius opened his eyes and looked at the candlelight dancing softly before him with a small frown, "please provide me courage to face my brother and to forgive him for what he has and is . . . probably going to say. He doesn't mean it. I'm sure of it."

Kaius returned to the statue, pressed his lips to his index and middle fingers, and tapped them against the Mother's outstretched hand. "I promise to leave a proper offering at Your temple tonight." He stood and bowed with a hand over his heart. Continuing on his way, he entered a small hall beside the Mother and came to a winding stone stairway leading up.

Kaius' stomach churned into a knot. "Here goes nothing." Taking a deep breath, he took his first step up.

The metal of his sollerets tapped against the stone stairs with every step he made. His heartbeat quickened as he climbed, his brother's words entering his mind once more: *I haven't seen you in almost a year, Kaius. A YEAR! And you tell me this!? That bastard barely allows me to see you as it is. What makes you think he will give you permission to be with his daughter?*

Kaius' brows furrowed, he took a nervous gulp and looked down at the steps. "It's not like I was going to act upon my feelings," he mumbled to himself, "I just . . . wanted to talk to someone about it. And why does he think King Cecilio is not *allowing* him to see me. I don't understand. Why would he think that? King Cecilio always told me that Vincent wanted to be left alone. What would he have to gain from lying?"

A door came into view and Kaius stopped, realizing he had come to his destination at the top of the tower. Vincent's chamber lay just before him, behind the mahogany door. He stared at it for a moment, hesitating. Kaius tried to compose himself and his thoughts, his gaze boring into the wooden surface.

Kaius took a deep breath and stretched out his fisted hand. "It's now or never." With two firm knocks against the door, Kaius waited for a reply from inside.

No one answered.

He sighed and looked down at the door handle. Beneath it Kaius found an iron key protruding from its surface, which he found to be quite odd. Now he found himself questioning whether the door had even been locked. Reaching for the silver handle, he lightly pressed against it and to his surprise, the door creaked ajar. Unsure if his brother was present, Kaius pushed the door further and stepped into Vincent's grand, neatly furnished bedchamber.

"I said I didn't want—" Vincent turned around, his voice catching and his amethyst eyes surrounded by dark circles, widening at the sight of his younger brother.

He slowly stepped away from his desk, his violet and gold robes wrinkled and his white hair disheveled. His snow-white skin seemed even paler than Kaius remembered. The briefest glimmer of a smile flashed on his face.

"You . . ." Vincent shuffled forward, approaching Kaius, his hand lifting ever so slightly, but stopped dead in his tracks. Vincent's posture shifted, still several feet away. "You actually did it. You became a knight in that bastard's kingsguard!"

Kaius startled. His body tensed at the foul language directed at the King. "Why . . . Why are you surprised? King Cecilio said you wanted me to join so that I could be closer to you. I joined because of you. I-I thought you would be happy."

"Happy!? Dammit Kaius, have my words seriously fallen on deaf ears this whole time! He's using you, Kaius. Using us both! Now that you're in the damn kingsguard, he's—" Vincent's words abruptly ceased. With teeth bared, he trembled. "Dammit! He's going to place you in danger. I *have* no choice, I *have* to do what he says! I have to . . . to keep *you* safe." His last words were faint, but just audible enough for Kaius to hear. "AGH!" Vincent screamed, turning his back to his younger brother and slammed his fists against his desk. "I thought I still had time!" He yelled with a croak.

Kaius tried to calm his own aggravation by taking a deep breath, eyes locked on his older brother. "Time? Time for what? King Cecilio knighted me on my sixteenth nameday just a few weeks ago, per *your* request. Vincent please, I don't understand your ire toward King Cecilio. Why won't you talk to me?"

"Because I can't, you fool!" Vincent spat, his words dripping with anger.

"Don't call me a fool!" Kaius clenched his fists. "What do you mean you can't? Just—"

"I CAN'T!" Vincent whirled back around, sending a gust of wind toward Kaius and pushing him back. He just barely caught himself in the doorway. Vincent's eyes glossed as if holding back tears. "Don't you know I would if I could, Kaius? I can't tell you anything. I'm a prisoner in this place, with a brother who doesn't believe ANYTHING I say, instead hanging on the whims of that stupid shit who—"

"Stop using such language when you speak of King Cecilio! We were orphans living on the streets. He provided us food when we had none. He took care of us when no one else would. He even gave us a home, Vincent."

"Locking me in a tower and sticking your dumbass in the Servants Quarters barely equates to a home, Kaius!"

Kaius clenched his hands. He locked eyes with his brother, flashing him a challenging gaze as he pointed to the key in the door. "Vincent, the door was unlocked. You're no prisoner here. I don't understand how your memories have warped so. You were just as sick as I when King Cecilio found us—"

"I wasn't sick Kaius, I never was! You were so weak you couldn't even open your eyes. I was terrified of losing you after . . . our parents, our home." A trembling breath escaped Vincent's lips, but his violet eyes looked at him as if pleading for Kaius to listen. "I stole medicine, but I was seen. I ran back to you, hoping to give you what I found, but that bastard found us first. I was so angry, so terrified that my magic awakened." Vincent glowered at Kaius as his hands clenched at his sides. "*That's* why Cecilio took us in. *That's* why I'm living here, without my younger brother beside me as he should be." He pointed at Kaius. "Instead, you stand across from me, as if you were a stranger. Cecilio orchestrates everything, manipulating things to his favor. *He* likely left the key there to further divide us! *He* is the key's owner after all and he knows I long gave up trying to break the lock to this gilded cage."

Kaius' shoulders slumped, unsure of what to say, his heart breaking. He didn't know how to even begin to respond. What was he supposed to say to something like that? As much as Kaius wanted to believe Vincent, how could he when both stories contradicted each other?

His lips curled between his teeth.

"Vincent, please. I . . . his majesty has done so much for us. I may not remember much from when we were children, but we have this home a—"

"Our true home is in Valtivar. Not here. I'm just a weapon, and you a tool." Responding assuredly, Vincent straightened himself and rested his hands behind his back.

A loud ringing suddenly ripped through Kaius' head. He winced and grabbed the side of his helm, eyes tightly shut. Faint screams cut through the high-pitched sound, as though very far away. Kaius slowly opened his eyes, his vision hazy. He blinked, trying to refocus his gaze. Eventually, the ringing faded just as quickly as it had come.

What was that? Kaius wondered as his head slowly cleared.

"If this is the way it has to be, then so be it." Vincent stated bluntly as he turned away to his desk, laid his hands flat on its surface, and leaned over an old scroll. "I have no other choice. I must accept." His words sounded almost sad and were as soft as a whisper.

Kaius' brows twitched in confusion. He took a step toward his brother, hoping to better understand and reconcile their differences. "Brother, I—"

A sudden gust of wind whirled through the room, causing Kaius to lose his balance and nearly fall to the floor.

Kaius looked up and saw Vincent seemingly unaffected, standing as still as a statue. Kaius' heart thumped rapidly in his chest. The air felt different, oddly thin. A feeling of lightheadedness befell him, as his breath was shallowing.

He glanced over to the arched opening of the window and saw only the bright blue sky, not a single cloud in sight while the curtains flailed wildly. The torrent then immediately dispersed, his breath returning to him as the room went still.

"Where did that come from?" Kaius demanded.

"It's none of your concern." Vincent replied somberly.

Kaius returned his gaze to his brother. He then noticed the plant on Vincent's desk nestled within a clay pot next to several worn scrolls. Its bright green stem and short branches were covered in tiny hairs. Clusters of bulbs were nestled beneath the plants' sawtooth leaves. The sight of it was unsettling, especially as his mind flashed back to the symbol on the Mother's pedestal.

A slow chill crawled up Kaius' spine, that same foreboding sensation coming back. If only he could remember which deity that symbol belonged to. An unpleasant feeling grew within his chest, screaming for him to remember, or if he couldn't, to simply get rid of that nettle all together.

"Vincent, why do you have that nettle on your desk?" Kaius asked, trembling.

"What's it to you?" Vincent glanced back at Kaius, his violet eyes hardened and cold. "Leave, you're useless to me as you are. There's nothing left to discuss."

Kaius stared at his brother through welling eyes. A hollow ache weighed heavily on his heart. "Have it your way. I just wish for ONCE you could be proud of me instead of treating me as a nuisance!" He turned his back to Vincent and grabbed the door's silver handle, hesitating. "His majesty saw *some* worth in me, why can't you?" Kaius glanced over his shoulder as tears flowed down his cheeks, hurt and anger threatening to overtake his better judgment.

Vincent didn't respond. He remained at his desk, his back all Kaius could see, but his brother's shoulders seemed to tremble ever so slightly. "Anyway, King Cecilio awaits you in the throne room." With that, Kaius exited the room and slammed the door behind him. He couldn't bring himself to say anything else as hurt and disappointment weighed on Kaius' heart.

KAIUS

TO TELL OF NOT

KAIUS STORMED DOWN THE CASTLE HALLS, **trying to stifle the** tears flowing down his face. Doubt and confusion threatened to consume his thoughts. Vincent's words repeated again and again.

He's just using you, Kaius!

"No, he isn't. He wouldn't." Kaius mumbled.

I can't tell you anything.

"What does he mean by that? What's stopping him?"

I'm just a weapon, and you a tool.

Kaius stopped in the middle of the hall, groaning in frustration. "NGH! What does he mean!?"

His head fell back, blinking away the tears. He took a deep breath and counted to ten, then exhaled with a long steady sigh. "He's using me, using us both? But why would—" Kaius shook away the thought, hoping to rid himself of the doubt bubbling its way to the surface. "No. King Cecilio has been kind to us, given us a place in this city. Vincent is just—" He opened his mouth, but no more words came forth.

He just didn't know his older brother anymore.

His gaze slowly slid to the tiled marble floor. A pang of guilt filled his chest, spreading like an uncomfortable wrot seeping into muscle and sinew. Why did he feel this way? Vincent was the one shutting Kaius out. He was the one keeping secrets.

Yes, but you're not listening either.

Listening to what!? Kaius demanded, knowing full well arguing with himself wouldn't produce an answer and yet, arguing all the same. *The accusations he levies at the King? The whole royal family!? BAH!*

His fears could be justified. It's likely there are things they aren't telling you. Do you really know the family that well?

"SHUT UP! There are things Vincent isn't telling me either. I know them well enough!" Kaius shouted in frustration. He startled as a castle servant walked by, eyeing him warily, causing Kaius to stutter out an apology.

With a groan, he balled a hand into a fist and rubbed his face with the other. "Dammit, why am I arguing with myself? This is ridiculous, I—" He paused, noticing a glass doorway before him, tall and ajar, leading out to one of the castle gardens. Two knights stood guard at the entrance, one at either side.

Kaius took a few steps toward the entryway. A cool, salty breeze brushed against his face. "Am I already at the Valencia Garden?" He walked through the doorway onto the large, lush balcony. "I guess so."

He approached the twirling stone railing overlooking the garden, soaking in all of its beauty. The scent of roses, carnations, water lilies, blue bells, and many more flowers filled the air. A pungent sweet mixture of flora and sea salt wafted gently in the wind.

As he gazed over the garden, he spotted long strands of wavy brown hair and braids dancing in the wind behind a tree. Kaius' heart fluttered as a soft breath escaped his lips. "Alaia." Kaius jolted lightly, catching himself whispering the Princess's name. He looked around anxiously and was relieved to find the two knights hadn't heard him.

That was close. He needed to be more careful. Kaius took another deep breath and composed himself as best he could. He made his way to the right, walking down several steps and onto the peach-toned cobblestone path leading to the Princess.

It had been some time since he last had the chance to converse with the Princess, almost eight months now, only able to see her in passing. The day of his knighting weeks ago was the longest he had seen her, and even then their time was short. She smiled proudly at him, but they were unable to speak freely due to her status as a royal, save for simple greetings or to answer direct commands.

In spite of this, they had managed to become quite close. Serving under the King allowed them to get to know one another. Their conversations were usually brief, often cut short by King Cecilio for bordering on familiarity. Due to those stolen moments, his heart was set a flutter every time she crossed his mind. Over time, he saw her less and less. He wondered if they had pushed their luck, if the King had taken steps to keep them apart, but knew better than to ask.

As he drew closer to the Princess swinging behind the tree, he cautiously navigated his way through the surrounding shrubbery, careful not to crush the flowers beneath his sollerets. Kaius looked down at the gazania flowers around the tree, recalling the Princess's fondness for them, and stepped lightly.

"What's with that frown mi caballero de brillante armadura?"[1]

Her voice startled Kaius, his breath catching in his throat. Princess Alaia sat comfortably on the vine covered swing, dressed in an extravagant pink and white gown, its edges decorated with gold filigree patterns. Her copper skin, although lightly shadowed by the mixed colored leaves of the tree, was radiant in the faint sunlight.

Surprised, he noticed the whites of her green eyes were reddened and the surrounding area was puffy. "Princess Alaia, is everything okay?"

Her smile grew a little wider, her head tilting against the rope of the swing. The loose strands of her hair slid off her bare shoulders. He saw an uncharacteristic weariness in her typically bright demeanor.

She exhaled softly and closed her eyes while slowly rocking on the swing. As her pink painted lips began to tremble, she stood and

1   Spanish for *My knight in shining armor.*

turned her back to him.

"It's been a while, Kaius. Since the day of your knighting, correct?"

He found the sound of her voice soothing. Her tone was soft, though seemingly more reticent than when last they spoke.

Kaius' gaze lingered on the Princess, taking in her beauty longer than one of his status should. Realizing this, he stiffened and looked away. "C-Correct, Princess." With a faint chuckle, she embraced herself as one would in a chill air, rubbing her biceps. "Princess—"

"Kaius, a moment, please," she said with a turn, now in profile to Kaius. Princess Alaia's eyes lingered on the flowers before her, and her expression somber. "Padre[2] enjoys reminding me of my standing. As Princess and heir to the throne, I must uphold the image of royalty . . . Nobility *must* respect me and commoners *must* obey me. I'm not to have casual conversations with servants. Not even to ask how they're doing, todo porque soy una maldita princesa!"[3]

Kaius winced, having never heard the Princess so frustrated, and unsure of what to say. She glanced at him, and their eyes locked. Her glare then softened, and she bowed her head.

"Mis disculpas,[4] Kaius, today hasn't . . . gone as well as I'd hoped." Looking away to the flowers again, she crossed her arms loosely over her chest. "Malditas reglas.[5] If it's alright with you, Kaius, can we drop the formalities and titles when it's just the two of us? I'm . . . in

---

2   Spanish for *Father.*
3   Spanish for *All because I'm a damn princess.*
4   Spanish for *My apologies.*
5   Spanish for *Rules be damned.*

desperate need of a friend, not a servant nor a knight. You're all that I have."

Kaius jolted at the Princess's request, his cheeks blushing brightly red. What could he say? He knew he should decline. The King had been quite clear on the subject. His place was to serve, and after everything King Cecilio had given him and Vincent, it would've been dishonorable to go against the King. But how could Kaius say no? How should he proceed?

"Is my request truly so odd?" She asked with a giggle, flashing him a warm smile.

He chuckled nervously. "A little. I remember those lectures from your father. You wanted a friend to play with, to talk to. So did I. He was quick to remind us of our stations, you as Princess and me as a servant. I felt sorry for getting you in trouble."

"You shouldn't feel sorry, Kaius. I was worried what Padre might do to you afterwards, but Madre⁶ assured he would never lay a hand on you. He didn't . . . did he?" Her brows curved upward in concern.

Kaius smiled softly and shook his head. "No, just scolded me."

His brow twitched suddenly after he answered, Cecilio's past words washing over him: *I'm growing annoyed, Kaius. I will not remind you again. You are not of the same station as my daughter. You are not nobility. You are a servant. You wouldn't want something unfortunate to befall your brother now, would you? Be mindful of your place, for the both of you.*

Kaius pressed his fingertips to his stinging forehead, his heart quickening and head ringing. What was that memory? Did the King

6   Spanish for *Mother.*

really say that? Kaius must've heard. At least, he hoped he had heard because if he had interpreted the insinuation for how it appeared on the surface, well . . .

Something gently squeezed both his arms. The scent of lantanas and Valencia roses filled his nostrils. Alaia stood just before him, a look of concern on her face.

"Kaius what is it? Qué está mal?⁷"

His hand slid away from his face, his eyes wide and body trembling. "I-It's nothing. I've just been dealing with a headache today, that's all." He looked down at the grass between him and Alaia. "Alaia, did you get into another argument with your father?"

Her concern then grew somber, her body straightening and standing nearly taller than him. She squeezed her left forearm nervously. "Did you have another argument with your brother?"

Kaius, not expecting her to answer with a question of her own, stumbled over his words. "Uh . . . Yes."

"Hmm, I'm sorry to hear that. I wish you would tell me what it is that's causing this rift between you two, but I know it's of no use. Just know I'm here if you need someone to listen." Princess Alaia smiled fleetingly, the expression quickly fading into a frown. "I, on the other hand, am having a similar situation with my padre . . . lately. I'm not sure if he's changed, or perhaps I never really saw who he truly is." Her fingers tightened around each other, pressing deeply into her skin. "He and I don't think alike. Not even close. I've learned so much about him. My family. It's . . ." She returned her gaze to Kaius, worry and

7   Spanish for *What's wrong?*

curiosity mixing in her green eyes, she continued. "Kaius, be honest with me, do you . . . really believe you owe my padre for taking you and Vincent in?"

Taken aback, he stared at her silently for a moment, dumbfounded, and finally answered. "What—How do you—"

"Just answer me, Kaius, please. I must know."

"Well, yes." Kaius' lips stretched into a smile. "He called for a healer for my brother and I when he found us. He gave us food, bedding, and allowed us to work for him. I owe him so much—"

"You don't owe my padre a thing!" Kaius startled at her sudden change of tone, hearing the anger behind her words. Alaia's brows furrowed heavily over her trembling eyes. "Kaius, I know this will be hard for you to hear, but you need to understand. He isn't who you think he is. Don't trust him."

"What? Why? Ala—"

"Promise me!"

"I'm not going to proe that, not without an explanation. You sound just like Vincent."

Alaia turned her back to him and pressed her fingers to the sides of her head, massaging her temples. "No, no! This isn't right. Why can't you . . . I should speak to Vincent—"

"Vincent! Why speak with him? Why is everyone keeping secrets from me!?"

Alaia paused. Her hands dropped to her sides and she straightened her dress. "Kaius, why did you come to see me?"

Stunned by the sudden change in subject, he balled his hands into fists, trying to control his aggravation. "I . . ." Kaius released a deep sigh, "have a message from your father."

"I'll consider listening to the message on one condition," Alaia positioned her hands behind her back, intertwining her fingers, and turned to him with a small smile. "It's been so long since we last spent time with one another. Why don't we play a game of chase?" She gathered together large folds of her gown, lifted it up, and hopped over the flowers encircling them. "Catch me, and then *maybe* I'll listen to his message."

He startled forward after her with an outstretched hand. "Pri— Alaia, wait!" She rushed off and disappeared into the small garden maze before him, her head bobbing in and out of sight behind the floral trimmed hedges.

Kaius sighed in frustration and rubbed his forehead with vigor. "I swear, she was like this even when we were children. Avoid a conversation unless . . ." A smile snuck its way onto his face. "I play her game."

He looked down at his attire. There was no way he'd be able to catch her in all that armor. Instead of giving chase, Kaius carefully stepped over the flowers and leisurely made his way into the garden maze.

He placed a hand on his waist and tapped an index finger on his chin, pursing his lips with deliberation. "You know," Kaius exclaimed, "it may have been a while, but I distinctly recall *never* being able to find you in here."

Alaia's muffled giggle sounded from behind the hedge at his side. He turned his head and looked over, just barely spotting the top of her head peeking over. "Gee, I wonder which way I should go?" Kaius announced playfully.

As he rounded the corner of a hedge, he quietly peeked out and saw Alaia push away from the trimmed bush. She must not have been able to see him. He had to be quick before she rushed off again. Hopping out, Kaius gently grabbed her around the waist and Alaia let out a squeal, dropping the gathered fabric of her gown.

"Gotch—AGH!" Kaius, having lost his footing, accidentally stepped on the long fabric of Alaia's dress.

The two frantically stumbled back. Kaius landed hard on his back, his helm sliding clean off his head. Alaia fell forward, landing on his chest with a soft thunk, and lay as still as a statue.

Kaius stared up at the bright blue sky wide eyed, the fall leaves rustling in the wind. His arms remained wrapped around the Princess. Kaius' heart fluttered wildly, feeling as though it could fly up and soar through the sky above.

He slid a hand off her and to the ground to get up. "We should really—"

"Don't," Alaia whispered, pushing him down, and laying her head on his chest. "Not yet. Let's just . . . lie here a little longer. Please?" She pleaded, her voice cracked and dripped with melancholy.

He felt an unusual heaviness build within his chest and simply embraced her as he gulped. The two lay there, undisturbed, and silent for a time.

Can I . . . Should I tell her how I feel? He asked himself, his question echoing repeatedly in his head.

I don't see why not. Her smile. Her laugh. I can't help but—

But she's a Princess.

So? What's the worst that could happen, she says no?

She could laugh, or worse, tell her father.

Don't be such a coward. Just tell her. His mind chastised with a sternness that took him by surprise.

"Kaius?" Alaia called to him, interrupting his contemplation.

He jolted, terrified that she may have somehow heard his thoughts.

"Please, I'm not keeping secrets because I don't trust you. Very far from it." She slowly lifted her head off his chest, her eyes glossy and breath shallow. "It's because I need to confirm something first. I need time. Do you . . . Do you understand me?"

She lifted herself lightly and leaned over him, her eyes meeting his. His breath was shallow and his heart drummed faster and faster. Alaia began to move, but not away, instead drawing closer to him.

Her wavy brown hair cascaded down to her sides. The sunlight bathed her in its glow, making her appear as though Bamiya, the Goddess of Beauty, had blessed the Princess in her radiant light.

His breath caught in his throat, just barely managing to swallow, and their noses were mere inches apart. To his surprise, she stopped and withdrew a little, holding herself above him.

"Kaius, I have to ask, is there . . . something you would like to tell me?" Her voice was soft and sweet. Gold and pink gemstones hung from her neck and ears, sparkling in the sun's rays.

He parted his lips, wanting desperately to tell her everything. How he enjoyed her playful demeanor, her tenderness when tending to orphans, how she twirled about to music playing in the streets of Rosado, and regularly going out of her way in seeking herbs and oils for the sick and wounded. However, the words never came, never escaped his lips. Kaius closed his mouth, lifted himself up, and helped the princess to her feet.

He turned around and retrieved his helm from the cobblestone path, inwardly calling himself a coward. Kaius slid the helm atop his head, trying his best to ignore the ache in his heart and the nagging regret filling his thoughts.

He turned to her with an outstretched hand. "King Cecilio wishes to speak to you in the throne room. Would you like me to escort you, Princess?"

Kaius hesitantly mustered the courage to look her in the eyes and there he saw it. Disbelief and hurt. Alaia averted her gaze, raising a hand to her face.

The moment was short, but to Kaius, it felt as though it stretched on for ages. It was as if the wind stopped blowing, the rustle of leaves and songs of birds fell deathly silent. Nothing he had weathered compared to the pain he felt, the regret and sorrow filling his every fiber. Just as it began, the moment ended.

The Princess gently took his hand, but refused to look at him. "Thank you, Sir Kaius, that would be nice."

KAIUS

CROSSROADS

KAIUS MADE HIS WAY THROUGH THE QUIET CASTLE HALLS with Princess Alaia in tow. Neither had broken the silence since stepping out from the garden. An uncomfortable tension hung in the air.

He glanced back, catching a glimpse of the Princess' expression, a mixture of disappointment and sorrow clear on her face. The look was as a dagger twisting in his heart. He hadn't meant to hurt her. It was just—

You're a coward. The thought came abruptly in a chastising, mocking tone. His fingers curled defensively into fists.

SHUT UP! I'm not a coward. She's better off with someone worthy of her.

How would you know?

Because I'm not —, Kaius' mind fell silent. He raised a hand to his face and rubbed his eyes in frustration. There was no sense in arguing with himself. Besides, what in Mortale was going on with him? Since last night his mind had been unsettled, to say the least. Ringing, dreams, and now visions? Kaius lightly shook his head, ridding himself of that train of thought. Perhaps it was just stress. Hopefully, this would pass.

As they passed through a bisecting hall, they came to two open sets of grand doors, one to their left and one to their right. To their left lead out to the castle's courtyard and to the right the throne room.

Kaius turned right and paused as he watched the servants scurry about. They worked quickly to decorate the throne room, scattering white and pink flower petals across tables and twisting lines of flowers about large cylindrical pillars. A few of the servants lit candles atop tall, silver candelabras dotting the hall.

A wide, blush-colored rug surrounded by flowers stretched from where Kaius stood all the way to a tall dais with three thrones atop it at the far end of the room. He looked back to Princess Alaia before entering, her gaze low, lingering on the flowers below. Where sorrow had been moments ago, now anger shined.

He winced at her expression, wondering if he were the cause or if her anger stemmed from her father. Hesitant to continue, and a little worried she may snap at him, he remained quiet and awaited her command.

After a few moments, she shook her head and unclenched her fists. Meeting his eyes, she softened. "It's nothing. We can continue."

Kaius, still struggling to find the right words, simply responded with a nod and continued inside.

As they proceeded to the thrones atop the dais, servants stretched to light massive candles set in large silver chandeliers hanging from the ceiling above. The firelight sparkled within the dangling crystals decorating the chandeliers, little rainbows dancing within.

Banners representing the various noble families hung from the ceiling on both sides of the hall. Their symbols ranged from an iguaca to a coquí, even to a leatherback sea turtle, and many more. All twenty banners paled in comparison to that of the one hanging over the castle's three thrones, belonging to the Ligera royal family. A crest depicting a large pink maga flower rested in the center upon a crimson field. Beneath the flower lay a golden crown, both symbols encircled by two gray manatees.

Standing before the thrones were the King and Queen themselves, Cecilio Ligera and Edurne Ororosa Ligera, talking with a few of the servants in charge of the decorations and seemed to be in jubilant spirits. The King and Queen both carried themselves with a poise and deportment that commanded respect.

As Kaius neared the dais with Princess Alaia not far behind, he eyed the King and Queen. Alaia was growing to look more and more the spitting image of her mother every day, save for her father's bright green eyes and thick brown hair.

Queen Edurne donned a simple yet elegant emerald dress, fitted more for comfort than for form, with gold pomegranate flowers painted about the fabric. Her wavy, ebony hair was loosely braided and fell long down her back.

King Cecilio donned a crimson tunic decorated with golden lace about his shoulders and tassels hanging long to his elbows. His short brown hair was neatly pulled back and held by a ruby ribbon.

Catching Kaius by surprise, neither the King nor Queen wore their crowns. That was interesting, he thought, as that had never been the case before with so many people around.

As Kaius and Alaia reached the dais, King Cecilio glanced their way and stretched out his arms lightly from his sides, greeting them with a small grin on his face. "Ah nuestra invitada de honor finalmente ha llegado.[1]"

Alaia didn't respond. Kaius glanced back and quickly felt unsettled by her intense glare, not directed at him, but at her father. What had the two of them talked about to make her so angry?

"Espera, Alaia es tu vestido de onomástica?[2]" Queen Edurne stepped forward to her husband's side, her hands resting on her hips and lips pursed.

"O-Oh, right." Alaia responded with surprise, eyes softening and looking down to inspect her extravagant pink and white gown. She looked up at her mother with a small apologetic smile. "Lo siento,

---

1   Spanish for *Ah our guest of honor has finally arrived.*
2   Spanish for *Wait, Alaia is that your nameday gown?*

Madre,[3] I . . . have had a rather trying morning and forgot I was still wearing it." She raised her shoulders and tilted her head lightly. "I'll go change."

"No, that's alright." Queen Edurne responded, her accent quite a bit thicker than her daughter's. "While you're here, echémosle un vistazo a tu vestido."[4] She took a few folds of her dress in hand, lifted it up and rushed down the steps of the dais. Kaius bowed his head and stepped aside. The Queen stopped before her daughter and proceeded to circle her, looking her up and down. "Te ves hermosa,[5] but how does it fit? Is it comfortable?"

Alaia groaned as she playfully rolled her eyes. "Sí, Madre."[6]

The two giggled as Queen Edurne gently slapped Alaia's shoulder and reached out to lift handfuls of Alaia's brown hair. "Now, what to do about your hair."

"Whatever you decide, make sure it doesn't obstruct her tiara. I want our subjects to remember just who she is." King Cecilio answered, making his way down the steps with his hands behind his back and a stern expression on his face.

Kaius snuck a glance at Alaia again while standing at attention. Her bright green eyes blazed with fury once more as she met her father's gaze. She abruptly turned away from him, facing her mother who appeared just as surprised by her daughter's anger as Kaius. It

---

3   Spanish for *I am sorry, Mother.*
4   Spanish for *Let's have a look at your dress.*
5   Spanish for *You look beautiful.*
6   Spanish for *Yes, Mother.*

appeared that even Edurne didn't know what had gotten into Alaia. Just what—

"Kaius."

"Y-Yes, your majesty." Kaius held himself as straight as he could, nervous to be before the King in his kingsguard armor for the first time. He hadn't seen King Cecilio since his knighting and didn't have any help in putting on the armor. Kaius hoped the King would approve.

King Cecilio glanced at him up and down and flashed him an approving smile. "Thank you for fetching my daughter. I trust she wasn't . . . too much trouble."

"No, not at all your majesty."

"Good." King Cecilio stepped closer, startling Kaius. He leaned in, close to his ear. "Tell me Kaius, how have you been feeling today?"

Kaius' stomach churned lightly. "Your majesty?"

The King leaned back, standing tall and towering over him. "Come now boy, you can be truthful with me. If something is amiss, I *need* to know. As a member of my kingsguard you must be in perfect physical health to complete your duty. Nothing seems out of place? Nothing out of the ordinary?"

Kaius stared at the King, unsure of how to respond. Should he tell him about the headaches? No. He was the King. Kaius couldn't bother him with such a trivial matter. His brows curved as a bead of sweat slid down the side of his face. "Out of the ordinary? N-No sir . . ."

King Cecilio turned his head slightly with a scowl. "Well, that's . . ." He started with a sigh, his tone momentarily harsh before becoming cordial once again, "Good to hear. Kaius, I've decided to place you in the División de Cazadores."

Kaius' eyes widened in shock. "T-The Hunters Division? Your Majesty, please. I've only been through basic combat training for fighting humans, there's no way I'll be able to face monstrous beasts like manticores and vejigantes!"

The King waved a hand with an eerie smile. "Nonsense. The División de Cazadores are aware of your abilities and will aid you in furthering your training so that you may face the beasts plaguing our lands. Besides, it's a great *honor* to be in their ranks. You should be thankful."

"I . . . It is?"

"Most definitely, Kaius. As you know I care for the people, and I *know* how much you want to help me safeguard our home. Don't you want to make these lands a safer place?"

Kaius stared up at him with softened yet trembling eyes. "I-I do, but—"

"CECILIO!"

The commotion in the throne room came to a halt, everyone turning their attention to the hall's entrance. There stood a man in violet and ebony robes. A hood casted his face in shadow.

He shifted his weight and adjusted the hood, revealing his face. Vincent's furious eyes radiated an unnatural violet glow, his hands balling into fists and jaw clenching.

King Cecilio puffed his chest in frustration. "Hmph, there you are, *boy*. I don't like being kept waiting."

"Like I care!" Vincent answered venomously.

Kaius looked at the King, Cecilio's posture stiffening and annoyance clear on his face. No one in the hall dared to make a sound as Kaius' hairs began to stand on end.

"What was that?" The King growled angrily.

"No matter what I did for you. All the blood I've shed. All the voices I've silenced. You would still place my BROTHER in danger. Try to force his magic to awaken! So be it, I've had it with you and your family tearing mine apart!"

Vincent's hands ignited in a glittering violet glow. In a flash he drew his arms into an X over his chest and thrust them outwards in an arc, sending a gale of wind across the room. The force sent servants, guards, and nobility flying back a great distance.

Kaius crossed his arms over his face, hoping to shield himself from the wind, and stood his ground but to no avail. His feet left the floor and a sensation of weightlessness overcame him. The wind sent him hurtling back. Kaius crashed into the steps of the dais, gasping loudly as he slid down the stairs and landed on the floor at the bottom. Flower petals rained down all around him.

There was only silence, save for the ringing in his head. He tried to say his older brother's name aloud, but all he could muster was a harsh cough and choked breath. His body felt heavy. He slid his arms under his chest and pushed himself up.

As the high-pitched hum faded, the sound of steps grew clearer.

He looked up and found Vincent approaching, walking along the blush-colored rug with such a glower it sent shivers up Kaius' spine.

His mouth hung agape, trying to speak, to plead with his brother to stop. Why was Vincent attacking? Why? Where was all this anger coming from? Vincent's words then raced through Kaius' mind with renewed clarity. What did he say before he attacked? Force Kaius to awaken? But . . . that was impossible.

He struggled through the cough as he regained control of his breath and yelled out, "V-Vincent, please! There's . . . a misunderstanding. There has to be! King Cecilio was just—"

Vincent stopped dead in his tracks, still several feet from Princess Alaia who cowered with her mother. "Going to place you in the Hunters Division, where you would be facing life threatening dangers, hoping that you would finally awaken to your magic, Kaius." Vincent turned his gaze to the King. "So that's your plan, you damn bastard. Why settle for one mage when you could have two, AM I RIGHT!?"

King Cecilio struggled to rise to his knees. His guards laid unconscious beside him. Small hair strands fell loose over his bright green eyes, which glared back at Vincent with a fury of his own. "You better watch yourself, you ungrateful little shit. You wouldn't want anything to happen to your younger brother now, would you?"

Vincent stared back, silent and seemingly disinterested. Kaius, upon hearing the thinly veiled threat, looked to the King with eyes wide. His heart raced as a terrible chill spread about his body. Had he . . . heard that right? A swarm of rushing metal footsteps and voices shouting in native Pacífican echoed through the halls nearby, jostling him from his thoughts.

"It won't be long till my guards show and arrest you both." King Cecilio straightened as tall as he could, a triumphant, smug grin spreading across his lips. "I can stop them, but only if you cease this foolishness. Right. Now."

Vincent showed no expression and slowly turned to his side, raising a hand glowing with glittering violet light. "Let them come." The hand traced an invisible circle midair and just as he reached its peak, a bluish white portal brimmed to life at his back. "The Princess and I will be gone before they arrive." Vincent then turned his still glowing hand to Alaia.

A black cloud swirled to life and flew toward the Princess, causing her to shriek. As her mother reached out to grab her, a black, misty sphere enveloped Alaia and thrusted Queen Edurne back. The Princess collapsed to the ground, falling fast asleep. Vincent raised his hand and called the sphere back to him.

"NO! Por favor, Vincent, devuélvemela!"[7] Queen Edurne's scream echoed through the hall. "If it's vengeance you want then take it on Cecilio, not Alaia. PLEASE! No mi niña."[8] She buried her face in her hands, sobbing.

Kaius stared at the trembling woman. "Take vengeance?"

"HOW DARE YOU!" King Cecilio stepped forward to threaten Vincent, but was swiftly sent flying back as a blast of wind crashed

7   Spanish for *NO! Please, Vincent, give her back to me!*
8   Spanish for *Not my baby girl.*

into him. The King landed on the steps of the dais and slammed hard to the ground.

"You should've listened to your wife. Using us. Threatening me and my brother. That is what forced me down this path. I swear to it, it will be your end. This *will* be the end of Rosado!" Vincent turned his gaze down to his younger brother, his eyes softening as he stretched a hand to him. "Kaius, come with me. It's time we left."

Kaius stared at Vincent in abject shock. His mind whirled with confusion and fear. Why was this happening? Why was Vincent doing this? They could've talked about this. Should've talked about this. They could've approached Cecilio together. Regardless of what Vincent thought of the King's motives, the man had been good to them. They could've talked with him.

Vincent wouldn't tell Kaius anything, nor would Alaia. Even Cecilio too had been keeping Kaius in the dark.

Who was he to trust?

"Kaius, we have to go!"

Kaius' eyes lingered on Vincent's hand. "Go where?"

"To where we belong."

Kaius' heart skipped a beat. Time slowed to a crawl. Cries and shouts faded to a whisper as he looked up at his older brother, meeting his gaze. Worry began to show on Vincent's face, his brows curving in distress and eyes darting between Kaius and the entrance.

Kaius, frozen in fear, his chest tight, and unsure of what to do, remained silent. Stand by the King or go with his brother? Save Alaia or let her be taken? Could Vincent really hurt her? The questions bombarded his mind so quickly he couldn't focus. His breath labored, coming short and fast. His heart pounded rapidly against his breast, feeling overwhelmed.

Vincent is your brother. The voice in his head, his voice, reminded. It should've been an obvious choice but as their relationship strained, so too did the trust between the two brothers.

But the King has provided for us since we were children.

He was only trying to use you.

You don't know that!

Are you sure? The evidence is there. You just need to look.

The air was thick, so thick he could barely breathe, barely think. Vincent startled and looked behind Kaius, urgency flaring in his eyes. His gaze returned to Kaius with furrowed brows and bared teeth. "Kaius, we need to go NOW!"

Kaius winced. With eyes locked on his older brother's, Kaius began to raise his arm. His hand trembled and hesitated mere inches from Vincent's fingertips. Should he? Had what Vincent was saying all this time been true? Was the King—

"Death will await you both! Put my daughter down right now!"

Kaius startled, his pulse racing impossibly fast, his heart thumping in his chest as his hand hovered over Vincent's fingers. He was terrified. More than anything, he was afraid of the King's wrath. Kaius' eyes blurred while hot tears streamed down his cheeks. "Vincent, please don't do this. You can set this right. Y-You have to. It's not too late!"

His voice cracked as he pleaded with his older brother.

Vincent's eyes slowly widened. His lips lightly trembled and his breath steadied. He straightened his posture, his eyes glossing, and his features softened. "I . . . It's alright. You're frightened. That's all. I'm sorry, little brother."

His eyes suddenly hardened and a flash of fury ignited within his piercing glare. He glanced past Kaius, back to the throne. The air grew heavy just as it had in Vincent's tower.

Vincent turned to the portal and sent the Princess through. Queen Edurne screamed out, begging through heavy sobs for him to bring her back, but Vincent ignored her. He then turned to the King. "This will be your end, your *majesty*. The barriers between realms have weakened since the fall of Kunnagar. Little by little, the demons of Velkran have broken through." Vincent raised a hand high in the air. "Summon your minions, Mykronvan!"

Dark spheres appeared, forming in thin air, and grew into a swirl of purple sparkling hues. Many still trapped in the room screamed and scurried toward entrances as the kingsguard began to pour in.

Loud, shrill screeches sounded from within the orbs. Kaius scrambled to cover his ears, but to no avail. The screeches pierced his eardrums. As the cacophony of cries reached a crescendo, they suddenly stopped.

Creatures the size of small children poured forth from the orbs with skin as black as a starless night. Curled horns protruded from atop their round heads. Sharp claws and pointed hooves scratched against the marble floor and glowing orange eyes stared hungrily at the knights slowly surrounding the dais to safeguard the King.

"Kaius."

Hearing his name through all the commotion, Kaius turned to Vincent standing before the portal. A tear rolled down his cheek. "When the world is at its darkest, it will be the end of Rosado. Be gone from here by then."

Kaius shook his head and balled his fists. "Vincent? I don't understand!"

"I don't have control over these creatures. They'll continue to pour forth until Rosado is no more. Please, don't throw your life away for *him*." With that, Vincent turned away and disappeared through the portal.

Kaius desperately reached out for his brother. "Vincent, wait! Don't go, PLEASE!" The portal vanished in a wisp of smoke and glittering light before Kaius could reach it.

KAIUS

GLIMMER OF HOPE

K AIUS KNELT THERE ON THE GROUND. His hand hung in the air, still reaching to the empty space where his brother once was as the monsters lurked all around. Their attention was slowly beginning to turn toward him. Vincent's name softly escaped his lips.

A searing heat suddenly exploded within Kaius. His hands flew to his breastplate, clinging to his chest and gasping for air. His heartbeat thumped as though it were a war drum.

Cackles and screams grew louder and louder around him, pulling his attention from the pain. He attempted to look up, barely able to raise his head. The knights of the kingsguard roared as they charged and crashed into the creatures. The strange dark monsters giggled at their attacks, dodging out of the way with ease.

What were these things? Well, whatever they were, he had to get up. He couldn't just sit there and wait for death. Through sheer determination, Kaius forced himself to stand, his knees quivering, threatening to buckle and send him back to the ground below, but he persevered.

He tried to keep his focus on anything but the feeling in his chest. Kaius quickly looked about as people rushed past him. One of them crashed into his shoulder, nearly knocking him forward to the ground.

A woman's scream sounded beside him. He spun around and saw the Queen cowering as one of the creatures rushed toward her. She tried to stand or crawl back, but her heels caught in the fabric of her emerald dress, trapping her where she lay.

The world slowed down around him once again and his hands trembled at his sides. He had to do something. He had to move and cursed at his body to heed his commands. With that, his legs finally sprung into action, pushing him forward.

Kaius roared as he raced toward Queen Edurne and the monster. There wasn't much time. Without a moment to lose, Kaius rammed into the creature as hard as he could, driving his shoulder into its large head and sending it tumbling back.

His breath labored. He stared at the monster, watching it fumble to stand, dazed and shaking its head. Kaius glanced down to his waist, remembering his longsword and drew it, readying himself to fight.

"Kaius?" He heard the Queen and glanced down, she was laying on the floor and still struggling with her dress. "You saved me?"

"Well, yes. Why wouldn't I?" He immediately returned his attention to the monster now recovering, wobbling lightly, but regaining its bearings.

The creature turned to him, brandishing its claws and fangs. Opening its mouth wide, it hissed like an angry, starving cat ready to attack.

He positioned himself between it and the Queen, ready to guard her with his life if need be. It then cackled and pointed in a fit of laughter.

"What?" He watched the creature in confusion, but kept his guard up. "I've had it with . . . with whatever you are!"

Kaius charged at the beast, sword raised high, roaring fiercely. He brought his sword down upon it as hard as he could, however, his blade passed right through, as though he had attacked the air itself. The sword crashed into the marble, sending a painful aftershock reverberating through the handle, and into his hands.

He stared a moment, dumbfounded at the monster. It simply giggled again and pointed at him while dancing left and right. Kaius jolted back defensively. He pointed his sword at it with a determined stare. "H-How can I beat such a thing?"

A gurgled scream nearby startled Kaius. He looked to his left and saw a knight stumble. The man dropped his sword and heater shield and fell to his back. His hand clutched his neck as blood coated his armor and spilled to the floor. The man stared up at the ceiling wide eyed, shallowly coughing and gagging as blood spilled from the corners of his mouth.

Kaius' breath hitched and his body tensed. The man's eyes rolled back, his convulsions stilling within moments. Kaius' hands trembled. He struggled to hold his sword straight. His knees shook and he was unsure if it was from fear or exhaustion. What in all of Eldara going on here? Why would Vincent—

More screams sounded about the hall. He looked around as knights fell, one by one. The scent of iron hung in the air while blood splattered the floor and walls. A chandelier lay broken and shattered on the floor. Several banners were torn while the Ligera's banner was ablaze over the thrones.

A ringing pierced his mind in full force. He shut his eyes and gritted his teeth, his grip on his sword weakening by the second. Beads of sweat slowly slid down the side of his face. The loud ringing drowned out the pounding of his heart and the screams of the men and women falling to the beasts that had before echoed all around him.

"Kaius, mira!"[1]

Hands slammed down on Kaius' shoulders, pulling him back. He opened his eyes just in time to see the monster before him lunge forward, a claw raised in the air. Kaius reflexively raised his sword, expecting the claws to pass clean through, and braced for his imminent end. To his surprise, the claws crashed into the blade. He then parried the blow. With a hard shove using the face of his sword, he forced the

---

1   Spanish for *Kaius, look out!*

creature back, sending it airborne.

It dropped onto another knight and caused her to stumble forward. The creature attacked, cutting deep into the knight's face and throat, and toppled her to the ground.

"NO!" Kaius screamed out in horror. Holding his sword high he readied to charge the creature once more.

"Kaius, venga!"[2]

Queen Edurne grabbed him by the arm and pulled him to the dais, toward King Cecilio who was shouting orders to the remaining kingsguards. Kaius quickly looked down to the deceased knight who had fallen beside him and his eyes drifted to the man's heater shield. He quickly whispered a silent apology and without another moment's hesitation, he dashed forward, slid his arm through the leather straps, and drew the shield to his chest to guard himself and the Queen.

The two carefully retreated to the dais. Reaching the base, rushed footsteps came thumping down the steps and a hand grabbed hold of his clasped cape. Forced to turn, he found himself face-to-face with King Cecilio's fury.

"What is the meaning of this!?" Cecilio shook Kaius vigorously. "After everything I've learned of your people, an event like this should've awakened your magic by now. So why—"

"Cecilio, STOP!" Queen Edurne pushed herself between Kaius and her husband. "He saved me! Stop this foolishness."

Hearing a loud hissing while the Queen tried to yell some sense into Cecilio, Kaius turned at the ready for another attack. A monster

2   Spanish for *Kaius, Come on!*

stretched its fanged mouth open wide, revealing a void of darkness within. A spark of violet magic began to take shape, growing larger and larger into a spherical mass of energy.

Kaius hopped forward, instantly placing himself before the King and Queen, and raised his shield. With his vision obscured, he braced for whatever form the attack would take and heard a strange, ear-piercing howl barrel toward him. The magic collided hard into the metal shield with a thunderous boom. A haze of violet fumes burst in all directions as sparks crackled in the air. The force was as strong as a horse's kick and pushed him back, nearly sending him stumbling to the ground.

He glanced at the front of the shield and found its surface cracked and the metal deteriorating before his eyes. "Oh shit!"

Kaius heard another howl and looked up in fear to see a second violet sphere spiraling straight for him. He raised his shield just in the nick of time. The blast slammed against the shield and shattered it completely. The explosion sent him flying back. He landed against the steps of the dais, just barely missing the King and Queen.

Kaius let out a loud gasp and slid down the steps. His head spun, exhausted, his limbs trembling. He tried to open his eyes. The burning sensation in his chest swelled. Kaius' vision blurred. He could only hear muffled sounds through the ringing in his head.

"This . . . ridiculous!"

". . . all your doing! If—"

Were the King and Queen arguing?

As Kaius' sight faded in and out, he turned his head and found Queen Edurne kneeling over him. King Cecilio's face turned beet red.

"Don't you DARE speak to me that way! I did what I had to do to get us where we are now. The methods don't matter, so long as things get done!"

"And where has that gotten our daughter?" Edurne returned a furrowed yet challenging glare.

The King's eyes narrowed and his jaw clenched. He lunged for her hand. "Tsk! He's a lost cause. We need to leave!"

Queen Edurne fought to free herself of his grip. "NO! You can't—"

As the King and Queen argued, the knights behind them were slowly being picked apart one by one by the dark monsters. Flashes of blood spurted with every slash of claw, rip of fang, and clomp of taloned hoof. Kaius' body trembled uncontrollably, and bile rose in his throat.

An echoing scream resounded within his mind. His vision faded again, filling with darkness and fire. A wooden ceiling bowed overhead, splintering and ready to burst. Furniture and potted plants burned as ash and gray smoke filled the room. Kaius' chest tightened and panic started to set in.

Where was he? It looked familiar, but—

He spotted a boy with blond hair knelt before a flaming boulder. Kaius' head began to throb. A voice then entered his mind, soft and undistinguishable at first. The voice suddenly became clear, thundering and commanding.

RUN! YOU HAVE TO RUN! TAKE YOUR BROTHER AND GET OUT OF HERE! IT'S TOO LATE FOR US!

What was this? Who—

Kaius jolted awake. Queen Edurne pulled desperately on his arm with tear-filled eyes.

"Kaius! You have to get up. You ha—"

"LEAVE HIM!" King Cecilio commanded, grabbing his wife's arm and forcefully pulling her toward the side of the dais. Try as she might to fight his grip, she couldn't break free.

Kaius tried to reach out for the Queen, turning with all his strength to face them. His body was just too heavy, limbs too exhausted and too sore.

No. No this wasn't right. Why was everything turning out this way? Why?

Shouts rang out in Pacífican from the front of the throne room. In the distance, small explosions of bright white light scattered about the hall. A flash of light zigzagged left and right at such a speed, Kaius could barely keep up. It shimmered and looked to be coming toward him, though his vision was obscured by the remaining kingsguard.

A group of knights before the dais parted ways and a small light hurtled toward him, stopping mere feet before Kaius. It instantly dispersed, revealing a creature the likes that Kaius had thought he would never see in his lifetime.

From head to toe she was no taller than the size of his head. She had radiant umber skin and thick, tight white curls held away from her face by a silver beaded band. Her sparkling silver and white wings fluttered quickly behind her as she floated in midair. Tattered ribbons of cloth hung from her white clothes and waved about. Was that one of the fae folk, he wondered.

Glaring at the monsters slowly moving to surround her, the little fae took a deep breath and crossed her arms into an X. Her hands glowed brightly white. With a quick exhale, she thrusted her hands forward releasing several volleys of light spiraling around her, striking the creatures in quick succession. With a wail, the creatures ignited before fracturing and disintegrating, the particles dissipating as they floated weightlessly upward. The creatures were dispatched one by one before Kaius and the knights.

Silence filled the grand hall. Kaius stared at the little fae floating about, zipping left and right like a hummingbird, seemingly searching for any remaining monsters that may have escaped the attack. His mouth hung agape, words unable to pour forth.

So that was the power of one of the fae folk, he thought in amazement. Her magic was indeed incredible. She could actually kill the shadow beasts. She could help the people of Rosado. The burning in his chest and ringing in Kaius' head began to subside. He slowly lifted himself, just barely able to kneel.

King Cecilio, however, rushed forward with a disgusted frown. "Kill the abomination!" He ordered.

The little fae jolted with a gasp as the knights pointed their swords at her.

Kaius' heart leaped into his throat, and a surge of energy filled him. He lunged toward her, shielding her with his body. He turned to the King with concern in his blue eyes. "What is wrong with you? Didn't you see what she did to those monsters? Regardless of how you feel about the fae folk, she can help us! She has helped us!"

"These . . . *beings* by law are to never step foot in our city. It's the reason we don't pass through their borders. By breaking this law, her punishment is death regardless of this perceived aid." King Cecilio's eyes narrowed with resentment. The little fae retreated and hid against Kaius' chest as he shielded her with his hands.

"Still, you saw what she can do! You *saw* what she did to those monsters. We didn't stand a chance. Just give her a moment to explain, please."

King Cecilio stared at Kaius with a stern gaze. He then nudged his chin toward the little fae.

Kaius looked down to her, releasing the protective embrace. Noticeably shaken by the threat, her four wings slowed as she floated down to his cupped hands, her breath heavy.

He flashed her a warm smile, trying to show he meant her no harm. After a moment of hesitation, she lowered her guard, sliding her hands down to her hips.

"Is that how Pacíficans say thank ye?" She asked coolly, her accent unfamiliar, but beautiful in its short, lyrical tones.

Kaius' smile wavered. "I'm sorry. Today hasn't been a terribly good day." He looked around the hall. Not a single monster seemed to have survived her attack. "It looks like you've dealt with all the monsters. Thank you little fae, or is it fairy?"

She remained quiet for a moment, staring up at him with lips nervously curled inward. Softly exhaling, she answered. "I'm sorry, but no. I've only dealt with the ones in here. I saw many more scattered about the city as I was flying overhead."

"What!? Vamos! Aquí solo se necesitan algunos de ustedes. Todos los demás, enfóquense en proteger a las personas!"[3] King Cecilio commanded. His guards pounded their fists to their chests and many rushed out of the throne room. The few remaining placed themselves at the entrance.

"By the way, I'm a fairy of Eylowen Forest, not a fae of Valtivar. I'm . . . unfortunately not as powerful as them, no matter how many spirits I have on my side."

"Wait, Eylowen?"

"Bosque Encantado!" King Cecilio responded, his words dripping with venom. "The damn creature means Bosque Encantado."

The fairy's face flushed dark with anger as her hands closed into tight fists. "NGH! No I don't! Ye humans have yer names for things, and we have ours. Now I came seeking aid, but saw you needed help and so I did what I could. Do ye want my aid or not?"

King Cecilio glared at the fairy, but didn't respond. Kaius turned

---

3   Spanish for *Go! Only a few of you are needed here. Everyone else, focus on protecting the people!*

his attention back to the fairy. "Please, tell me what I need to do."

She stared up at him for a long moment, then placed a hand on her chin and looked him up and down. "Actually, I think ye'll do just fine as ye are."

Kaius cocked his head to the side, raising an eyebrow in confusion. She pointed to his sword lying on the ground beside him and whispered something in a language Kaius couldn't understand. He looked down to his blade, unsure of what to do, and saw it slowly begin to glow. Kaius leaned down and grabbed the sword. He raised it to inspect it, and his eyes went wide as he took a deep breath.

"Oh trust me, we aren't done yet lad. This sword is linked to ye and ye alone."

"What do you mean?" Kaius raised a brow.

"I mean only ye can use the sword. Now hush hush for a moment."

He watched the fairy as she clutched her hands over her chest and continued to recite the spell. A small, round, bright blue crystal gem, the size of a coin, materialized in midair and floated in front of her. She placed her hands beneath it, raising it high in the air, and thrusted it into his left gauntlet. As it made contact, the gem affixed itself to his armor as though the bottom were coated in honey.

"And . . . there we go." The fairy exhaled a labored breath, her wings fluttering erratically, struggling to keep her in flight. He raised a hand for her to land on his palm. "Thank ye, flying all the way from Eylowen and using so much magic really tired me out." She pointed at the gem. "I'll just need some time to rejuvenate." In a flash, she became a ball of light once more and disappeared into the gem.

Kaius startled at the spectacle and raised the gem to have a better look at it. *"Don't trouble yerself trying to understand my magic. Just raise yer arm as though ye would if blocking with yer shield."* Her voice echoed from within the gem.

He nodded and readied to try out the magic. Just as he was about to raise his gauntlet, more dark spheres formed, and hissing again filled the hall. The creatures came pouring forth, ignoring the few remaining guards, and rushed straight toward Kaius with claws raised, causing him to jolt in fear.

"Do it! Raise yer arm, NOW!"

Holding his breath, Kaius raised his arm. A large shimmering barrier of light instantaneously surrounded him. The little creatures jumped and ferociously attacked, clawing and biting at the dome. As each attack landed, the light sparked to life and repelled the monsters, hurling them back, and sending each tumbling to the floor like balls bouncing off a wall.

He watched as the monsters got back to their feet. Hesitant and seemingly confused, they retreated back ever so slightly. Kaius exhaled and his mouth fell open in surprise. He knew it. They could beat the monsters.

Twirling his glowing sword about and lowering his left arm, dismissing the barrier, Kaius took a quick breath to calm his nerves and rushed toward the beasts, striking at the closest one.

At the touch of his blade, the little monster fractured and dissipated in a burst of black dust. He could stop them. Kaius launched his attack on the other monsters in their moment of panic, one by one striking them down where they stood.

Now he could save—

The piercing ringing returned to his mind, the pain sending burning waves through his limbs. Momentarily stunned, he ceased his attack. The remaining monsters retreated toward the castle exit. He had to. He had to save them. Vincent. Alaia. He had to help—

"What is it? What's wrong?" The fairy's voice broke through his rattled thoughts.

"I-It's nothing. I—"

"Well, why are you still here?" A chill crawled up Kaius' spine. He turned to find King Cecilio standing tall with hands held behind his back and watching him with a stern glare. "Quit your dawdling, Kaius. You have a duty to uphold. Now push these creatures from my walls!"

Kaius' heart beat hard against his chest, his nerves causing his legs to tremble. He glanced at Queen Edurne standing behind her husband. She looked at him with concern and tearstained cheeks.

In her he saw Alaia's face. Kaius relaxed his tense muscles and forced himself to bow. He then rushed out of the throne room to dispatch the retreating monsters.

Passing through the castle's entrance, he looked out over the vast courtyard. There, many people tried as they might to flee from dark monsters. The kingsguards and the city guards banded together to fend the creatures off as best they could. His lips quivered as he watched the guards slowly succumb to the creatures.

"There are so many."

"Hit them with yer sword mister knight. Ye can beat them!"

Kaius shuddered as the mayhem unfolded before him. People were mauled, sliced open, stabbed, and blasted. His eyes widened and his breath quickened. All of this, for some reason, felt eerily familiar. Too familiar.

"Mister knight? Are ye okay? Ye have to help them." The fairy called out, her voice soothing, but filled with urgency.

"No, I'm terrified. I'm not sure I can do this on my own." Kaius' feet were frozen in place atop the steps to the courtyard, unable to move forward.

"Ye're not alone. I'm here with ye. We have to do something. If we don't, more people will die. Come on now, ye have yer sword and my shield. We CAN do it. Now move!"

Kaius' brows furrowed as he tried to calm his racing heart. He looked down at the steps before his feet and then back to the monsters rampaging through the courtyard. With a few deep breaths, he commanded his legs to move. After a brief pause, he found himself rushing down the stairs and onto the cobblestone courtyard.

A few monsters near the massive fountain centered in the courtyard took notice, growled angrily, and rushed toward him. While still running, he raised his sword to the side, ready to strike, and swung his blade as the monsters came into range. The blade sliced right through their necks. Just as before, they fractured and turned to dust where they stood.

Kaius' spirit began to rise as a smile snuck its way onto his face, feeling relief and his confidence returning. "It worked!"

"Of course it worked! Ye had doubt? Besides, ye already slew some in the castle, remember?"

Kaius chuckled nervously. He looked around to the monsters now slowly surrounding him. "Yeah, but there weren't this many in there." Kaius raised his blade to the monsters to continue his assault and without hesitation, unleashed a flurry of attacks.

One by one they went down, but there were still so many. His body was tired. Muscles ached and were bruised, hurting from being hurled into the stone steps of the dais more than once. Kaius' sword whistled through the air as it laid waste to the enemy numbers.

He couldn't believe this. Kaius could do this. He could actually do this.

The remaining beasts began to step cautiously away, holding their distance as they hissed and clawed defensively in his direction. They all suddenly threw their heads back and roared in a cacophony of horrible sounds into the sky.

"What are they doing?"

"HEY LOOK OUT!"

Kaius looked down at the fairy's gem. A growing shadow fell over him as though the sun itself had fled beneath the horizon. Something crashed with a boom into the ground behind him, causing the entire area to quake. Water splashed against him as he struggled to keep his footing. A great roar washed over the noise and chaos of the courtyard.

He slowly turned, terror threatening to once again take hold within him. His eyes flashed wide, but before he got a good look at the creature, a force slammed into the right side of his body, sending him flying. Kaius hit the ground hard and tumbled several feet. The air in his lungs escaped as he rolled and settled onto the grass.

Lying face down and his body aching, he fought to remain conscious. Mustering his strength, he opened his eyes and looked to see what had struck him.

A tall, thin creature lumbered in the fountain. It lifted its hocked legs up and over the fountain's ring, dropping its large hooves with a loud thud to the ground. The creature's unnaturally long arms stretched to the cobblestone, its knuckles dragging behind it as it moved about. Its claws were long and sharp. With one swing of its massive hand, it shattered the statue of manatees dancing in the fountain. Its horns stretched high and curled like willow branches behind its angular head. Rage burned within its bright orange glowing eyes. Sharp fangs protruded from a gaping maw as drool trickled down its chin.

"Hey! HEY! What's going on? The gem is facing down so I can't see anything. Come on, answer me!"

Hearing the fairy's voice, he slid his arms underneath his chest, wincing in pain, and pushed himself up. His arms shook with strain, but didn't falter. Spotting Kaius, the creature bellowed out a tremendous roar and charged at him.

Kaius jolted as the monster raised a massive, clawed hand high in the air. Not wanting to be lying still when it came crashing down, Kaius pushed with every ounce of strength he had left to stand and dodged back, just barely evading the deadly blow.

"*LOOK OUT!*"

His vision was still fuzzy. Kaius didn't notice the second attack in time as the back of the creature's hand smashed into his side and sent him flying once more. Hitting a stone wall hard, he let out a loud gasp and landed face down on the grass, feeling his grip on the waking world wavering.

The world was dark, and his head spun. His body at once felt both lighter than the air around him and heavier than all the stones comprising the courtyard. Kaius' mind raced, though his thoughts were jumbled and erratic.

Memories flashed to life as though they were not in the past, but happening this very instant. Vincent told him that he would be King Cecilio's Grand Mage in their living quarters. Then Vincent passed through the portal in the throne room. Now he was meeting Alaia for the first time and served the King a chalice of wine. Then the King and the royal quarters vanished and Alaia was sitting over him in the garden.

What was he to do? All Kaius' life he wanted to show his worth. Repay the kindness given to him. Had he been a fool all this time? What was he—

"Get up! Ye can't just end here. I'm here with ye. Come on, ye have to

get up!"

The fear in the fairy's voice pierced through the jumbled memories, reeling him back into the present. The visions faded as the present became clear, his sight and senses slowly returning. He slid his left arm back, trying to push himself up from the ground again.

Heavy stomps thumped louder and louder, causing the ground to quake as the monster approached. Kaius quickly slid his right arm back while using his sword for balance, pulling himself up. Once he got to his feet, he raised his sword toward the sounds of the footfalls.

His vision was blurry and head ringing from the previous attack, but he knew he must fight. As a shadow loomed over him, Kaius looked up in a panic and saw the creature's hand high over his head, about to come down to end his fight for good.

"SHIT!"

Remembering the fairy's shield, he raised his left arm high and summoned the barrier. With a loud crash and flash of sparkling light, the clawed hand slammed down, the force sending dust and debris flying in all directions.

Kaius stared on in disbelief. The barrier held. Relieved and happy to still be alive, his spirits began to bolster.

The monster's hand bounced and hung in the air. The barrier's magic reverberated through it and threw the creature off-balance. Kaius exhaled a shallow breath as his brows furrowed deep over his eyes.

Now was his chance. He had to end this. Quickly. Kaius lowered his left arm, dismissing the barrier, and rushed toward the monster.

He struck its legs with his sword, the blade glowing as it passed clean through. The bottom half of the creature's legs burst into a cloud of dust, sending the creature toppling. Kaius' heart leaped into his throat, fearing its weight would crush him. He drew his right arm back and swung his blade upward, piercing the creature's chest with the point of his sword.

The creature let out a pained wail, its cry echoing even to the outskirts of the city's walls. A haze of black dust washed over him and vanished into the air. Seeing this, the smaller beasts shrieked and retreated to the exit of the courtyard.

Exhausted, his legs gave way and he fell. Dropping his sword, his hands landed firmly on the ground, catching himself just before hitting the grass. Through labored breaths, he tried to steady his racing heart.

"Hey, hey! Don't go collapsing on me. We still have a lot to do."

"I-I know . . . I ju-I just need a moment . . ."

"I'm sorry lad, but I don't think ye have a moment."

Marching sollerets clanked in the distance, growing louder as they approached. Kaius looked up and his heart sank. King Cecilio rushed toward him, glaring angrily, and his kingsguards followed close behind.

Kaius lifted himself off the ground and stumbled to his feet. His stomach churned, a sense of dread filling his gut. Before Kaius could speak, King Cecilio raised a fisted arm and punched him square in the jaw, knocking Kaius to the ground.

Kaius lay there for a moment with wide eyes, his body trembling in exhaustion and confusion. He slowly looked up to the King, his cheek stinging and body bruised. The King met Kaius' gaze with a furious yet stern glare.

"Twelve years. Twelve years spent on you and your *ungrateful* brother. Wasted."

Kaius jolted, the words a knife in his side.

"Now I have to clean up this mess." The King turned to his kingsguard. "Arrest the boy and throw him into a cell until I know for certain he's not in league with his brother."

"No wait!" Kaius pleaded, pushing himself to his knees.

Everything was falling apart. What should he do? What could he do? Kaius knew now there were many things he hadn't been told, but he couldn't believe everything had been a lie. The life he and Vincent had was good, wasn't it? There had to be something Kaius could do.

King Cecilio stopped and looked at him with a disinterested stare.

"I-I can fix this." Kaius exclaimed through choked breath. "Please, just give me the chance to prove my worth to you. If you allow my leave, I can speak to Vincent. Convince him to stop all this and return with your daughter. Please!"

King Cecilio remained silent for a moment, then crossed his arms over his chest. "We would be left defenseless. Only you wield an enchanted weapon."

"I can go to the forest. To the fairies!" Kaius held up the gemmed gauntlet. "She said she came seeking aid. If I can help the fairies, then they can help us be rid of the monsters. I just . . . I just need a chance, your majesty. Please," Kaius bowed his head low to the King, trying to hide his trembling. "Give me a chance to rectify this."

Kaius kept his eyes to the ground, awaiting the King's response. He desperately hoped King Cecilio would let him have this.

Just say yes, the thought repeated in his mind, trying to will it into being. Maybe he could bring Vincent back, talk him down peacefully. They didn't have to lose the life they built there.

"Bring this boy a horse."

Relief washed over Kaius. He raised his gaze to the King, whose expression had gone from stern to something wholly more intimidating. The eerie intensity in the King's green eyes sent a shiver through his body.

"I will give you this one chance and *only* this one chance to convince your brother to stop this foolishness and return *with* my daughter, unharmed. Succeed, and you will escape punishment. Your brother on the other hand, I make no such promise. He will be lucky to have the mercy of the whip should I not find a more creative punishment, but when I'm done, he will have his life." King Cecilio raised a hand to Kaius. Thinking he would be struck again, he flinched, but to his surprise the King gently tousled his hair. "I suggest you not dawdle."

A knight stepped forth with a black and white mare in tow, set with a saddle, side satchels, and reins. "Oh, and Kaius," the King turned, swiftly plucking a sword from one of the guards' sheaths, and pointed the blade to Kaius' throat, "if my daughter is returned to me injured or worse, dead, know that *you* will meet the same fate."

KAIUS

THE SPIRITS

KAIUS' STEED FLEW OUT THE GATES of Rosado with haste. He struggled to wrap his head around the day's events as they played out over and over in his mind.

The statue of the Mother. Arguing with his brother. The flowers in the garden and Alaia's distant expression. The disappointment in her eyes when met with his deflection. The awkward silence between Alaia and him as they made their way through castle halls to the throne room. The King's prying question and news of his joining the Hunters Division.

From there everything was a blur. It all happened so fast, fell apart so swiftly. Vincent and Alaia vanished through a portal. The little monsters. So many of them. Fallen servants and guards. The beast in the courtyard. The King's thinly veiled threat.

Kaius glanced up and peeked over his horse's head. A vast, dense forest sat at the end of the single dirt road just beyond the split in the path leading left, its leaves still a vibrant green. To the right led North.

His brows furrowed as he thought of the quest now thrusted upon him. Pleading with the Mother, he hoped to be granted the strength he'd needed for such an undertaking. Even asking for courage to face Vinc—

As though suddenly struck by an arrow, a strong pain and loud ringing bored into his mind. With a loud groan, Kaius pulled the reins, making his horse rear and bray at the sudden tug.

Once the creature's hooves stomped back down to the earth, Kaius lunged forward to catch himself with hands firmly grasping the side of his helm. His face scrunched, and his teeth clenched. Kaius' breath fell heavy and short. Slumping to one side, he slid from the saddle and toppled hard to the grass. His helm slid off and rolled a few feet away.

"A-Ah! W-Why—"

A short chime sounded and the little fairy emerged from the gem fixed to Kaius' gauntlet. "What is it? What's wrong? Are ye in pain from the fight, or maybe that asshole King hit ye harder than I thought."

"H-He was just angry. It's not his fault!"

"Are ye seriously defending him, after what he did? What he said?"

"H-His daughter was—AGH!"

"One moment mister knight!"

The excessive ringing intensified, pain clouding his thoughts, and made it hard to focus. He felt something tiny and warm touch his forehead. Kaius winced at the sensation, the ringing seeming to draw toward that spot. The cool touch of a gentle wind swirled about him. He slowly opened his eyes and saw the little fairy lean in, her forehead resting against his.

"We're not close enough to a source of water to ask the spirits for help, and I'm still struggling to communicate with the spirits of earth, so I can't heal ye, but the wind spirits are great at relaxing the body's muscles. Just focus on steadying yer breath. This will only be a moment."

Kaius took a long, deep breath and exhaled slowly. As he drew in another one, the painful ringing began to lessen, quieting to a minor ache. Kaius slowly sat himself straight while trying to focus his sight on his hands just past the fairy. He curled his fingers a few times, his sight clearing, and even his stiff, sore muscles relaxed.

The fairy let out a quiet breath and the winds around him calmed once again. She slowly withdrew and hovered in front of him. "There, hopefully that helped."

"What did you do to me?" Kaius looked at her, mouth agape, and delighted by the magic.

"As a fairy of light, I can speak to many of the spirits within the elements of nature. Fire, water, earth, and wind. As my mother's heir,

I must master and commune with the spirits of the four elements. Each spirit can assist me with tasks such as healing, defending, and even attacking if they choose to answer my request."

"Wait a moment, heir? Are you a . . . Princess?"

"Hm? Oh right, I never introduced myself, did I? My name's Adhnis, daughter of Queen Throstnie, Princess of Eylowen Forest, Heir to blah blah blah, all that stuff. Are ye feeling better now? Can ye continue on?"

"Wait! You can't just drop that kind of knowledge on me and then move on as if it isn't a big deal. I have questions."

"I'm sure ye do, but my titles won't matter if we don't save my kin. We're pressed for time. Besides, the faster we save my mother, the faster she can help that asshole King of yers." Adhnis' brows furrowed hard over her glittering silver eyes.

"Don't speak that way of the King!" Kaius met her expression, his fists clenched.

"And why not huh? He tried to have me killed, almost had ye arrested after ye fought back those creatures, and threatened ye."

Kaius winced. "His . . . His daughter was taken by my brother. He was just angry—"

"So what, that gives him the right to take it out on ye? The way I see it, he's a terrible King and the son of a monster who tried to eradicate my kin—"

"STOP IT! JUST STOP IT!" Kaius' hands flew to his ears and his eyes shut tight, not wanting to hear another word.

His heart thumped fast, his mind a whirlwind of doubt. After a few moments, he slowly opened his eyes, trembling slightly as he stared down to the grass below. "I . . . I can't. So much has happened today and I don't know what to believe. Who can I trust?" He lowered his hands and squeezed his biceps. "My brother . . . Vincent took Alaia. I know not where. I have to save them both. I just became a knight, and yet I have to save the fairies of your forest AND save Rosado from those monsters. I have to do this for a man I don't even know if I can . . ." Kaius stopped himself and gulped, unsure if he would regret his next words.

Adhnis remained quiet. The wind blew softly and in the distance, the stomping of hooves against dirt drummed ever so lightly. Kaius relaxed his grip and let his hands fall to his lap. His thoughts revolved around Vincent, King Cecilio, and Alaia.

What was he supposed to do?

Adhnis sighed heavily, drawing Kaius' attention. "Well, let me make it easier for ye." Slowing the flutter of her wings, she floated down, and landed on the grass.

"What are yo—"

She immediately raised a finger to her lips. "Shush, I need silence. It's easier to hear them when it's quiet."

"Them?" Kaius tilted his head curiously.

"The spirits in the wind, remember." Adhnis said with a pouting glare.

"Oh right, sorry." He whispered and tightly closed his lips.

With an approving nod, she faced forward and concentrated. Closing her eyes, she shook her hands in the air, and breathed in deeply. She released a steady breath as she raised her hands before her, palms to the sky.

Everything around them seemingly fell still, save for the horse now grazing nearby. After a moment, a strong breeze surged past him, startling him slightly. Soft indiscernible whispers sounded all around. A swirl of wind whirled to life about them, somehow feeling both warm and cool, and sent his loose blond strands of hair dancing around his face.

He looked down to the little fairy standing still as if she were made of stone, her white tattered dress billowed around her small, curvy frame and her white, tightly coiled hair waved about.

Kaius startled as thinly veiled, translucent green ribbons came soaring toward Adhnis in the breeze. As they reached her, they swirled around her at a swift pace. He wondered if those were the wind spirits Adhnis spoke of.

The green ribbons swirled faster and faster around her, stretching out to include him in the torrent. The whispers grew erratic, sounding similar to the soft howls of wolves echoing over the horizon at the birth of a full moon.

The wind and ribbons suddenly burst away, the surroundings fell still once again.

Adhnis opened her eyes, blinking a few times, and stared dead ahead. She then looked up to Kaius. "Okay, it looks like yer brother has taken the Princess to the ruined city of Kunnagar. It's just past the Pacífican border leading into Valtivar. Do ye know where that is?"

Kaius took in a breath, his brother's words now making sense. He slammed a hand to his face. "Dammit!"

"What? What is it?" Adhnis rushed to Kaius and placed her hands on his knees.

"Before my brother left he said he was going to where we belong. I'm so damned stupid for not realizing what he meant. I mean, earlier today he said our *true* home was Valtivar."

"Oh, I had a feeling ye weren't from Pacífica. After all, yer hair is so light and yer eyes are so blue. Anyway, the spirits explained that we still have some time, two nights to be exact. Your brother must wait for a new moon, when it's hidden from the world. Darkness is the key, I think is how they explained it. Also, ye need not worry about Rosado."

"Of course I have to worry! They're still dealing with those monsters. They don't have the magic to defeat them."

"THAT'S why we need to go to Eylowen. If ye help save my mother, she can place a barrier of light over Rosado to keep the monsters out. I wish we had the foresight to sustain such a barrier, but my people hadn't seen those monsters in centuries." Adhnis' eyes softened while her brows curved over them. "They ambushed us. By the time we knew what was happening, it was too late. So what do ye say, do we have a deal? Ye help us, and we help ye. Save my mother, then we head to Kunnagar. Together." She stretched her tiny hand out to him with a warm smile.

Kaius looked at her for a moment, then to Bosque Encantado. A shiver crawled up his spine. "Okay, but . . . I heard there *is* a barrier around your forest. Once a person enters it, they're lost forever."

Adhnis raised an eyebrow at him and planted her hands on her hips. "That's not what the barrier does." She raised a finger to him, as though one would if shushing a child. "If yer heart is just and ye are entering in peace without thoughts of harm, then ye'll be allowed entry. If not, the barrier turns ye around, and after a time, ye will find yerself outside Eylowen again."

"Oh, then why does such a rumor exist, and why were the monsters able to pass through?"

"As for the creatures, I don't know. The rumor though, it's likely yer *King* made something up to keep his people away from our border to honor the truce. The last time I saw him before today he tried to pick a fight with us, but Mother would have none of it. With the help of the spirits, the barrier was created, and try as he did, yer King could pose no threat. Hence the deal he spoke of in the castle."

Kaius shuddered. "Why . . . Why would King Cecilio pick a fight with your kin?"

Adhnis shrugged. "I was very young when he came with his soldiers, but I remember one thing very clearly; he had hoped to enslave us for our magic. Likely for some nefarious thing he had or may still have planned." She floated up into the air with a giggle, holding her stomach and trying to keep from bursting out laughing. "He had such a defeated scowl! Ye should have seen it, the stupid stinkhorn."

Kaius' heart weighed heavily in his chest. Was the King really so nefarious? Vincent and Alaia's warnings slowly started to sink in. Perhaps there was truth to what they said. However, King Cecilio's kindness toward him still shined the brightest in his memories. Whatever the King's reasons were, that kindness should've counted for something, Kaius thought. His brows furrowed a little in agitation. It wasn't like Alaia or Vincent had told him the whole truth either. What reason did Kaius have to believe any of them over the other?

"Hey." Adhnis floated before him. Her wings fluttered fast, her elbows resting on her knees, her expression still. "I don't know what happened in the city between ye, this Vincent, the Princess, and the King, but we can't dilly dally anymore." Adhnis' silver eyes softened. "I'm worried about my mother. Please, are ye ready to go?"

Kaius took a deep breath and exhaled steadily. He looked to the lush forest. "Save your mother and then we head to Kunnagar. Are you sure?" Kaius returned to Adhnis.

She nodded. "Aye. The spirits never lie and are *never* wrong."

He nodded without breaking his gaze. "Okay then." Kaius grabbed his helm and stood erect, sliding his helm back over his head. "You have a deal, Princess Adhnis." He flashed her a smile and stretched a hand out to her, palm up.

Adhnis smirked. "Hmph, call me Adhnis. I never really cared for titles." She hopped on his hand, and he raised her to his shoulder. She then hopped off and grabbed hold of his azure cape.

"Then you," he grabbed onto the horse's saddle, lifted himself up it, and prepared to ride, "can call me Kaius."

"Aww, but I like mister knight." She winked playfully.

He chuckled and answered, "I bet you do, little fairy." Kaius snapped the reins of the horse, and away they galloped toward the forest's edge.

6

KAIUS

THE FAIRY QUEEN

KAIUS STOOD SEVERAL FEET BEFORE the entrance to Bosque Encantado; Eylowen Forest to the fairies. The path leading in was unusually dark, even with the sun dipping low in the sky. The sun's rays were blotted out by the forest's vibrant green canopy. The only light emanating from within was the strange glow of mushrooms dimly bathing their immediate surroundings in a blue radiance. Each one was spaced a good distance apart, forming a path leading deeper into the darkness.

His heartbeat quickened, nervous as to what may await them should they continue forward. He looked to Adhnis resting on his shoulder, her silver eyes stared on with lightly curved brows.

"Princess—"

"Adhnis, remember? What is it? Yer Princess place so much importance on titles that ye're stuck using formalities?" The fairy's tone sounded chipper enough, but her trembling eyes betrayed her concern.

Kaius chuckled bashfully. "Um, sort of. The use of titles is important to King Cecilio, and thus, it should be to his subjects. That said, Alaia recently suggested that when it's just the two of us, we should forgo such formalities. However . . . I've been using titles for so long now, it's hard to simply drop them."

"That's interesting." Adhnis hopped off his shoulder and hovered in front of him.

Kaius watched as she moved ahead. He looked past her and into the forest, attempting to see what he could through the darkness. Nothing, save for the absence of light, seemed out of the ordinary. He took a deep breath, mustering the courage to push on. "So I just . . . walk right in?"

"Aye. As I said before, as long as yer intentions are true and just, the spirits of the forest will allow ye entry."

"Oh, so the spirits control the barrier? I thought it was the fairies that put it in place. Do they ever get tired?" Kaius cocked his head with curiosity. "I imagine keeping a spell active at all times must be quite draining."

"The spirits are a part of the world around us, they never tire, never wane. They are constant. They aren't tangible like ye and I. It's okay, I'll show ye."

"Okay." He responded nervously.

Adhnis flew further past the horse, heading toward the forest's border. On either side of the path stood two large trees. Overhead, branches were twisted and interlocked with each other, forming a natural archway. Watching as she reached the opening between the two trees, he spotted an odd flickering light briefly pulse and expand within the arch like ripples in a pond, then quickly fade from sight.

She looked back and waved for him to follow. "Come on Kaius!" Adhnis flashed him a wide grin.

"Right..." He tightened his grip on the horse's reins and hesitated, staring ahead.

Adhnis tilted her head lightly. "Kaius?"

"Why?" He asked in a whisper with eyes lowered. "Why did you pick me out of all the knights in the throne room? I . . . I'm not an experienced swordsman. Let alone—"

"Kaius." He looked up at Adhnis floating just beyond the entrance. She planted her hands firmly on her hips and looked at him softly. "This isn't some grand fairytale. Ye aren't some chosen one on a quest preordained by an all-powerful being to save a damsel in distress. Ye're overthinking things. Ye saved me from being murdered, so I chose you. Ye promised to save my kin, and in return, I will aid ye in saving yer brother and Princess. There's nothing else to it."

Kaius chortled softly. "It really is as simple as all that?"

"Aye." Her lips stretched into a smile again.

Kaius relaxed and let out a soft sigh. "Thank you, Adhnis."

"Hm? What for?" She raised a brow.

"Just, thank you." He rolled his shoulders back and gently kicked the sides of his horse, guiding her forward.

Kaius held his breath nervously as he passed through the archway. A strange, calming warmth washed over him. The memory of being held in his mother's arms, hugging him tightly and keeping him happy and safe. Once on the other side of the arch, the feeling faded, leaving him with an emptiness in his chest.

"Ye okay, Kaius?"

A tear rolled down his cheek followed by another and another, startling him. "What? Yeah," he answered while trying to wipe away the tears from under his helmet. "It's strange. I don't know where that came from."

She flew to him and placed a hand on his gauntlet, her eyes soft and warm. "When passing through the barrier and inspecting ye, the spirits' magic often brings yer happiest, kindest memory to the surface. So, whatever it was that ye remembered, ye should cherish it." Adhnis tilted her head with a kind smile.

Kaius returned the smile. The moment was abruptly interrupted as a slew of screams sounded in the distance. Frightened, his horse reared on her hind legs and refused to continue.

"Kaius, come on." Adhnis exclaimed. "We have to hurry!"

"I'm trying, but she isn't heeding me!"

"Then tie the beast up and leave it. My kin need us!"

"Dammit, okay!" Kaius hopped down and tied the reins to a nearby low hanging tree branch. As he turned around, he saw Adhnis' white glow slowly fading deeper into the forest.

He rushed forward, following her as fast as his legs would carry him into the darkness. Her light flickered on their passing surroundings. The mushroom path on the ground illuminated just enough of the roots and underbrush for him to avoid tripping as the two raced into the unknown.

Further and further they descended into the darkness. Screams and other eerie noises emanated in the distance, sounding louder as they continued in. Rushing straight down the path as fast as they could, both Kaius and Adhnis scanned the area as they ran, looking for any signs of movement in the shadows.

Stopping dead in his tracks, Kaius spotted something wiggling a short distance away. He quickly drew his sword thinking it could be one of the creatures he had fought in the city.

"Adhnis wait!" He exclaimed, causing Adhnis to turn to him.. "Look over there." Drawing closer, Adhnis' light chased away the shroud of darkness obscuring the mysterious figure.

A knee-high, egg-shaped pod pulsated irregularly. Its surface was covered in pustules, lightly oozing a foul substance the likes of which Kaius had never seen, and at that moment, never wanted to see again as bile slowly seeped its way into his throat. A faint violet light trickled through a structure resembling a web of bones beneath its translucent surface.

Adhnis flew about the pod, circling, and inspecting it. As she reached out to touch it, the thing suddenly jerked left and right, as though it were a boar caught in a net. Muffled screams sounded from within.

"By Gealach! Kaius, use yer sword to carefully pierce its surface."

"Are you sure?"

"Aye. I enchanted it, remember. Ye should be able to destroy anything created through this lesser dark magic with ease."

Kaius nodded and cautiously approached the pod. He raised his sword, pulled it back, and thrusted the blade forward. Piercing the dark things' surface, he slid the blade upward and rented it open.

A bright light burst from within. Many fairies hastily poured out, looking overjoyed and twirling about. The pod spilled from the cut all the way to the forest floor. It withered as if time had leapt forward and, with a puff, disintegrated before them.

The newly freed fairies shined in various colors of the rainbow, bathing the area in their combined glow. The darkness affecting the surroundings faded. Just then, the sunlight broke through the canopy and washed away the taint with its warmth.

The fairies quickly noticed Kaius and stared at him, the elation in their faces waned as alarm set in at the revelation that a human had managed to pass into their domain.

As Kaius opened his mouth to say something to settle their nerves, Adhnis swiftly flew in front of him to divert their attention to her. She flashed them a happy smile. "Thank the light of Grian! Ye're all okay.

Please, tell me ye have word of my mother."

"Princess, ye actually escaped! Thank the Sun and Moon." One of the fairies exclaimed.

"Princess Adhnis," another of the fairies interjected, "there's something ye should know about those . . . those pods. I think they're draining the spirits of their magic through us."

"What!?" Adhnis' eyes opened wide.

"That's not good, is it?" Kaius asked, stepping beside Adhnis.

She turned to him with worry. "No, it isn't. If the spirits are drained of their magic, they die. Their magic binds our fates together. The forest, the spirits, the fairies . . . we're all connected. If anything happens to one of the three pillars, it affects us all. If one falls, we all perish. That's it. No more fairies."

Adhnis' wings slowed, and she began to lower. Kaius stabbed his blade into the dirt, cupping his hands, and caught her as she slumped onto his palms. He raised her up. A defeated expression hung on her gentle face.

Kaius turned his gaze to the surrounding fairies, hoping to find out what else they may know. "What about her mother? The Queen. Is she safe?"

"She was captured as well." One of the fairies answered. "We all were. There's a strange creature now nesting deep within the queendom. It seems to be the source of all of this. Defeating it should free the forest from its hold."

"Okay, thank you. Try to find somewhere safe to hide. I will do what I can to free the rest of your kin and find the Queen." The fairies nodded and flew high up to find refuge in the canopy. Kaius turned back to Adhnis, raising her eye to eye. "Adhnis, I need you to try to focus. Are you ready to continue?"

She remained quiet for a moment. Adhnis took a deep breath and slapped her hands against her cheeks, reinvigorated. She hopped up and hovered above his hands, looking at him with renewed determination. "Okay, let's do this!"

Kaius nodded and raised his left gemmed gauntlet. "I think you'll be safer in here, to protect you from those pods."

Agreeing, she transformed into a bright ball of white light and entered the gem. He turned to his sword embedded in the ground and pulled it out, swung the dirt off the blade, and hurried further into the forest.

As they traveled deeper and deeper in, surrounded by an inky black darkness, Kaius' stomach filled with molten hot dread. Unease clawed at his thoughts. They had been in the forest for a while now and yet, they still hadn't come across any shadow beasts? He didn't like this.

On their way to the heart of the fairy queendom, following Adhnis' directions to the letter, Kaius found several more black pods filled with imprisoned fairies and freed them as they went. A feeling of dread deepened with every step he took, fearing a trap may lay in waiting. As he freed another group of fairies and grew closer to the center of the forest, a deep growl sounded from the shadows. Adhnis' kin fled into the leaves above.

He raised his sword, preparing to strike down anything that might come his way. The bushes behind him rustled. He quickly turned his head, spotting a small dark creature emerging, similar to the ones from Rosado. It jumped at him with claws raised.

Kaius swung his sword, cutting the thing in half, and watched as both halves dissipated into black dust floating in the wind. More creatures hopped out from the darkness, surrounding him on all sides. He swung his sword as fast as he could to quell their numbers. With each swing of the blade, more fell, sometimes two to three with each stroke, but their numbers continued to swell.

Kaius carried on with his assault. However, as the fighting lingered on, his limbs grew weary. His muscles still ached from the fighting at the castle.

He cursed as they just kept coming. If he didn't get them out of this soon, they were done for.

A series of terrible roars sounded behind him. He turned, and through the bramble of claws and teeth attacking him, he saw even more clambering down tree trunks and hopping out from the surrounding bushes. He began to wonder if their numbers were endless. They were going to overwhelm him.

Several of them suddenly slammed atop his back causing him to stumble forward. They viciously clawed at his armor and clothes. While swinging his sword, he reached back with his free hand and grabbed them one by one by the legs, hurling them off himself.

"Yer shield, Kaius! I'm right here with ye!" Adhnis screamed, her words dripping with worry.

"Right!" Kaius quickly raised his gemmed arm and enveloped himself in a dome of white light. Just as the light flashed to life, several beasts slammed against the barrier and fell onto the surrounding monsters. The creatures clambered to their feet and glared at him.

His breath fell heavy and sweat slid down over his brow, the salt stinging his eyes. He looked around, using the moment of pause to plan his next move. The monsters covered the forest in all directions, stretching out past the shroud of darkness. Kaius' eyes slowly widened in shock, unsure of what to do.

"Run Kaius, run!" Adhnis bellowed from the crystal. *"Follow the balgan-buachair, they will show ye the way!"*

"The what!?"

"THE MUSHROOMS!"

"Got it!"

Kaius scanned over the horde, searching for the mushrooms' light. Small flashes of a blue glow peeked past the creatures as they scurried about. Spotting a small path through, he dismissed the light shield and made a break for it.

Kaius rushed as fast as his tired legs would carry him, slicing enemies and pods as he made his way down the pathway. Running on and on, he broke through the monsters' ranks, hearing the creatures angered hisses and growls fading in the distance.

Continuing on, he spotted small white lights shimmering not too far ahead. Reaching the small glimmers, he skidded to a stop. The area felt cold, sending gooseflesh up his neck.

Little crystals dotted the ground while others hung in the air, each emitting a dim white light. The blue mushrooms littered the ground here, more plentiful than they were on the path. The blue and white lights mixed together and softly bathed the nearby trees in their glow. Though it was still fairly dark, he was glad to have the extra illumination.

Kaius squinted his eyes in an attempt to peer through the darkness, trying to make out the forms encircling the trees. Small openings, resembling doors and windows, were carved into the bark.

He started to wonder if this was how the fairies lived, but the moment of respite was interrupted as a great weight slammed down into his back, nearly dropping him to the floor. Large hands wrapped around him, threatening to restrict his arms to his sides. He managed to free a hand and grabbed hold of whatever it was behind him, hurling it with all his might over his shoulder.

Without a moment's hesitation, Kaius stabbed his blade into the thing's muscular chest. "Wait, this one seems different, broader and taller than the ones in the castle. Are they changing?"

Deep growls rumbled loudly around him, guttural and cacophonous. Try as he might, he was unable to see anything that could be looming in the shadows. Glowing orange eyes started popping into view, shining with a dim glow. "Dammit, Adhnis I can't see. This forest is just too dark!"

"Use my shield and run. Let it light yer way!"

"I didn't think I could move when using it."

"AYE! Of course you can, you dummy. It's magic!"

He startled. "Okay I'm sorry!"

Kaius raised his left arm and summoned forth the light barrier once more. The light of the barrier illuminated around him and made clear the creatures before him.

Their forms were wide and heavily muscular. Their long, thin biceps lead down to massive, monstrous forearms and hands. They were taller than those he first encountered in Rosado, but smaller than the looming brute he faced in the castle's courtyard.

"Wha-What are these things!?" Adhnis exclaimed, her voice dripping in horror.

The barrier around Kaius shifted and flickered. Could her fear interfere with her magic? "Adhnis, I need you to remain calm. I think your worry is affecting the barrier. Breathe deep."

"How are ye not scared!"

"Scared isn't the word, more like terrified." He chuckled nervously. His heart raced with the intensity of a war drum. Kaius couldn't give into his fears now. Taking a deep breath, he looked at the monsters gathering around him and exhaled, trying to calm his nerves. Everyone was counting on him. Alaia. The fairies. Even Rosado. He couldn't falter now. Kaius could do this. He had to.

The creatures started to draw toward him, shifting about, and encircling him. There was no opening. Kaius cursed with a sneer. Were they inspecting him? Perhaps they were looking for a weakness.

"Why aren't they attacking?"

"How much you want to bet they're waiting for one of us to falter. For our shield to waver." Kaius gulped nervously. Sweat poured down the side of his face. He spread his legs apart, readying himself to sprint. "Adhnis, I'm going to run straight ahead with the barrier up. Hopefully they'll bounce off just as the smaller ones did. Are you ready?"

"Hmph! Please, I just have to sit here, not lifting a finger." Adhnis boasted, her tone now seeming more confident.

Kaius dashed forward, the barrier repelling many of the muscular creatures as they smashed into it, their blows nullified by the shield. A feeling of relief budded within him as he put some distance between himself and the creatures.

As he looked back, one of the monsters landed with a loud thud in his path, its hooves planted firmly and hands raised. The monstrous hands clutched onto the front of the shield. Its hooves dug deep into the dirt and stopped Kaius dead in his tracks.

"SHIT!"

"Quick, drop the shield and hit it with your sword!"

Kaius dismissed the shield and held his sword toward the creature's chest. The monster stumbled forward and fell into the blade. As it dissipated into wisps of dust, Kaius was surprised to find he could see without the barrier. A large pod a few feet away glowed with an eerie violet and azure light, illuminating a small area around him.

He cautiously proceeded, taking a few steps toward it, and heard a strange pulse emanate from within. "What is that—" Loud roars sounded far in the distance behind him, causing him to jolt. "Whatever!" Kaius raised his blade and thrusted it into the pod, sliding the blade upward.

The pod spilled over as its light faded, revealing a faint white light. He peered inside and saw a fairy lying within. Her skin was of a deep umber with silver makeup painted over her eyelids. Thick, white tight curls were pulled back, fastened into a cloud-like ponytail. Beads of glowing crystals encircled her head. Her regal white dress sparkled in the faint light as the crystal jewelry twinkled about her.

"MOTHER!"

KAIUS

IMPRISONED MAGIC

STARTLED, KAIUS REACHED OUT TO GRAB HOLD of the Queen, but just before he could get her secured, something slammed into the ground before him, lumbering over the dissipating pod, and let out an ear-piercing roar. Not having a chance to react and summon his barrier, something rammed into him with such a force it sent him hurtling into a tree. The air escaped his lungs.

He fell to the ground hard, his chest tight with pain and his breath raspy and coarse. Kaius heard faint sounds about him. A scream rang out, followed by a pounding noise. He struggled to open his eyes and saw a blurry dark world around him. Kaius shook his head, his vision slowly clearing. He then discovered the origin of the noise and the thing that had hit him.

The creature looked to be some sort of combination between the muscular monsters and a spider. Its body was black, orange, and yellow. Eight legs protruded from its waist, tipped like that of spears and covered in thorns. Long, thin arms stretched from broad shoulders, punctuated by unusually thick forearms and hands. Its posterior was as bulbous as a black widow's while four jagged horns jutted from atop its head.

It pounded its monstrous hands on the ground and roared, then it charged toward him. Kaius jolted, pushed himself up, and rolled to the side, just barely dodging the creature's attack. With a swipe of one of its massive hands, it hit Kaius, knocking him back a good distance further from the Queen.

A loud cough escaped his lips, the taste of hot copper filling his mouth. "Dam-Dammit—Ugh!" Kaius attempted to lift himself up off the ground, but his arms trembled under his weight and he fell to the dirt.

"*Kaius!*"

"Ad-Adhnis . . . fly to your mother a-and get her out of here!"

"*Are ye kidding me? I'm not leaving ye!*"

"I-It's okay, your mother needs you. Take her somewhere safe. Please, Adhnis." Kaius' voice was soft and trembled.

He winced, but managed to stagger to his feet. The spider beast skittered restlessly from side to side, growling and cautiously moving to close the distance between them.

After a moment of silence, Adhnis reluctantly groaned in defeat. *"Dammit, why do ye have to be right! I'll come back for ye. Just hold on."*

Kaius chortled, feigning confidence. Adhnis flew in a streak of light to her mother. The beast roared and began moving toward Adhnis. Seeing this, Kaius jumped toward the beast and rammed it with a shoulder tackle, pushing it as far back as he could.

Reaching the Queen, Adhnis picked up her mother and fled, their light disappearing into the darkness, leaving Kaius with only his glowing blade for light.

"Okay, n—" Pain coursed through his overworked, battered body.

Kaius' muscles locked up as the pain shot through his joints. The spider beast got back on its tarsi and loomed tall over him. Kaius' eyes widened with concern. The beast then slapped Kaius with the back of its hand, causing him to crash into the ground again.

As he landed and rolled to a stop, he let out a plethora of bloodied coughs. His muscles tensed and his head rang.

He cursed through clenched teeth. Was it toying with him? Kaius demanded for his body to get up. To fight. The fairies were counting on him. Rosado was depending on him. Vincent and Alaia . . . They needed him. So he had to get up. He had to.

He slid an arm under himself and pushed off the ground. His limbs trembled under the weight, but he managed to get back to his feet. Kaius pointed his blade at the monster, his free arm clasped over his armored stomach, and he continued to cough. More blood spilled out over his lips.

Kaius spat the blood from his mouth. "Okay you beast, let's end this!" He glared at the creature in the dim light.

It tilted its head for a moment, as if confused, then roared and charged. Kaius dodged quickly to the side, the creature nearly trampling him as it passed. Seeing an opening, Kaius swung his sword with as much strength as he could muster. The beast moved with almost imperceptible speed and with a loud thud, the blade slammed into the creature's hand.

Kaius' breath caught in his throat, stunned. The blade had been able to cut these creatures down with ease so far, so why not now? His eyes widened with fear.

Adhnis' words from earlier echoed in his mind: *Aye. I enchanted it, remember. Ye should be able to destroy anything created through this lesser dark magic with ease.*

Kaius took a troubled gulp and his heart dropped into his stomach. The creature raised the sword with a roar and punched the flat part of the blade with its free hand. It shattered completely.

Shock set in as Kaius stumbled back with mouth agape. Looking at what was left of the broken sword, the light faded and despair hung heavy in the air.

No way. This couldn't be happening.

His body trembled and seized as darkness engulfed him entirely. Frantically looking around, he hoped beyond hope to find any source of light, however, he found nothing but darkness. Kaius' knees grew weak. The area was still. Silent. He tried to quiet his breath, hoping the beast was as blind as he was in the darkness.

His muscles burned and a hollow weight filled his chest. Cursing repeatedly, what in Helgad Inferis was he to do now? He couldn't die here. Not now.

The thumping of something scuttling behind him sounded in the darkness. He turned to face it, but the sound faded away as quickly as it had come.

Kaius struggled to control his thoughts in his panic.

You're out of your league.

Shut up. He retorted to himself.

If you can't stop this beast, how can you save Alaia and Vincent?

SHUT UP!

He slowly moved about, trying to add distance between himself and the creature lurking in the shadows. Stumbling on something loose under his footing, he started to fall. He braced for impact, but something grabbed him and pulled him from behind.

"DAMMIT!"

Slamming into the creature's chest, he struggled to break free, but its arms held him tight in an embrace and began to squeeze. Kaius' armor screeched and popped, pressing into his chest and arms as it buckled under the pressure. He screamed out in pain.

His hands tingled and arms numbed, causing his grip to weaken. Kaius' broken sword slipped from his fingers and fell to the ground with a soft thud. Rising higher and higher into the air, he braced himself as best he could, expecting next to be thrust down into the earth and crushed. Instead, the creature sent him soaring through the air.

Slamming into the ground with a hard thud, he rolled a short distance and lost all sense of his surroundings. Kaius gasped, trying to catch his breath as he attempted to turn over to his belly.

He pushed himself off the ground as best he could, trying to ignore the pain surging through his limbs. With every ounce of strength he had left, he crawled forward, hoping the direction would take him further from the creature, to buy himself some time.

This was bad. He was defenseless. No sword. No magic. Nothing. What could he do? He . . . He didn't want to die. Not here. Not like this.

The ringing in his head erupted and a raging inferno burst to life in his chest. Cursing with a pained groan, Kaius desperately demanded to know what was going on with him. Mourning what at that moment seemed like his inevitable end, he let out a cry so loud it echoed through the trees and into the darkness.

Something then caught his eye. Kaius looked up and briefly spotted a bright spark through the shadows. It hurtled his way. Closing the distance so fast, he didn't have a chance to react. The beacon of light stopped before him as a gust of wind whipped by. The light then exploded in all directions, revealing Adhnis' mother, the Queen of Eylowen Forest.

She stared past him with anger burning so intensely in her silver eyes, he wondered for a moment if perhaps she wasn't there to help him. Did she see him as an intruder? No, that couldn't be. Kaius was sure that Adhnis told her mother about him.

The creature could be heard lurking a short distance behind Kaius, its legs thumping erratically as though hesitant to attack.

Kaius' eyes were locked on the Queen's radiance. Her light bathed the surrounding in her brilliance, seemingly impervious to the darkness.

She brought her hands close together. Stringing a slurry of words in a language unknown to him, a bright light sparkled between her palms. The Queen raised it in the air above her head. As her arms locked straight, the light exploded outward, blinding Kaius.

He covered his eyes with his arms and a loud screech pierced his ears. Kaius heard the creature's hurried steps as it scurried away. While the light dimmed and he opened his eyes, to his surprise, an elegantly made sword floated in the air before him in colors of silver, gold, and bright blue.

"Use this sword to defeat the creatures. I was unaware of just how weak the barrier between the Mortal Realm and the Shadow Realm had become. This weapon is said to have been forged on high. I entrust it to ye. Use it, and keep us safe."

Kaius was taken aback by the soothing, gentle voice of the Queen in contrast to the energetic cheer of Adhnis'. He looked at the hand and a half longsword floating before him. He reached out, and a strange yet wonderful warmth radiated from its grip. It washed over him, easing the pain in his head and chest.

Kaius wrapped his hands around the hilt, taking hold of it as tightly as he could, and felt its warmth flow through his limbs. The sword suddenly dropped, no longer floating in air as its weight rested in his hands.

He was left in awe. What was this power he felt coursing through him?

Adjusting his grip, he was surprised at how light the weapon had become. In awe of the glowing sword, he pushed himself up off the ground. A soft sigh escaped his lips. He turned around and spotted the creature just barely poking its head out from behind a tree.

It noticed Kaius' gaze and roared out, dashing toward him with claws raised. Kaius lifted the blade high in the air, held his breath, and swiftly brought it down toward the creature's head, hoping it would not break as his last sword had.

Once the blade met its mark, it sliced clean through, cleaving the creature in two. The monster fell and faded into black dust, dissipating as it touched the ground.

Kaius exhaled harshly, happy to be free of the beast, but felt his wounds intensely. A weight lifted from his shoulders and a tired chuckle escaped his lips. His knees buckled as exhaustion set in, his eyes fluttering nearly to a close. With that, he fell to the ground, dropped the sword, and breathed heavily with harsh grunts.

He slid his helm from his head and let it fall to the dirt. His blond hair fell over his face, no longer held neatly back by his hair tie.

A warm light slowly seeped through the leaves above him. Kaius looked up, feeling the cool air embrace him. He closed his eyes, trying to calm his labored breath, and felt a strange rumbling beneath his legs.

Kaius looked at the magical sword as it rose from the ground, levitating before him. It radiated a pulsing light, slow at first, but pulsed faster and faster. The light exploded out in golden rays, startled him, and caused him to fall on his backside.

The light spread throughout the forest, chasing away the dark taint. With the fairy queendom now fully restored, the light of the setting sun bathed the forest in its warm radiance.

The glowing sword dimmed, and it fell to the ground, now appearing no different than a normal sword. The Fairy Queen hovered beside him, placing a hand on his pauldron, her soft light commanding his attention. "That's it young one, take a breath. From what my daughter told me, ye've had quite the day. If there's anything ye need from us, tell me, and it shall be done."

"H-How did those things get in through that barrier of yours?" His brows pushed against each other as he struggled to keep his eyes open.

"They crept in through the shadows cast by the forest, stowing away until a true threat could enter. They launched a sneak attack so swiftly, the fight was over before it had begun. Anything else? That can't be all?" She smiled warmly.

Tired, Kaius forced the words from his lips, "R-Rosado. The city needs help . . . the monsters . . . Please. I-I know what Adhnis—"

The Queen pressed a finger to her full lips, shushing him. "That's enough on that. I'll do what I can regardless of my feelings for that King of yers, but first I must see to ye."

Kaius tried to slow his thoughts, but the Queen's words popped into his mind. "You said the sword was from on high, but then why was it here, in your possession no less?"

"Originally, the sword was protected by *yer* people, Kaius. That's yer name, isn't it?"

Kaius' eyes widened. "My . . . My people?"

She nodded. "Aye. Yer ancestors were the only ones brave enough to face off against the monsters, those who come from what my kin call the Shadow Realm. The Kunnagarians struggled to defeat the creatures until someone from on high gifted them that weapon. They used it to seal the beasts away. Sadly, since the fall of yer city—"

"The barrier between realms weakened . . ." Kaius answered softly, his brother's words becoming clearer.

She nodded. "Aye."

Kaius' head felt light. His eyelids fluttered as he lowered his head to the ground, his breath shallow.

"Kaius?!"

"Adhnis . . ." He turned his head to the Queen. "How is she? Is she okay?"

The Queen laughed softly. "She's fine. I asked my daughter to see to our kin with the help of her lover and protector, Leona. Adhnis has proven quite the steady young woman with all that has happened. Oh! Adhnis also said something about checking on a horse?"

"O-Oh, right . . . I was forced to leave my horse tied by the forest's entrance." Kaius tried to lift himself up once more, but fell back on his bottom. "Your name, what was it?"

"It's Throstnie, Queen of Eylowen Forest. Is there . . . something else ye want to ask me?"

Kaius eyed her for a moment. His arms trembled, trying to keep himself up. "I . . . I don't suppose you know what's wrong with me." He chuckled, doubting the Queen could possibly know the answer.

She fluttered to one of his knees and landed atop it. Queen Throstnie looked him up and down, and her eyes lingered on his heaving chest. "I may have an answer, but I'll need to inspect ye further to know for certain."

Kaius' eyes widened. "Oh, seriously? I was joking."

"This isn't something ye should joke about, Kaius. Ye're from Kunnagar, correct?" At Kaius' hesitant nod, the Queen continued. "Those born with Kunnagarian blood have an innate ability for magic. Some simply awaken to it faster than others. It has been a long while since I saw an awakening, but nevertheless, it happens to everyone. Yer hair will go as white as the clouds and yer eyes violet. Ye are connected to something called the Cosmics."

Kaius blinked at her, dumbfounded. "No, you have to be mistaken. I-I can't be—"

Queen Throstnie hopped off his knees and glided down to the grass, placing her hands firmly on her hips. "Ye're quite the timid one it seems. Come now, remove yer armor. The trek won't be long, but I'd like it to be easy on ye."

He looked down at his armor, then to the small clearing encircled by trees with rich red-banded polypores spiraling around their trunks. Bright crystals hung from the branches, small entryways, and the canopy. Crystals also jutted from the ground like tiny swords, shimmering with rainbow sparkles as sunlight kissed their surface.

Kaius then glanced at the golden sword beside him resting on the earth. "You just . . . want me to leave my stuff here? Out in the open?"

"Aye, of course. Don't worry yerself, everything'll be fine. Now come on, I have much to do and very little time to do it, as do ye." With a flutter of her wings, Queen Throstnie rose into the air and hovered before him, arms crossed.

Kaius let out a long sigh and acquiesced. She was as impatient as Adhnis. With a soft chuckle, he removed his armor and placed it on the ground by the sword. Though free of the weight of the armor's burden, his body ached all the same. Kaius then slowly pushed himself up to stand with a loud groan.

Stumbling forward, he clutched his stomach, feeling a painful pinch in his side. Cursing through clenched teeth, he now realized the beast must've hit him harder than he thought. Everything was hurting. Pain soared through his body.

"Kaius, come this way! Rest here so I can heal ye." With that, Throstnie flew toward a thin path covered in white petals.

Kaius struggled to push his battered body forward, fumbling his steps and dragging himself over to a tree to help keep him on his feet. He shuffled after the Fairy Queen as best he could, occasionally stopping to regain his balance on the passing trees. As they reached a sizable, circular area, curtains of vines brushed over Kaius' shoulders, leaving white, pink, and lavender petals in his blond hair. A small flowing river surrounded the area. Moss coated the ground so thickly he mused it could be used as a bed.

"Lay down here, Kaius." Queen Throstnie gestured toward the moss with a kind smile.

"O-Oh, okay." Kaius sluggishly nodded and cautiously made his way to the mixture of green and purple moss. His feet sank slightly with each step.

Once at its center, he lowered himself with a heavy grunt and a sigh of relief. The moss was surprisingly comfortable, its surface soft against his back. Closing his eyes, he breathed in deeply the scent of earth and wisterias, calming his aching body and troubled thoughts.

The flutter of wings sounded beside him, most likely Queen Throstnie, but he was unsure. Strands of his hair gently slid away from his face. "How're ye feeling, Kaius?"

"So . . . tired."

She giggled softly. "Understandable. Can ye open yer eyes?" Kaius winced, and though struggling, managed to open his eyes, and saw the Fairy Queen through a haze. "With the aid of the spirits, I'll be inspecting yer magical center."

"My . . . what?" He asked groggily.

"Yer magical center. Although ye're born a sorcerer of Kunnagar and I a fairy, our magics flows from the same place. Right here." She tapped the very center of her chest with her long fingers.

"Our hearts?" Kaius' eyes narrowed.

"Aye. Think of it like this. We both have a chamber in our being that allows us the use of magic. For my kind, this chamber is a gateway that allows magic to flow into us. Our magic originates from the spirits of nature who use this chamber as a conduit for their magic. For ye, if I remember correctly, the chamber acts as a well. This well is self-sustaining, meaning ye alone are the source of yer own magic."

Queen Throstnie grabbed the folds of her gown and lifted up the fabric, her bejeweled feet glittered against the lowering sun. "Try to remain still. It should only take but a moment."

She glided over Kaius' chest. Her footsteps were so light against his skin he could just barely feel her at all. Upon reaching the center of his chest, she knelt down, and extended her hands to him. She took a deep breath, and as she exhaled a round, bright white light appeared in her palms.

Kaius lightly gasped at the sensation. A chilling surge spread through his chest into the rest of his being, slightly unnerving him. His heart raced and his breath quickened.

"Kaius, ye must calm down. I promise, I'm only inspecting, nothing . . ." Her gaze remained fixated on his chest, her brows furrowing.

Queen Throstnie's sudden silence caused him to worry. "Is-Is everything okay?"

The glow of her hands dimmed and vanished. She raised a hand to her chin. "That's interesting."

"What is?" Kaius' brows curved over his eyes.

"I sense yer magic . . . is being blocked. It's impossible for ye to awaken it using the normal method of yer kin." Queen Throstnie looked at Kaius, her silver eyes softening with worry.

"What's it being blocked by?"

The Fairy Queen remained silent for a moment, then placed a hand flat to his chest. "Ye."

Kaius winced. How could this be? He didn't even know he could do magic like Vincent. How could Kaius have locked something away he didn't even know he had?

He recalled the few times he was allowed to see his brother. They usually spent their time arguing about the Ligeras. His heart panged with guilt. Kaius' eyes stung and his sight blurred. "I . . . I never once thought to ask my brother if I too could use magic. Should I have? Would he have been able to help me? Maybe—"

"Kaius, listen to me. Whatever ye experienced in yer past, that is why yer magic is blocked. Yer people used a method long ago to force open another's magical center. This method allowed one to traverse another's mind to help summon forth their magic. This method over time was deemed too dangerous to the caster and was ceased. The magic within would often fight back and attack the traveler, considering them a trespasser. Once the aforementioned method had ended, the standard practice became to place the individual in dire circumstances."

Kaius parted his lips, wanting to say something, but the words didn't come. He looked at the leaves far above him, hearing the wind gently rustle through the trees. His mind traveled back to Rosado when he was ten falls young. The waves slid on the beach's sands as his brother performed amazing spells. Vincent commanded fire to whirl around him. Afterward, he guided water into a pillar stretching over ten feet high and smashed it down, creating a large splash.

His brother then stood as still as a statue, the winds brushing his white hair strands back as he stared out into the ocean. The water gently splashed against his ankles. Vincent's face was so somber. Kaius didn't know why his brother looked so sad, but now, he slowly began to understand.

Queen Throstnie smiled warmly at Kaius. "I wouldn't dare attempt the method myself, but I think I can send ye to yer magic. Have ye meet it yerself. That should be safe."

Kaius' heart skipped a beat. "What . . . What will it look like when I see it?"

She shook her head. "I don't know. All I can do is send ye to it. Once there, it will be up to ye. Don't be afraid of it. Don't run away from it. It is a part of ye, and most likely wants to be free, to help ye, but ye must accept it."

"What happens if I don't?"

She looked at him for a moment, grasping her chin with brows furrowed, and then answered. "I don't know."

Kaius' head fell back onto the moss and his gaze drifted to the trees again. He took a deep breath and exhaled gently. The sun's rays twinkled in through the leaves, harking back to when he was six or seven and resting under a kapok tree with Vincent beside him.

His brother had just created little purple light fireflies with his magic. Kaius watched wide eyed with wonder. They were then visited by Alaia. Like Kaius, she was small and full of joy.

Kaius recalled Vincent's hesitation, how guarded he was with her. She handed him a white maga, a symbol of peace. Vincent was taken aback by the gesture, holding the flower and simply twirling it in his hand. Her smile was so wide. Alaia's mother then called her and so she left, curtsying a goodbye.

Vincent, after a moment, handed Kaius the flower. His words were still clear to this very day: *Here, Kaius. I . . . don't think I'll ever find peace here.*

Kaius' chest twisted tightly. A pang resonated throughout his entire being. His brows furrowed and resolved burned within him. "If my magic can help save Alaia and Vincent, then I must accept it." He looked to Queen Throstnie. "Send me to my magic."

She nodded in affirmation and stretched her hands out to his chest. "Close yer eyes and calm yer mind, Kaius." Kaius nodded and situated himself on the mossy bed, closing his eyes. "To help quiet yer mind, focus on the wind blowing overhead and the flowing waters of the river around ye."

The wind blew with a soft whistle and the water gently splashed against rocks and banks. He took a deep breath and felt his body fall.

Kaius' eyes jolted open, and he found himself surrounded by darkness.

He scanned the void, finding a neverending stretch of nothingness. Taking a step forward, a ripple of violet light flashed across the ground in all directions. A glowing, glittering violet path came into existence as the ripple passed over it. The once dark void quickly filled with twinkling stars.

His heart raced nervously and his stomach churned. He assumed he had to move forward, so he did.

Without any other clues to go by, Kaius strode up the somewhat winding path. He walked for what seemed like miles. His hands trembled as he massaged them. Reaching the end of the path, he stopped, and examined what seemed to be folds in space forming something resembling a doorway.

The creases began to glow brightly in an orangish-red light. The face of the door looked no different than the night sky around him.

He tilted his head to the side. "That's odd."

Kaius stepped closer and placed his hands on its surface. Surprisingly, it felt no different than any normal wooden door. He slid his hand down its rough surface and to the side, hoping to find a handle. Instead, he found a small rectangular indentation.

He gulped and pushed the door. As it opened, a powerful blast of heat engulfed him. Kaius let out a scream. The world around him changed, morphing into a fairly large empty room. A few windows dotted the walls, but no doorways could be found. Fire raged around him. The ceiling bowed inward and the floor creaked and dipped down where he stood.

Kaius shielded his face from the flames with his arms. Sweat poured down his face. "Wh-What is going on!? Your majesty? Queen Throstnie? Anyone!? PLEASE—" He let out a harsh cough as he breathed in the black smoke filling the room. His eyes stung.

A child's cry suddenly rang out amongst the roaring of the fire. A portion of the ceiling collapsed, sending cinders soaring. "Hello? Whe-Where are you?"

The child's cry continued, growing louder and louder, echoing through the room. Kaius tried to find its source, narrowed his eyes, and peered through the flames, but saw nothing. The cries grew deafening.

A ringing in his mind pierced him to his core. He fell to his knees and grasped the sides of his head. "AGH! What is this? What's going on!? Please, someone, anyone! MAKE IT STOP!"

The world around him immediately fell silent. The roaring of the fire, the child's cry, and the ringing all vanished without a trace.

He opened his eyes and found he was still in the room. The fires still burned, but no longer made a sound. The thick smoke didn't choke or sting him, while a bright white figure stood before him.

Kaius stared up at the glowing being, its silhouetted form familiar, however, he knew not why. He sat himself straight, his mind racing with questions, but only one escaped his lips. "Are you . . . the magic within me?"

The figure was quiet. It leaned forward and stretched a hand out. Kaius stared at the glowing hand. It radiated a gentle coolness that was both unnerving, and somehow soothing. Although his chest tightened, Kaius felt a familiarity toward the figure, as though it had always been with him, something he had known for a very long time.

The memory of Vincent standing before him with a hand outstretched flashed into his mind. Kaius just couldn't take his hand. He was too afraid of the King. If Kaius took it now, would his magic awaken? What consequences awaited him if he did? What awaited him if he refused? Kaius' brows furrowed. Vincent, how betrayed his older brother must've felt. He couldn't make the same mistake twice.

He slowly brought his hand toward the light, hovering over it for a moment. Kaius' hand trembled, nervous, and unsure if he was making the right choice.

Then the hand covered in light stretched closer, startling him. He had to do this.

He took a deep breath and grasped the hand. The figure's glow intensified, growing brighter and brighter. Kaius shielded his eyes with his free arm. The light grew so bright it enveloped everything in sight. The room, the fire, the sky, and the darkness outside, all gone. Everything was white.

KAIUS

AWAKEN

"HOW DO YE FEEL? Can ye feel yer magic? Do ye—"

Kaius raised a hand and dismissively shooed Adhnis with a smirk. The little fairy giggled and playfully dodged with a flourish. "Come on Adhnis, that's enough. I told you I don't feel any different. Let me eat in peace." He chortled uncomfortably while taking a bite of a delectable fairy fruit which grew only in this forest, gifted to him by Queen Throstnie.

Adhnis rested her elbows on her knees and cupped her face in her palms. "Are ye sure? Ye must be feeling *something* by now. Ye slept all night. Undisturbed too, yer welcome by the way. Ye looked so adorable sleeping." She grinned mischievously from ear to ear.

Kaius' jaw tightened, his cheeks heating up. Bashfully, he looked away with pursed lips. "Oh come off it."

Adhnis kicked her tiny legs in the air and burst out laughing, which made Kaius' lips tremble with embarrassment. Instead of choosing to argue, which was no small effort, he quietly shoved several fruits into his mouth and glanced away to his horse that was grazing nearby. It had been retrieved by Adhnis and her guardian lover, Leona if he remembered right, while he slept, to which Kaius was thankful.

"Anyway, do ye reeeeeally not feel anything, Kaius?" Adhnis rested her chin on the back of her hands and stared at him intently.

Swallowing, Kaius briefly glanced her way before looking back into his now empty hands. He stared at his palms, his back against the trunk of a tree. Kaius rolled his shoulders back, happy to be free of pain thanks to the Queen's healing while he rested. As he moved his arms about, his elbows lightly knocked into something next to him.

His gloves and armor rested beside him on the grass. Kaius looked over to his silver and azure armor, the only signs of fighting left on its surface were tiny scratches here and there. The dents had been flattened out and the metal wiped clean, shining brightly in the sunlight.

He smiled softly. "Adhnis, remind me to thank the fairies who cleaned and fixed my armor, okay?"

"I will, but stop trying to change the subject. Feel it. Dig deep. Tell me. Now." Her face was still, her eyes locked on his, and carefully inspected him.

Kaius' lips thinned as he chewed the inside of his cheeks. "As I said, I don't feel any different. Did your mother say something before she left this morning for Rosado?"

"Hmmm," she glanced up to the trees, "no, she just asked me to keep an eye on ye and to help ye with yer magic. So, how about this: try to conjure something."

Kaius raised an eyebrow. "Uh, like what?"

"Anything. Try to summon fire in the palm of yer hand."

"Okay, but don't our magics come from different places?" Kaius cocked his head to the side, unsure of what to do.

"Where our magic comes from is different, yes, but how we bring it forth should be similar. Reach deep inside yerself, to yer center, and call it forth. Visualizing what ye want helps too. So, just try it. Call for fire," Adhnis raised a hand, palm up, "on the palm of yer hand."

With a long sigh, Kaius raised a hand, and focused. "Just call it, huh. It's that easy?" He stared at his palm for a moment longer, then closed his eyes.

He quieted his thoughts and focused, picturing the flame. A gentle breeze flew around him, rustling the leaves of the nearby trees, and lightly brushed his hair against his cheeks. Kaius took a deep breath and exhaled softly.

Calling upon the fire within him, he waited and waited for something to happen, feeling sillier by the moment as nothing happened. Was this really going to work? No. He couldn't think like that. It had to work. Kaius called for the flame once more and to his surprise, a warm sensation sparked to life in his chest.

Kaius startled. Was that it? Was that the magic? He focused his concentration with a renewed resolve as the warmth grew and stretched to his shoulder, down his arm, and to his hand.

His heart raced, pounding against his ribcage as the heat collected in the center of his hand and continued to grow. He took another deep breath, trying to calm himself, and spread his fingers wide. Kaius' face scrunched as he tried to concentrate.

"Come on—"

"Yer highness! Yer highness, are ye still here?"

Kaius jolted, immediately dropping his focus. The heat dwindled and dispersed, leaving only a tingling sensation in his hand. He cursed inwardly as the traces of magic faded away. It felt so strange to him. Kaius rubbed his hands together, massaging the point where the heat had gathered.

He looked up to see where the voice had come from. Some fairies, decorated in green, enter the small clearing.

"Princess Adhnis, there ye are."

"Is everything okay?" Adhnis asked and turned to the fairies. As they reached her, they all bowed low.

"Has Queen Throstnie made it back already?" Kaius asked, tucking his trembling hand between his bicep and ribcage, arms crossed, hoping the pressure would stop the tingling under his skin. The fairies in green looked at him, confused, and then to each other, falling quiet.

"It's okay, he saved us from those Shadow Realm beasts." Adhnis interjected. "Ye can trust him."

"If ye're sure, yer highness." A fairy with bronze skin, monolid emerald eyes, and braided green hair looked to Kaius, hovering closer. "Queen Throstnie should be working on the barrier there by now. It'll still be some time before her return. Actually, we came here for another matter."

"And what's that, Guardian?"

"Guardian?" Kaius looked at Adhnis curiously.

"Oh right, fairies like these," Adhnis gestured to them, "born with green eyes and hair, have a strong connection to the earth. Because of this, they can easily speak to the spirits of the forest and everything connected to it."

"That's why we are here, yer highness. It's the spirits, they're terrified."

Adhnis turned to the Guardian with curved, concerned brows. "Of what?"

"Those shadow beasts have amassed atop the hilled lands by our borders."

Adhnis visibly shuttered. "How-How many?"

"Too many to count yer highness, but what's odd is that they don't really seem to be moving. They're just . . . standing there."

Kaius stared at the small group with eyes trembling. "I'm sorry, but what do you mean by hilled lands? Do you mean Costa De Egale?"

The Guardian gave him an agitated look. "I don't know the names humans have given these lands, but it's the land connecting to the massive cliffside North of us."

Kaius' heart skipped a beat. North of this forest was Kunnagar. Was Vincent building a wall to keep people out?

He placed the tip of his thumb between his teeth, nervously biting at the nail. Cursing to himself, he wondered what his older brother was planning. Kaius turned to his armor and hastily began strapping the pieces on, one by one.

Adhnis, surprised, turned to him. "Kaius, what are ye doing?"

"I've rested long enough. I have to find my brother in Kunnagar."

"No ye can't! Princess, please talk some sense into him. Those creatures' numbers stretch from where the cliffs overlook the sea, all the way to the forest in the West. For all we know, they may have spread their darkness there as they did here. They may as well be an army."

"Be that as it may, I can't stay here and do nothing. I'll go on my own if I have to." Sliding on his helm, Kaius picked up his new golden sword and strapped its sheath to his belt side. He looked at Adhnis, her brows curved, mouth agape, and her silver eyes trembling.

His lips quivered lightly, betraying his projected determination. He forced a small smile. "Adhnis, why don't you stay here. What's coming next is my fight to overcome, my duty is to rescue Vincent and Alaia. Yours is to this forest, your kin—"

"Oh come off it!" Adhnis gave him a hard glare with glossing eyes, catching him off guard. "I promised I would help get ye to yer brother and Princess. I'm not about to break that because I'm scared. Besides, ye don't even know how to use yer magic yet. Ye should at least wait for my mother to return."

"Adhnis, after tonight, we only have one more day to stop Vincent from doing whatever it is he's planning. What if he intends to sacrifice Alaia? I can't wait anymore." He turned to Adhnis and gestured to the sword at his side. "I'm sure I can break through their lines with this. I don't need my magic right now, just this sword. I can learn how to wield my magic later."

Kaius started walking to his horse still grazing in the clearing. He patted the creature on the side of her neck. The horse shook her head, her golden mane flapping from side to side. With a chortle, he climbed up the saddle.

Before leaving, he looked at the fairies. "Seeing as I have no idea which way is which from here, can you tell me where the North path is?"

Adhnis exasperatedly crossed her arms and looked away in protest, sticking her nose high in the air. Kaius sighed. "Adhnis please, Alaia aside, I'm worried about my brother. I . . . I need to speak with him as soon as I can, or we'll all be in great danger. Please?"

Adhnis remained quiet for a moment. A shudder ran through her shoulders, and she scrunched her face in anger, letting out a loud groan of frustration. "FINE! But if they start to overwhelm us, ye better make a run for it back to the forest. On my word. Is that clear!"

"Yes ma'am." Kaius flashed her a thankful smile. "Well Princess,

I'm going to assume you're older than me."

"Hmph! I've been in this realm for eighteen seasons. I'll have ye know, spring cycle . . . and ye?" She glanced at him with pursed lips.

"Sixteen falls myself." He raised the gemmed arm to her.

"Tsk! That explains yer stubbornness. Fall children are *known* for being frustratingly stubborn, just like the earth." She flew to him with arms still crossed and a sullen expression on her face.

"If my wanting to stop all this impending doom and gloom makes me stubborn, then so be it. I suppose I'm stubborn," he said with a warm smile. Adhnis glanced at him with darkened cheeks and raised shoulders. "Anyway, you should stow away in this gem for now. Scold me all you want from in there where it's safe and please, save my dumb ass if it comes down to it. Okay?"

Adhnis rolled her eyes and let out a groan. "No promises." A faint grin creased on her lips. She turned to look back at the Guardians over her shoulder. "When my mother gets back, inform her that we're heading to Kunnagar and that I'll do what I can to help Kaius with his magic." They all hesitantly nodded. She then ignited into a glowing ball of light and entered the gem.

With that, Kaius snapped the horse's reins and they followed Adhnis' directions. After a while, the trees numbered less, and the edge of the forest came into view. Passing through the threshold, there in the distance, beyond the rolling hills and gray clouds overhead, waited the army of dark monsters all lined side by side just as the fairies described.

Kaius' heart dropped into the pit of his stomach. As he scanned the horizon, despair threatened to set in. "Oh shit, your Guardians weren't kidding. I was hoping their intel was exaggerated."

"*A-Aye . . . Kaius, are ye sure ye can't wait? There's still ti—*"

"If we wait any longer, there's a good chance their numbers will continue to grow." Kaius took a deep breath, trying to calm his nerves. His mind turned to the ancient sword hanging on his side. "I don't suppose you know how this sword works?"

"*It's the same as using yer magic. Ye must command it to do what ye want. Ye just need to make sure to focus. That's it.*"

Kaius stared out at the line of muscular monsters, all of which stood firm, flailing their massive claws and roaring wildly. His hands tightened around the leather reins.

"Okay, just have my back, and we'll get through this." Kaius kicked the horse's sides to continue on. The creature bucked and neighed in refusal. Kaius tugged at the reins once more. "HEY! You're supposed to be a freaking warhorse, right? You've been trained to go through shit like this. If I can suck it up and face these creatures, then so can you. Now come on!" He snapped the reins and kicked the creature's side. At that, the horse reared up, and as her hooves met the earth with a thud, she dashed forward at such a speed, the wind stung Kaius' eyes.

They passed over hill after hill as the thunder overhead drowned out the waves crashing against the cliff face below. Kaius, after a deep breath, reached for his new sword and drew it. The gold and silver blade gleamed as the faint sunlight shined through the booming clouds above, kissing its surface. Growing closer to the line of monsters, he let out a fierce roar of his own.

He slashed clean through the first monster he saw. Beast after beast, he hacked away at their numbers from atop his horse. Having never trained at mounted fighting, he struggled to hold on while dispatching the attackers. All he could do to avoid hitting the horse was strike back and forth, side to side, attacking only those that came his way.

Kaius cursed; there were so many. His horse suddenly stopped and reared up, throwing him completely off balance. Kaius' grip loosened and he slipped off his saddle to the ground below. He landed hard on his backside and looked up with his mouth open. His mount bucked and bounced around, trying to avoid the monsters. The horse kicked a few in her panic and sent them flying as she fled.

Kaius jumped up and reached out for the horse, missing the reins by what must've been less than the length of his index finger. "No wait, come back!" His hand hung in the air, his mount running further and further away.

"KAIUS LOOK OUT!"

Kaius startled and hurriedly looked about. A monster rushed up beside him, its massive clawed hands high, and ready to strike. Without hesitation, he swung his blade in a vertical arc, cleaving the creature in half. Fearful for his life, he slashed away again and again, his limbs growing heavy with every strike. Sweat slid down the side of his face. His eyes stung.

"Shit! There's too many. ADHNIS!"

"Don't worry I got this!"

Kaius raised his gemmed arm in the air, summoned forth the barrier of light, and shielded them from the monsters now pounding away at the dome. He let out several heavy breaths, and his chest heaved beneath his chest plate, his heart thumping fast.

The shadow beasts clawed and attempted to bite their way through, but the shield held. Though the light repelled each of the beasts' attacks, sending them flying back into the sea of black, more and more poured forward to take their place.

"Adhnis," he let out a heavy breath, "how are you holding up?"

- *"I'm fine. So long as I'm in this gem, my energy is limitless. The barrier will stay up for as long as your arm can hold out."*

"That's good to hear . . ." He looked down at the magical sword, wondering what to do. "I just need to focus and command. Focus and command. Focus, and command!" He closed his eyes and tried to clear his thoughts of the muffled pounding of the monsters just outside.

They were darkness. Shadows incarnate. He recalled when he had first met Adhnis in the Rosado throne room, how quickly she had defeated the monsters with her light magic.

Kaius' eyes flashed wide open. "That's it! Dark is weak against light."

"Well aye, even fairy children know that! Command the sword to summon forth light and swing away."

"Okay. Here it goes." Kaius closed his eyes once again and thought of the bright light that Adhnis and her mother had conjured. He pictured the light enveloping his blade and held onto that image, trying to will it into being.

A sense of joy built within him. His chest swelled with love, happiness, and contentment. He could almost feel his loved ones by his side, their strength flowing into him. His muscles relaxed with renewed vigor.

The skin on his sword arm prickled and the hairs stood on end. A surge of energy ran down his arm and into his hand. Kaius opened his eyes, looked at the sword, and was taken aback. The very edge of the blade glowed brightly white.

"Incredible!" He looked up to the monsters and shot them a determined glare, startling them back.

Kaius lowered his gemmed arm in an instant, dismissing the barrier, and swung the sword in a horizontal arc. A massive wave of light flew from the blade and swept across the battlefield, leaving nothing but a cloud of black ash where the monsters stood. Without delay, he turned on his heel, and swung the sword again, this time dispatching the beasts behind him.

The remaining beasts shrieked in fear and started retreating North. Kaius released a heavy huff of breath, followed by another. Watching the beasts flee, he began to chuckle, relief washing over him.

"I did it. Adhnis I did it!" He raised his arm to look at the bright blue gem on his gauntlet.

Adhnis let out a warm giggle. *"I saw, now how about—"* Just then, they were cast in shadow as something massive flew overhead, giving her pause. *"What . . . was that?"*

A sudden, ear-piercing screech rang out in the sky, calling Kaius' attention upward to the gray clouds overhead. Though he could see nothing above, he heard the loud flapping of wings. It sounded like that of a bird, but much larger than anything he had witnessed before.

Kaius scanned the area. Two massive black wings suddenly emerged briefly from below the cliff's edge, sending a powerful gust of wind across the plateau. They disappeared, then reappeared again, each time growing higher as more of the beast came into view, and larger gusts of wind slammed into him. With a few more flaps of its wings, a pitch-black bird-like creature rose before him.

A wispy black smoke danced upon its feathers and quickly dispersed in the wind. Four glowing orange eyes glared at him intensely. Its beak was sharp and jagged, resembling a bundle of mountain tops. Its talons were long and sharp.

Kaius' heart dropped into his stomach as he stared wide eyed at the massive beast above him. Fear took hold and made his limbs quiver under his weight.

"Shit . . ." Spotting his horse in the distance, he burst into a full sprint toward her. "By the Mother's Light! I didn't think anything THAT big existed. It's even bigger than a dragon!"

"This isn't good! If something that big is out here, the tear is MUCH bigger than we realized. Run faster!"

"I'm trying—"

The massive monster flapped its wings toward Kaius, sending an incredibly powerful gust of wind hurtling all around him and nearly causing him to lose his footing. The creature let out a cacophonous shriek, making even the ground under him tremble. Kaius, regaining his footing, scanned the skies for the beast. With eyes focused upward, he didn't notice a shadow expanding under him.

"KAIUS WATCH OUT!"

Kaius looked directly above him as he continued to run and saw hundreds of dark violet spheres raining down toward him. He skidded to a stop and jumped as far back as he could. The dark globes pummeled the earth where he stood, each exploding and sending bolts of lightning streaking through the air. The once green blades of grass withered and turned dingy brown. The soil dried, becoming gray and cracked.

The dead, brittle grass crunched under the sharp hooves of many groups of dark monsters joining the fray. Innumerous monsters barred the way to his rightly panicked horse, now rearing and neighing on the other side of the blockade. Kaius quickly searched for a path through the monsters as they growled and roared, readying to strike.

"Kaius! We're . . . We're surrounded!"

"I know, I know!" Kaius glanced to the monsters approaching at his rear, then back to those at his front. He briefly closed his eyes and took a deep breath, raising his sword and readying himself. Thinking of the light, he commanded for it to come back, hoping it would work as it had before.

Another surge of energy poured through his arm and into the sword. Opening his eyes, the blade brimmed to life with a bright white glow. "Okay, here we go again!" He changed his stance and charged forward.

He struck quickly, each swing of the sword sent blades of blinding light through the dark creatures all around. Kaius twirled the blade left and right, dodging and distancing himself from the monster's attacks. Even with his newfound magic, there were just too many, and their numbers were seemingly endless.

Kaius continued his assault. His lungs burned and his body was heavy. Kaius dropped to a knee. Sweat flowed down his face. He looked about, the world growing hazy as exhaustion started to set in.

He cursed through gritted teeth. Unless Kaius could take out that bird, it would keep summoning those monsters and eventually overtake them. He needed to do something. Anything. He needed more power.

"*LOOK OUT!*" The blue gem on his left gauntlet flashed and out flew Adhnis disappearing behind him. As he turned, a bright explosion of light burst in a cascade of isolated flares across the enemy lines.

Adhnis turned back to him, light faded from her hands while concern shone in her silver eyes. "Kaius, ye need to be more careful. If—"

As the light vanished, a monster jumped through the cloud of dust left by his fallen brethren, a clawed hand raised.

Kaius' eyes widened as his breath caught in his throat. Before he could act, Adhnis was swatted out of the air with a pained shriek and hit the ground beside him, motionless.

His heart skipped a beat and the world slowed to a crawl around him. The monster's movements were barely perceptible, almost as though they were frozen in place.

He took a deep breath and called out, "ADHNIS!" His heart beat louder than any drum he had heard before. The inside of his chest felt tight, like it was caving in.

Anger at the sight of his fallen friend burned within him. He raised his hand to his face and there was a bright golden light radiating as bright as the sun itself. Kaius closed his eyes and stood, taking a deep breath. His head fell back as tears streamed down his cheeks, letting the anger boil over, and he released a blood curdling scream. Golden light exploded out in all directions, vaporizing the enemies around him.

He then turned his eyes upward to the bird-like creature above. Letting out a quick screech, it spun to fly away.

"You're not going anywhere you bastard!" His voice boomed, echoing across the cliff. Kaius raised his sword to the sky, pointing the blade at the massive creature now making a hasty retreat.

With another deep breath, Kaius let out another piercing battle cry. Power channeled into the sword, causing it to hum with destructive force. A beam of light burst from the blade, racing toward its mark, and skewered the creature, ending its escape.

The great monstrosity dissolved and the light vanished. The glow around Kaius faded as well.

Out of breath, he dropped his sword arm, his grip loosened, and he released the sword to the earth. It landed with a ping against the rejuvenated ground around him. He felt something inside him wither, like that of a dwindling fire in a fireplace.

Kaius' knees trembled and buckled under him. He fell back, but instead of hitting the ground, he was caught by something and lowered gently to the soft grass below.

Kaius heard someone scream his name, but couldn't make out who the voice belonged to. An ever-encroaching darkness shrouded his vision. His eyelids grew heavy. Giving in to his exhaustion, he closed his eyes and allowed sleep to take him.

9

ADHNIS

HIS LIGHT SO BRIGHT

ADHNIS, REGAINING CONSCIOUSNESS, shielded her eyes from the bright golden glow beaming around her. At its center, she faintly saw Kaius screaming. A blast of light shot from him and after a moment, it faded away. Slowly lowering her arms and shocked by what she had just witnessed, she stared at him, silently.

The gray clouds above drifted gently through the sky. Nothing, save for the grass dancing in the wind moved in the hilled lands surrounding them. No sign of the shadowy beasts lingered in the beautiful lands.

Adhnis suddenly startled hearing something hit the grass. She looked at Kaius. His arms slumped down to his sides as he swayed uneasily from side to side.

"K-Kaius?" Just as his name escaped her lips, he dropped to his knees, starting to fall backward to the grass. She jolted upright. "KAIUS!" Adhnis thrusted her arms high in the air and called for the wind. "Please Gaoth, ease his fall!"

By her plea, the winds swirled around them both. The spirits, taking on a corporeal form like a translucent cloth, swarmed behind Kaius and stopped his fall, gently lowering him to the grass. As his back met the ground, the spirits faded away, and the winds calmed once more.

A lump formed in Adhnis' throat, her heart heavy. She used every ounce of strength she could muster to flutter over to Kaius. Adhnis hovered just before his face. "Kaius, are ye okay? Please, say something!"

Dropping down and landing on his shoulder, she climbed his blond hair strands up the side of his head. She knelt on his cheek and brushed a few hair strands from his face. His eyelids hung low, nearly obscuring his striking blue irises.

Adhnis gently patted Kaius' cheek. "Hey, Kaius? Can ye hear me?" His eyelids slowly closed, causing her stomach to churn in worry. "Kaius? Kaius! Come on, please respond!" Kaius remained silent, his body unmoving.

Adrenaline rushed through her, she leapt upright and looked him up and down. "I-I don't know what to do. What can I—" She gasped as an idea popped into her mind. "That's it!"

Adhnis hopped off Kaius' cheek to the ground below, dropped to her knees, and slammed her palms flat to the grass. "Domhan, please hear me! I desperately need yer aid. I-I need to save him. I need to know he'll be okay!" It's hard to believe a moment ago he glowed as brightly as he did. Her mother wasn't kidding when she told Adhnis stories of his people and this sword.

The soil shifted just beneath her fingers. Adhnis jumped up, nearly losing her balance as the dirt squirmed to life, and moved about Kaius. The earth built under Kaius' helm and slid it off his head.

Adhnis released a breath of relief as the tears welling in her stinging eyes retreated. "Thank ye! Thank ye thank ye thank ye!" She repeated the sentiment vigorously and rushed toward Kaius, joy rising within her.

The spirit turned Kaius' head to meet her. Placing her hands just under his nostrils, a soft, warm breath blew against her palms.

She sighed. "Oh thank all of Talamh, he's okay." Adhnis touched her face to Kaius' cheek with a smile and wiped the tears from her eyes as the dirt continued to shift wildly beneath them both. "Yes," she chuckled graciously, "thank ye too."

Adhnis laid still on Kaius' cheek, her mind racing. He had unleashed so much magic just now, but that power had likely intimidated him greatly. It was just too much power for one person to wield. That had to be why he was like this. She turned from Kaius and looked down at the ground.

"Domhan, can ye carry him away from the edge? It would give me some peace of mind. Please?"

The dirt shifted wildly once again, bundled beneath Kaius, and carried him a short distance from the cliff's edge. She smiled, tension lifting from her shoulders. "Thank ye D—" Before she could take another step, her feet sank into the soil. She looked down curiously, wondering if the earth spirit wanted to converse with her.

She knelt down on one knee and laid a hand flat on the ground. An electrical surge rushed up her arm and then back down to the ground, causing Adhnis' breath to hitch. She took a deep breath and closed her eyes.

A pulse emanated from her hand. Kaius appeared in her vision and lit up in a green glow. There she could see his center thanks to the aid of the earth spirit. The magic within him resembled a swirling mass of stars and energy.

It . . . looked so small. She cursed softly to herself. Adhnis needed to help him learn to conserve his magic. If he used too much—Adhnis paused, shaking away the thought. No, she didn't want to think of it. She just needed to tell Kaius after he woke, make him aware of the dangers before he did something like that again.

The spirit then sent her attention elsewhere. It took her hurtling through the earth, her vision of the world becoming a disorienting glowing blur of green. It crashed to a stop before towering mountains that stretched far to her sides. At the foot of the mountains rested a city in ruins. She wondered if that was Kunnagar. The vision then suddenly faded away.

Adhnis' eyes flashed open and stared at the ground. "Wait, Domhan, are ye trying to warn me about something?" Her question was met with silence. Adhnis rolled her eyes. "Mother said ye're frustratingly cryptic." She stood up and placed her fisted hands on her hips. "Okay fine, keep yer secrets. Thank ye for tending to my friend at least."

The ground went still. Kaius laid peacefully on the grass, his breath soft, but steady. She rolled her shoulders back and fluttered over to her friend. Landing beside his face, she placed a hand on his cheek. His fair skin was cool to the touch.

"Oh, ye must be cold. One moment." Adhnis turned around and traveled a short distance away. "This should be a good spot."

Earth spirits may be stubborn, but fire ones were even more difficult. Incredibly unpredictable. If only there were a red fairy nearby, they were so much better with Dóiteáin than she was. Oh well, Adhnis thought with a sigh, she just needed to have confidence like her mother.

Adhnis took a deep breath and closed her eyes, stretching her arms far in front of her. "Dóiteáin, heed my call. I ask for a fire large enough to bring us warmth, and nothing more."

Her chest brimmed with warmth. She released a trembling breath as the sensation worked its way through her shoulders, down her arms, and to her hands. Then an explosion of heat swirled to life around her.

Opening her eyes, a small flame flickered before her. Adhnis let out a soft sigh. She was hoping for a little more than—

Just then, the little flame erupted and grew into a fire large enough to befit a human campsite. "Okay OKAY! That's good!" With the aid of her wings, Adhnis quickly fluttered away from the roaring flame and accidentally crashed into Kaius' shoulder.

Sweat slid down the side of her face. Her brows furrowed in annoyance. Adhnis hopped off Kaius' shoulder and angrily crossed her arms over her chest. "Really!? Ye could've singed my wings off ye know!" Though scolding the spirit, it simply danced before her exuberantly, almost looking as though mocking her. She rolled her eyes, too tired to be upset. "Aye aye. Just keep him warm for me, okay?" The fire swayed unnaturally and continued to dance and crackle playfully. She nodded in thanks all the same.

Adhnis walked around Kaius' shoulder, making her way to his cheek again. She placed a hand on his skin, feeling it begin to warm. "That's good, just rest for now." Adhnis reached down to the dirt beneath them, scooped some up, and placed it against his skin. "Okay now, let's see how ye're doing."

She closed her eyes and concentrated to call for the earth spirit once more. "Domhan, how's my friend? Anything I need to heal?"

A chilling feeling stretched from her hand and pulsed through Kaius' body. His limbs were sore and muscles worn, but nothing seemed to be broken nor bleeding. "Okay, nothing that rest alone can't fix." She wiped the dirt from Kaius' cheek, collected it, and placed the clump back on the ground.

Clapping her hands together, brushing the remaining dirt from her palms and looking up at Kaius. He let out a soft moan. Sighing, her mind turned back to the ruins in the North. That must be Kunnagar, she decided. Why else show her that place? Was something waiting for them there? Or maybe . . . Adhnis looked up at Kaius with wide eyes. What if something was waiting for him?

Her heart dropped into her stomach, startled from the thought as his head lolled lightly. "I'm . . . sorry . . ."

Adhnis' gaze rested on him softly. "Oh Kaius, I'm sure ye have nothing to be sorry for. Whatever happened, I'm sure we can figure it out . . . Soon, I hope."

KAIUS

BY A BLAZING FIRE

"**D**AMN THIS POUNDING IN MY HEAD." Kaius gently rubbed his fingers against his temples, hoping to soothe the pain, and sighed. "If I knew this is how I would feel after using my magic . . ." He groaned through gritted teeth. "It's my own fault, I should've listened to Adhnis and let her mother teach me."

Kaius looked up to the night sky above. The fire before him swayed as if almost alive, dancing impossibly on the open earth with no wood or straw to keep it alight, bathing him in its warmth while the cold fall winds blew.

A silver illuminated crescent peeked through the sea of star speckled darkness. "A new moon is almost upon us . . . I hope I can get to them in time."

Kaius rested his arms atop his knees, hands clasped together, and stared North to the lightning screeching wildly across the sky. A shudder crawled up his spine. His stomach churned. Lowering his gaze to the fire, thoughts of Alaia and Vincent haunted him. "Regardless of his reasons for taking you, Vincent *better* be treating you with care, Alaia."

A sharp pang of concern shot through his heart, followed by the pounding in his head threatening to flare again. Massaging his temples to slow the pain, he glanced down to his helm, gloves, and sword beside him. His eyes narrowed as they set on the magical weapon. "That magic I unleashed, was it . . . really from me, or was it you?" A wave of pain washed through his head. Each throb struck as intensely as a smith's hammer to an anvil inside his skull, stealing his attention from the blade.

His tense jaw muscles relaxed as the throbbing subsided, the waves breaking on the shore of relief. Kaius shifted his position and turned his gaze toward the cliffside. "Adhnis has been gone for a while. I hope she's—" As though manifested by his thoughts, the fluttering glow of silver-tinted white wings appeared in the distance. A smile broke on his face. "There you are, I was beginning to worry."

"Aye, sorry. The ocean waves were pretty violent. It was harder to call upon the water spirits there than say the ones that reside in the rivers of Eylowen." Adhnis fluttered to him holding out a somewhat flat disc of stone filled with water. "Healing can take a lot out of a person. So instead, I'm just going to activate the gem to hold the spell for me."

"Sure, no arguments here." He chuckled with exhaustion. "Is it like the barrier magic? Do I have to do anything for it to work?"

Adhnis flashed him a smile. "No silly. You don't have to do a thing, just rest. I'll activate the gem and link it with the water spirits. Since the gem's magical center is endless, the spell will only end when either the water spirits or myself break the link."

Kaius raised his arm to her, the blue gem shimmering in the firelight. "That's incredible! Is there any way I can use the gem's center, so I don't drain too much of my own?"

Adhnis glided down and pressed the gem with her foot. "Cute as ye are, yer no light fairy, so no."

"Oh. That's too bad."

After a moment, the gem brimmed to life, glowing softly with a blue light, and then illuminated the rest of his arm. "Wow!" Kaius' mouth hung ajar, watching the light spread.

Adhnis giggled. "After everything that's happened, what ye just did, ye're still this amazed? Ye're a silly one, Kaius. Palm up please." She sang the last few words in a chipper tone.

Kaius placed his palm under Adhnis, and she poured the contents of the disc onto his hand. The water pooled in his palm, not a single drop spilled out. It glowed too in a hue similar to that of his arm.

"Amazing, now what?"

"Now, place yer palm to yer head. Ye should feel a nice cooling sensation when ye do."

Kaius pressed his hand gently to the side of his head. Just as Adhnis said, a cooling sensation soothed the pain. He smiled with relief. "Thank you so much, Adhnis."

"Ye're welcome." She said with a wide grin, her gaze lingering on him.

He chuckled with confusion. "What?"

"Oh it's nothing. I'm still in awe of the display of magic ye showed earlier. It was amazing." A light grumble came from her stomach. "Let's eat. I'm starving."

Kaius chuckled again, feeling a little nervous about his magic. "Well, I'm glad one of us is. Here." He grabbed the satchel of food left to him by Queen Throstnie.

Adhnis unclipped the bag and dove in, searching for something. After a short while, Adhnis' muffled voice broke the silence. "Yay! I'm so happy she packed these!" She climbed out of the bag pushing out two large, greenish raspberries. "Here Kaius, these will rejuvenate yer energy. We're especially lucky to have these, given what ye unleashed."

"Right . . ." Kaius stared at the fruit in his hand, recalling the sensation he felt when he unleashed the blast on the shadow beasts. Power. Raw, untamed power. He had felt his chest burst, consumed like a dry forest in a wildfire. It was exhilarating, but terrifying at the same time.

"Something on yer mind?"

Kaius glanced at Adhnis sitting on his helm while holding onto a piece of her fruit. He took a deep breath and sighed. "Yeah, I . . . I don't know. As helpful as that was, it was really . . . scary, experiencing all that. The monsters, the magic, your . . . all of it." He crossed his arms over his knees and rested his chin on his forearm. "I thought you were dead. I can't lose you too."

"I'm sorry I worried ye, Kaius. I'm fine. I'll be more careful. Ye do the same. I don't want to lose ye either." Adhnis responded, her eyes softening. "And I understand yer reluctance about using that magic. Although I felt differently when wielding my magic for the first time, I've met others of my kin that were . . . unsettled, as ye are now. That feeling always comes when yer first time is in great stress or danger. That's why I pressed to have ye learn yer magic first, but because of what's going on, I understood why ye needed to leave."

"Y-Yeah." He buried his face in his arms.

"Anyway, ye need to eat to regain yer energy before facing yer brother tomorrow."

"My . . . brother."

Kaius' brows twitched. He still had no clue of what to do once he finally came face to face with Vincent. Would he listen to reason? Listen to his younger brother? Or would Kaius be forced to fight Vincent, or worse . . . Kaius violently shook away the thought. No. No it wouldn't come down to that. It shouldn't. It couldn't. Kaius released a heavy sigh as he grabbed hold of his hair, his heart heavy in his chest.

"So . . . *Do* ye know why yer brother took the Princess?"

Kaius hung his head low and let his arms drop, hanging over his knees. He stared quietly at the dirt for a while. Everything said between him and his brother came back to him in full force.

"I . . . I don't know. I don't know why exactly, but something you and your mother said, back in the forest, it made me think everything my brother has been telling me about King Cecilio may be true after all. Perhaps I shouldn't trust him." He raised the green fruit to his face and twirled it between his fingers.

The blood in his veins began to boil, and his muscles tightened. "I just—" He let out a loud groan. "I wish I had answers. Both he and Princess Alaia were behaving oddly, keeping secrets from me. Before yesterday, every time I tried to ask about the Ligeras' past, I was told to keep my mouth shut, head down, and to forget it. They behaved as though their lives depended on their silence."

"Ye . . . are from Kunnagar, right?"

Kaius looked at Adhnis and raised a brow. "Yeah, you know that. Why?"

"Do ye not remember what happened?" Adhnis' eyes softened, confused, yet curious to hear his answer.

"Remember what? Kunnagar falling under attack? No, I was way too young to remember. Vincent, on the other hand, said he remembered everything, but would never talk about it with me. He said he couldn't." Kaius rolled his eyes in frustration. "Something about an oath."

"A magic oath!?" Adhnis exclaimed, startling him.

"A what?"

"A magic oath. It's a binding pact between two or multiple people. Those who undertake the oath are bound to it and must adhere to the rules set during the pact, else they face the agreed upon consequences. If he were sworn to secrecy, the magic could've made it impossible to divulge the secrets of his pact. These oaths, however, are not so easy to cast. One wrong word could have dire consequences for all involved."

Kaius stared wide eyed at Adhnis. "Are . . . Are you serious?"

She nodded. "Aye, and another thing, Kaius, I have wondered why ye would be on the Ligeras' side in the first place, but I think I'm starting to understand the situation now."

"Understand what!?"

"The Ligeras were the ones to instigate the attack on yer home of Kunnagar."

Kaius' heart leapt into his throat. He sat frozen before Adhnis, speechless. Kaius suddenly jumped to his feet. The world spun lightly around him. Clutching at his chest, he only felt the cold steel of his armor. A loud ringing enveloped his mind.

"Kaius? Stay calm, ye have to take a breath!"

It hit him all at once. His memories surfaced. He saw images of a city, small, but built of stone with colorful banners strewn about. On them were beautiful knot designs of dragons, horses, wolves, griffins, and all sorts of animals both magical and otherwise, woven with both gold and silver strings.

Blurry faces of what could've been his parents came into view.

They picked him up off the ground, watching a magical spectacle in the middle of a square. Fire in the shape of birds soared through rings of earth twirling about in the air.

In a flash, the memory changed, darkness, and fire burned all around. Screams rang out as people fell into view, dead, some burning and others pierced by arrows raining from above.

"NO!" Kaius fell to his knees as his hands flew to the sides of his head, wanting the memories to stop. His eyes shined wide with fear. Heart sinking into his gut, it was causing it to churn dangerously. Kaius' body trembled.

Adhnis flew to him, placing her hands on the tip of his nose. "Kaius, it's okay! Try to take a deep breath. Come o—"

"Why!? Why would they do that? We were peaceful people . . . weren't we?" He asked, his voice quivering.

She looked at him with concern and sorrow. "It was the King who preceded Cecilio, his father. Everyone knew that man hated everything having to do with magic. He died soon after the attack. No one knew how, but didn't care. Many rejoiced, some even rather openly."

Kaius' body slowly relaxed, his breath calming as the visions ceased. He raised his head to Adhnis, her light lifting his spirits. The scent of cedarwood and something else, something unknown, but as wonderful as Valencia roses wafted over him. He cupped her in his hands and brought her close to his cheek, wanting for her comforting embrace which she happily offered.

"So the late King ordered the attack, but what of . . . King Cecilio?

Was he involved as well?"

"All I know is that yer King aims to *use* magic users, not kill us. I don't know what role he played in Kunnagar's demise or how they even snuck up on yer people, but once we reach yer brother he . . . might be able to explain himself." Adhnis was quiet for a moment, but he felt her hand slide softly against his skin. "At least I hope so. I hear oaths made with magic are pretty powerful and are difficult to break unless specific circumstances have been met." She pushed off of him. "I'm sure we will have answers soon enough."

Kaius looked over her tiny frame in his hands. His eyes welled with tears, but instead of fighting them, he let them flow freely.

With a flutter of her wings, Adhnis floated up into a hover as Kaius lowered his hands. Looking down to his side, Kaius realized, in all the commotion, he had dropped the fruit. He picked it up and walked back to the fire, taking a seat next to his things on the ground.

Watching the flames dance, he scoured his memories of life in Rosado, the people welcoming him and Vincent with kindness and care. However, one day stuck out.

Vincent was called upon by King Cecilio and was gone for most of the day. When he returned, something in his older brother's eyes felt different, he looked worried. Soon after, Vincent began training with masters of magic. Kaius never had the chance to meet them. Then there were Vincent's mysterious tasks undertaken for King Cecilio. Vincent grew distant, angry.

"It seems . . . that kindness was simply a mask hiding the truth.

My brother was right about everything, and I . . . turned my back on him."

"Kaius, I'm sure yer brother still loves ye."

"No he doesn't. How could he? If you saw how he looked at me when I refused to take his hand . . ." Kaius dropped his head, burying his face in his arms crossed over his knees. "I would feel betrayed too. I'm such a shitty brother!"

"Kaius."

"If I actually listened to Vincent, confronted the King and demanded the truth, maybe things would be different. I might've even stopped him from taking Alaia. Stopped him from doing anything this reckless!"

"Do ye think Alaia lied to ye?"

Kaius jolted, having not before considered the possibility. He stared silently at the fruit still in his hand. Did she lie to him too? When Kaius found her on the swing she looked so . . . upset. What could her father have told her? Why hide it from him?

Silence hung heavy in the air. Adhnis quietly glided to him, stopped at his side, and took a seat on his helm. "Kaius, are ye in love with Alaia?"

"What!?" He quickly turned to Adhnis with heat building in his cheeks.

She watched him with a warm, curious smile plastered on her face. She bit her fruit, her eyes not once leaving him. "N-No! She's a Princess and I'm . . . just a lowly knight only fit to be used by the King."

Kaius' elbows rested on his knees, glaring at the fire before him.

"I bet yer Princess doesn't feel that way." She said, her tone sincere.

Giving her a glance, he asked, "And how would you know how she feels?"

"How would ye?" She returned with a playful yet challenging look. Caught off guard, he averted his eyes, trying to hide his burning cheeks. "Ye'll never know how she feels unless ye ask."

"Yeah yeah, little Princess. We'll see."

"We better."

Kaius laughed weakly at the demand. He wanted so badly to tell Alaia how he felt, but never thought he should due to his station. Now, with everything that had happened, he wasn't sure what to do or how to feel. There were still more secrets left to uncover and questions needing answers. Kaius looked at the strange raspberry-like fruit and raised it to his lips, finally taking a bite.

11

KAIUS

THIS IS MY HOME

KAIUS RODE SWIFTLY ON HIS HORSE. A thick mist hung heavy in the air and gray clouds darkened the chilled surroundings. Riding ever forward through the mist, eventually he and Adhnis came across large shadows looming in the short distance. Kaius pushed the beast to gallop faster, hope and fear swirling in his heart as he drew closer to his brother and Alaia. Breaking through the shroud, Kaius pulled hard on the reins for the horse to stop. His eyes shot wide with disbelief.

Adhnis flew forward and hovered just before him, her mouth agape in amazement. "Wow, look at the size of this place."

A ruined city of stone lay before them. Tattered banners waved lazily in the howling winds, blowing through the empty streets. Lamp posts rested, fallen and covered in rust on the dry, barren ground. Large cracks told of the ravages of time and conflict upon every stone. Buildings that once reached high and touched the sky, lay toppled. Remnants of statues depicted creatures of many forms: drakes, direwolves, even krakens dotted the area.

"This . . . This place was something to behold back then, wasn't it?" Adhnis asked, turning to Kaius with softness in her silver eyes. He remained silent, his gaze lingering on that which was once his home.

Kaius gently kicked the sides of his horse, signaling her to continue forward. Kaius continued cautiously through the empty roads, following the straight and beaten path. Adhnis flew about him, peering through broken doorways and shattered shutters, finding nothing but darkness, save for that which was illuminated by her light.

"NGH!" Pain brimmed to life in Kaius' temples. His hand flew to the side of his head, almost knocking his helm clean off. Kaius' head throbbed as memories flooded back to him again, all filled with fire, screams, and his brother's terrified face pulling him as they ran.

"Kaius, are ye okay?" Adhnis glided to him, trying to get a look at his face.

"I'm-I'm fine. It's the memories again. They've been steadily returning, more frequent as we draw closer." Kaius slid his hand down his face and signaled his horse to continue again.

"Do ye want to stop and rest?"

"There's no time, Adhnis. The faster we find my brother and

Alaia, the more likely we'll be able to stop him from doing whatever he has planned." Kaius focused his sight on the neck of his horse, wishing to no longer look over the remains of his shattered home.

Adhnis nodded, but startled as lightning screeched across the sky. As he followed the main path, ignoring the side streets, he glanced up to a tattered blueish gray banner. Most of its decoration had faded, however he faintly made out the knotted symbol of a horse-like creature through the muck. He wondered if it was a unicorn.

A flash of light engulfed his vision, the surroundings changing to that of white, clean stone. He no longer sat atop his horse. Colorful confetti fell from the sky, and a beautiful blue banner flapped gently in the breeze, a gold knotted symbol of an alicorn at its center. He looked to his left and started walking, but was suddenly picked up and swung playfully through the air.

"Kaius? Kaius!? Come on, wake up!"

Kaius jolted, not realizing he had stopped. He looked at Adhnis with worried eyes, his breath labored. "By the light of Grian AND Gealach Kaius, don't scare me like that."

"I'm . . . I'm sorry. I think we need to go this way." Kaius tugged his horse's reins and nudged her sides. He guided her down the path to the left as the vision had shown him, drawn to whatever lay at the end.

"Really? What for?" She hovered beside him, keeping pace. Her concern was clear in her voice, but curiosity shined in her eyes.

"I think . . . I think my hom—" Kaius' voice caught in his throat as wood creaked, followed by the light pattering of debris thudding to the ground. Dark monsters suddenly jumped down from the rooftops of the surrounding buildings, landing about him with deafening roars. His horse startled and reared up.

Kaius pushed forward on his mount, helping her back to all fours. Once situated, he scanned for an opening in their formation as his heart beat against his chest. With nowhere to go, he felt frozen in his saddle.

Catching him by surprise, instead of charging as he had come to expect, all the beasts retreated down alleyways and peered through gaps in the debris.

Adhnis clung onto his azure cape. "Why are they . . . just standing there?"

"I don't know, but let's tread cautiously." He raised a hand, shielding her from their sight, and glanced at Adhnis with an assured nod. She returned a hesitant nod back and tried to tuck herself further into the cloth by his neck. He snapped the reins of the horse, having it continue onward.

Lightning bolts screeched across the clouded sky wildly, illuminating the world in bright flashes. Kaius watched the monsters as he passed them by, their glowing orange eyes simply staring back at him, sending shivers through his nerves. Their guttural growls caused his body to quiver. His breath quickened.

Why weren't they attacking? Was it Vincent? Was he keeping them at bay? The questions raced through his mind as though he himself could possibly begin to know the answers.

Then he heard a small gasp from Adhnis. "Kaius look out!"

Something scratched the back of Kaius' helm, the force knocking him against the neck of his horse. He caught himself and quickly looked up, seeing creatures similar to the monstrous winged thing he faced just the day before. These, however, were much smaller, only about the size of a common crow.

The creatures cawed at him as they swooped by, taunting him from above. One by one they swooped down on him from out of sight, attacking with their sharp talons. Kaius tried to swipe them away with his arms, but only succeeded in scratching up his gauntlet. "Dammit! What should we do?"

"I don't know. The others are still just—" Adhnis jumped.

A cacophony of short growls echoed the street around him, as though the creatures were laughing at him. His brows furrowed over his eyes, anger swelling within him. He was sure that they were taunting him and his aggravation was fighting to get the better of him.

Energy in the center of his chest surged and swirled. He wanted— No, needed to be rid of the flying beasts overhead. Kaius' arms tingled and sparked beneath his skin. His left hand tightened with fury and frustration. The bird monsters continued to flap, caw, and swoop at him, taunting him still.

Not noticing the violet glow emanating from his hand and the gasp from Adhnis, he reached his left arm back. "By the Mother's mercy, be gone with you!" Kaius thrusted his arm forward and out burst a volley of violet arrows streaming from the palm of his hand.

He let out a pained scream as the sparkling arrows hurtled toward the beasts, homing in on the creatures as they tried to flee and killing them instantly.

"Woah, what was—"

Kaius doubled over and clutched his left hand, startling Adhnis. "AGH! What the—Why did that hurt!?" His hand trembled, feeling thousands of needles boring into his skin. He tried to close his hand and released a trembling breath from the effort.

"What's wrong? Tell me?" Adhnis exclaimed.

"I-I don't know! I was just so angry with those creatures, at this whole stupid situation we're in, and I—"

"I think that magic ye just displayed is common only to yer people. I've heard it go by two names, both cosmic and arcane. Either way, that was amazing Kaius." She hovered down to his hand, touching the glove. He could barely feel her.

"If it's so amazing then why does it hurt!?" Kaius asked through gritted teeth.

She looked up at him with curved brows. "I don't know. It could be that ye lack the proper training to cast it, or maybe it has to do with yer feelings when casting? Let me help ye." Adhnis knelt on the center of his palm and raised her hand in front of her chest, palm up.

Something gently brushed against his cheek. A gust of wind began to swirl about and encircled him. A cool sensation filled his chest and spread to his shoulder, down his arm, and to his hand. He stared at his trembling hand. The wind swirled around him and his arm, the tremble slowing and eventually ceasing all together. His fingers relaxed and he released a long sigh of relief.

"Thank you so much, Adhnis."

She giggled. "Of course." With eyes closed, she continued to focus on the wind.

Shortly after, she exhaled steadily, and stretched her arms high above her head, interlocking her fingers. Opening her eyes, she looked up at him. "Better?"

"Yes, thank you, again." With a chuckle, he raised his hand to his shoulder, and Adhnis hopped off. Hesitating for a moment, she looked around.

"What's wrong?" Kaius asked.

"The shadow beasts . . . they're gone." She answered, looking uneasy.

He looked around and saw all the glowing eyes that had been there moments ago had now vanished. His pulse quickened. This was so strange. Just what was going on here? Kaius took a deep breath. "Let's move on. We should be careful, but . . . I think we're safe for now."

"Okay." Adhnis sat herself down on his shoulder between the folds of his cape as he snapped the reins and continued on.

The two traveled along the quiet street. The wind howled through the broken city, whistling through breeches in the buildings, and caused loose doors to clatter as they swung to and fro. Lightning flashed across the sky and thunder boomed in waves, echoing through the rubble.

Kaius soon reached a small building with a massive hole through its front, looking as though something had smashed its way in. He gently pulled back on the horse's reins to stop and spotted something hanging by the door. Kaius squinted as he examined the object. A small, familiar, worn-down wooden horse hung on a cracked wall. His eyes flashed wide as recognition set in.

He hopped off the saddle and ran to it without a second thought, reaching out with shaking hands. Then, just as before, a flash of light engulfed his vision, his surroundings fading. A pristine white stone wall and beds of colorful flowers rested before him. His eyes remained locked on the toy horse. Tiny hands tried to reach for it, but couldn't quite grab it.

Do you like it, Kaius? Mama carved it just for us, but it isn't a toy. If either of us ever get lost in the city, look for this horse hanging on the wall, and you'll know you've found your way home.

Kaius' hand flew to his mouth. His eyes stung with tears. With knees shaking, he fell to the ground. Kaius' lips trembled as he reached out once more for the horse figure, his tears flowing freely.

Adhnis rose off his shoulder and floated closer to look at the figure now in his hand. "Do ye know this place?" She turned and looked at him empathetically, her silver eyes soft and warm.

He scanned the ruined building before him, speechless. Colorful tattered banners swayed gently in the wind. The cold touch of a rain droplet suddenly kissed his nose.

"This is . . . This is my home." Kaius let go of the figure and turned his attention to the massive hole in the wall. "Come on, the hole is big enough to fit her through." He said while gesturing to his steed with his thumb. Adhnis nodded and headed through the hole in the wall first while Kaius grabbed the horse's reins, guiding her hurriedly into his home as the rain started to pour.

Once inside, he tried to shake the wet from his clothes, flapping his cape to remove the droplets before they soaked in and weighed him down. Taking a few steps in, he tripped on a downward dip in the wood boards.

Catching his balance, Kaius looked down and saw he had stepped onto the edge of a large crater embedded in the floorboards. The wooden planks were broken and splintered. His heart hung heavy at the sight, unsure as to exactly why. Looking over the debris, he scanned the floor to the right, noticing large, scuffed grooves etched into the ruined floor leading off to the side, at the end of which sat a massive boulder. That was so strange, he thought. Did Vincent—

"Everything okay?"

"Hmm? Yeah I . . . It's nothing." He carefully stepped around the crater and continued a few steps further into the darkness of the house. Kaius paused, unable to see anything, save for the small area in which his fairy companion's light touched.

He looked at Adhnis. "Hey, Adhnis—"

"Already ahead of ye." She saluted playfully and flew to the center of the room, increasing the brightness of her light to illuminate that which was hidden in shadow. Against one of the walls was a worn-out desk, covered in a mountain of books.

Kaius made his way to the desk and tipped over some of the books. Runes had been painted on the spines and covers of many of the books and journals. His heart fluttered uneasily as he picked one up and held it to Adhnis. "This is Valtivarian writing. Vincent taught me how to read these."

"What do ye mean?" Adhnis asked as she tilted her head with a confused expression. "Do Pacíficans and Valtivarians not use the same language?"

Kaius raised an eyebrow at her. "Are you really asking that?"

Adhnis' fists slammed against her hips as she pursed her lips. "Aye, I'm really asking! There's no need to be a big jerk. My kin and I don't know everything about yer kind. What makes ye think we know yer runes? I bet ye don't know ours!"

Kaius raised his hands up in defense. "Okay okay, I get it. I'm sorry." As Adhnis calmed, he returned to inspect the runes on the cover.

"So, what does it say?" She drew closer and hovered just over his shoulder, her light shining brightly on the cover.

"It has been a while, just a moment. It . . . looks like some of these are spell books, and these over here . . ." He leaned over the table and perused the titles. "History books? That's odd. Why would he be reading history books?"

As Kaius scanned the desk's surface, a blue leather journal lay at its center, catching his eyes. His chest grew heavy as he stared at it, entranced, as if it were calling to him.

Resting his hands flat on the table's surface, he felt a strange vibration coming from the wood. He was startled from its call as Adhnis lit a couple candles on two tapered candle holders nestled between the stacks of books.

"There, that should make reading easier." She let her light dim back to its natural soft glow and landed on the desk. The flickering flames of the candles washed them in a warm orange hue. "Okay, so what does—"

As she walked toward the blue journal, a translucent, crimson dome appeared and enveloped the book, causing Kaius to jump. "ADHNIS STOP!"

Stopping dead in her tracks before the dome, with hands raised, she released a trembling breath. "Oh wow, no way!"

"You know what this is?" Kaius looked over the faint crimson dome with a bemused look on his face. "What is it?"

Adhnis carefully moved to the edge of the dome, her palm lightly hovering over its surface. "I think it's a . . . seal? Some sort of ward?" She glanced up to Kaius and continued. "I think the best example I can give you is the barrier around Eylowen Forest. The one that judges yer intentions, remember? I think this is something similar."

He nodded. "I remember. Is this . . . dangerous?"

She was quiet for a moment, raised a hand to her chin, and scrunched her face. "Honestly, I don't know. I'm not that well versed in yer people's magic. Vincent likely placed the ward so that no one could grab the book. It could do anything from simply sending a jolt through yer hand to blowing up the house."

Kaius looked at her, puzzled. His eyes darted between her and the journal. "So what do we do?"

Adhnis took a few steps back. "I'm not touching it. He's yer brother. Ye do it. Just . . . don't die on me." Adhnis looked at him and shrugged.

"Thanks." Kaius' brows furrowed, hardening his glare at the dome shielding the journal. He curled his fingers into fists over the table, feeling the vibration fluctuate. His jaw tightened. "There has to be something important inside, something about his plan. Why else place the barrier on this one journal?" Kaius straightened himself. "I'm going to try."

Adhnis let out a soft sigh. "Be careful, please."

Kaius nodded and raised a hand to the crimson dome, fingers hovering just above its surface. A spark of lightning skittered across its surface, startling him. His breath caught and heart raced. Kaius then exhaled and proceeded. To his great surprise, his fingers broke through the barrier without issue.

"Huh, that's strange, it unlocked. I wonder . . ."

He looked at Adhnis as he grabbed the journal. "What is it?"

"I'll tell you if my hunch is right. Lift the journal for me please."

Kaius nodded and did as she asked. Lifting the journal uncovered a rune decorated circle beneath it on the table's surface, written in dried blood. His stomach churned at the sight. The barrier over the journal then faded.

"I thought so. It was a blood seal. I heard Valtivarians call their magic Seidr. Valtivarians outside of Kunnagar require runes to use Seidr. Most often, these Seidr runes and circles are drawn in ink. However, if they need a particularly powerful spell, they use a rather chilling method. Blood. Most likely, this seal allowed ye to take it because ye share the same blood as yer brother, Vincent. I've also heard that the faes far to the North can mix their elemental magic with that of Valtivarians Seidr runes, but that's about it. I'm not that well versed in their ways either. I only know what Mother told me."

"You seem to know quite a bit. Compared to me, you're an expert." Kaius opened the journal and was taken aback, seeing it too was written in runes. The handwriting was familiar to Kaius, so clean and succinct. After reading a few lines, it confirmed his suspicion. "This . . . It belongs to Vincent. I guess he wrote in Valtivarian so no one else could read it. At least . . . not the wrong people."

"Really?" Adhnis flew closer.

He nodded. "Yes. I recognize his penmanship. His strokes were always precise, almost artistic . . ."

Adhnis looked from the page to Kaius, wondering why he fell quiet. "What does it say? I can't read it."

"This journal was given to him after . . ." Kaius' mouth went dry.

"After he did the binding oath with King Cecilio. It's just as you said."

Adhnis watched him in silence, then landed on the page of the journal, and looked up at him. "Hey, are ye going to be okay?"

Kaius didn't respond, instead he placed the journal back on the table, and was quiet for a moment before answering. "This will most likely have the answers I seek. I have to be."

"Okay, if ye're sure." She floated up from the pages.

Kaius then flipped through them, soon reaching the middle of the journal. He jolted, surprised at the first word he saw.

"What? What is it, Kaius?"

He released a trembling breath as tears welled in his eyes. "This entry is after he'd gone on several missions chosen specifically for him by the King. It-It details how Cecilio used Vincent to remove certain individuals from his court and, oh shit . . ."

"Okay lad, when ye use that word, I can't help but be nervous."

"Cecilio threatened to—" He swallowed, "kill me if Vincent didn't do everything that was asked of him."

"Hmph! Not exactly asking if there's only one clear answer." Adhnis planted her hands on her hips with a frustrated frown.

Kaius' grip tightened on the book, fear and anger in his troubled thoughts. His heart raced, sure that each entry would only reveal more and more horrors. He had to tell himself that it was okay. That he could do this. It was for Vincent after all. Kaius had to continue. He gulped and forced himself to read on.

Scouring through several more pages, he paused, and tears began rolling down his cheeks. "He felt like a prisoner in Rosado, used for Cecilio's dirty work, and . . . was confused when I confessed my feelings for Alaia and felt betrayed as a result." Kaius felt a chill as his frown deepened. "That's when he told me about our home and what happened, that I shouldn't trust the Ligeras, let alone Alaia, but I refused to listen. I even had the gall to accuse him of being jealous. I don't even remember why I said that, but I did, and the disparity between us grew." He closed his eyes and leaned against the wooden surface. It creaked lightly, bearing his weight. "Dammit, I'm such a shit brother."

"Hey, no ye're not. Ye both just . . . needed to be more open. Miscommunication can be the downfall of any relationship." She walked to the right side of the book and placed her hands on her knees. "The end of the book is back here, right?"

"Yeah, one moment." As he was turning the pages, a set of runes caught his attention. He flattened the pages and began reading. A shudder ran down his spine, his stomach churning. His mouth was dry as a desert again.

"What is it Kaius, what did ye find?"

" . . . Sometime last year, after Vincent's seventeenth summer, he said he began hearing . . . a-a voice?" Kaius' brows furrowed with worry.

"A voice? What kind of voice?" Adhnis looked at him, concerned.

"I don't know, all he wrote here is that the voice was quiet, weak, yet tantalizing . . . powerful. It didn't give him a name . . . but it promised him help?"

"I don't think that's a good thing. Are there any more entries about this voice?" She stood up, wringing her hands together nervously.

"One moment." He glanced through a couple entries and found another mention of the voice and read it aloud. "It's odd . . . how so much clearer the voice has become. It scared me at first, but promised it was a friend . . . it's here to help me. The next time he comes to me, I will listen to what Mykronvan has to say."

"Mykronvan?" Adhnis exclaimed, jolting with worry.

Kaius looked at her. "Do you know the name?"

"A-Aye, but only from stories told by Mother. I . . . I didn't think he was real."

Kaius stared at her for a moment longer, then glanced away, thinking. "To be honest, that name is familiar to me too, but I just . . . can't remember why." He stood himself straight and clutched his chin, placing his index finger between his lips.

"Ye've probably heard a similar tale as I. Long ago he was a sorcerer who made a deal with the Shadow King—"

"And the demon bestowed upon him great power." Kaius finished. "I remember now, the tale was told during prayer at the Mother's temples every now and then. The sorcerer sought a means to defeat his enemies. Traveling down through the depths of darkness and violet flame, there he found sat upon a throne of bones, the foulest of all demons. The Demon King of Velkran, or something like that." Kaius crossed his arms, grasping hold of his biceps in discomfort.

"Why would Vincent accept the aid of someone like that?"

"Ye forgot the ending of the tale." Adhnis said nervously. "Mykronvan became an all-powerful sorcerer, but in the end, he was taken down by the sorcerers of Kunnagar, and imprisoned in, as you call it, Velkran." She rubbed her forearms, as though trying to rid herself of the gooseflesh showing on her tiny umber arms.

"Y-Yeah, but that doesn't explain why Vincent would accept his aid." Kaius' brows curved as he looked to Adhnis searchingly.

"Let's keep reading. I'm sure we'll find his reasoning."

Kaius nodded and continued reading through the pages of his brother's journal. Many of the entries he was unfamiliar with, such as his older brother liking some boy, but because of Cecilio watching his every move, he chose not to act out of fear of what the King might do to the boy. Some of the other entries were of familiar events, such as the brief meetings he and Vincent were gifted by the King, Kaius watching Vincent's training, and so on. A sharp pang swept through Kaius' heart as he read the entry regarding his nameday.

This is supposed to be a momentous occasion, the day my brother turns sixteen falls. I read that if his magic hasn't manifested before now, it should just come forth on this very day. I should be there, but instead, Cecilio has seen to it that I can't. My own brother. All because someone needs "taken care of". I swear, I WILL make him pay for keeping my brother from me.

Kaius' eyes stung and his jaw clenched.

"Kaius, is everything okay?"

"Yeah, it's . . . it's nothing." Kaius flipped to the next page and hesitated, noticing the tone of the entry was different from the others. "I think I've found it, one moment." He squinted his eyes and read, "I can't. I can't take this life anymore! Not for me *or* Kaius. Cecilio is planning something, I just know it . . . Some of my books on Kunnagarian History have gone missing. I think he intends to force Kaius to awaken his magic . . . Dammit! I've run out of time . . . and options. I have no choice. As suspicious as I am of Mykronvan, I must accept his aid . . . It's the only way . . ." Kaius' breath hitched in his throat.

"What? What else does it say? Don't keep me in suspense!" Adhnis leaned over the pages, trying to see where Kaius left off.

"It's about Alaia." His eyes trembled.

"Yer brother's not . . . going to sacrifice her, is he?"

"No, it's . . . one moment." Kaius leaned a little closer to the pages, squinting again, trying to focus his eyes, and struggled to remember the meaning of some of the runes. "He says it can't just be him, there must be another. Vincent wrote, 'Mykronvan says I need the Princess to open the door to free him. I don't know exactly how or what will happen to her, but if I want to be rid of Rosado for good, I need her. Once Mykronvan is freed, then and only then can he share my body—'"

"He's going to do WHAT!?" Adhnis exclaimed, her eyes wide and jaw dropped.

"Vincent is willing to go *that* far to take down Rosado?" Kaius pushed himself off the table. "No, I can't let him. I have to—We have to do something!"

"Desperate or not, yer brother is being stupid. Listen Kaius . . ." Adhnis fell quiet as she looked up at Kaius, undoubtedly seeing his body trembling. Adhnis rushed to the edge of the table, catching his attention. "I know this can't be easy. How are ye feeling?"

"Honestly, terrified. I just . . . I don't know what to do. I want to talk to Vincent, try to turn him away from this madness, but he seems set on this plan. If I can convince him to come back with me, Helgad Inferis, no . . . I have to convince him to set Alaia free and leave with me. Maybe then we can put all of this behind us and start a new life far from here."

"Leave!? What about yer feelings for Alaia?"

His heart fluttered, panging with grief at the thought of never seeing her again. "Adhnis, after everything you just heard, do you truly think it wise that my brother and I be anywhere near King Cecilio?"

"Well . . ." Adhnis released a defeated breath, glancing away.

"Look at me, Adhnis." She took a deep breath and looked up with glossy eyes. "You've been good to me, a caring and helpful friend. I don't know how I can ever repay you for your kindness, but I think this is for the best. If I can convince Vincent to leave with me for Valtivar, where Cecilio can never reach us, it'll be a start. Maybe you can visit us when all is said and done." He flashed a smile at her, hoping to ease the sadness of their soon to be parting.

Adhnis stared at him, trying to hide her quivering chin and lower lip. With a hesitant nod, she wiped the tears from her cheeks. "Okay then, but there's just one thing we *must* do before then."

Kaius tilted his head. "What's that?"

She looked at the stacks of books on the table and then returned to Kaius with a determined gaze. "Let's figure out how to save Vincent from that magic oath. There should be no more secrets between you two."

KAIUS

TO SAVE A PRINCESS AND A WIZARD

HAVING LEFT KAIUS' CHILDHOOD HOME, he and Adhnis continued deeper into the ruined city as the world grew slowly darker around them while the air was growing more colder. Mountains peaked over a tall, battered wall at the back of Kunnagar, towering ominously above. The walls' gates lay worn and rotted on the ground.

Continuing along the path through the gates, the two found themselves in a courtyard. Weather-beaten statues, likely depicting the Valtivarian gods, lined the path. At the path's end, just before the base of the mountains, were another set of gates, these tightly closed.

As Kaius walked the path, he glanced to one side and stopped in his tracks. A field of grave mounds stretched from end to end of the courtyard. Some were topped with small bundles of white poppies and lavenders, tied together by a black ribbon decorated with acorns. His heart hung heavy in his chest, his eyes locked on the mounds. White petals rolled in the chilly wind, drifting from mound to mound.

Adhnis hovered down from his shoulder to get a closer look at a few of the mounds. "Are . . . all of these graves?" She turned to look up at him.

Kaius responded with trembling hands and sorrow in his voice. "Did Vincent do all of this by himself? Bury all these people?" He scanned over the graves, his throat tightening.

"These flowers are lovely. I wonder if they have meaning to those who've passed?"

"Let's go." Kaius said wearily, quickly turning away and continuing down the path toward the mountains. He wiped away the tears that fell down his cheeks, the pain and hollow feeling in his chest worsening with every step. A curse escaped his lips as he languished in his own grief. If he had known Vincent was in this much pain, he would've—

He stopped and his gaze drifted down to the grime infested cobblestone path. Kaius wouldn't have known what to do. Where to even start. He probably would've shared his sorrows and perhaps, maybe . . . just maybe that would've been enough. Kaius sighed and blinked back his welling tears, his resolve strengthening.

"Based on the entries in Vincent's journal, this mausoleum houses

Mykronvan's prison."

"Is this place recognizable to you at all?" Adhnis flew up beside him, her head tilted to the side.

He looked up to the face of the mountain. Jagged spires hid amongst the rocks, its face peppered with arched openings, most likely windows. A large gateway was carved right into the base.

Visions of people shrouded in violet robes walking about flashed before him, but vanished as quickly as they appeared. "I remember people in violet robes, but I don't believe I ever entered this place as a child. I remember Vincent was excited. I think he looked forward to working here as one of the caretakers."

"Hmm, I wonder why it was referred to as a mausoleum? I've never heard the term before." Adhnis looked up at the monument.

"There are likely tombs resting beneath this place. Probably for those who worked here. Come on, we should hurry." Kaius picked up his pace down the path.

He walked up and stopped at the base of the steps before the stone gate led into the mausoleum. Carvings of robed figures decorated the gate's surface. Beams led from each of the figures' outstretched hands toward a monstrous creature at the top center of the gate. Its appearance bared a striking similarity to the creatures of darkness running rampant over the lands. It had many curling horns, four eyes on its face, and numerous tendrils stretched from its body spreading throughout the relief.

Kaius took a nervous gulp, climbed the steps, and stopped before the cold stone door. Adhnis floated along, but paused as she noticed Kaius' hesitation, and turned to him. "Kaius?"

He remained silent, his gaze falling to the floor. Closing his eyes, he took a deep breath and raised his hands to his helm. Kaius exhaled steadily as he slid his helmet off, holding it at his waist.

Adhnis looked at him in amazement. "Yer hair!"

Kaius responded with a soft laugh. "Not really the reaction I was expecting." He tossed his helm to the ground and brushed a few loose strands of hair from his face. "I noticed it this morning while you were still asleep and confirmed it while we were at my old home. My hair has changed at the roots, just as white as Vincent's, save for the small amount of blond left at my tips. I think this is because of the awakening of my magic." His eyes drifted downward, not focusing on anything in particular. With hands clasped together and lightly shaking, Kaius ran a thumb up and down his palm. "To be honest, I'm scared, Adhnis."

"Ye shouldn't fear yer magic, Kaius." She flashed him a warm smile. "Ye have *nothing* to worry about. Just remember what I said, concentrate—"

"And don't force it. Right." Kaius chuckled weakly.

"Ye have a good heart, Kaius. Listen to it and ye'll be just fine."

He stared at her for a moment, then nodded softly, and glanced away. "Adhnis, while I'm confronting my brother, I need you to find Alaia for me and get her out of here."

She blinked, puzzled by his request. Adhnis' mouth fell open, most likely to protest, but she stayed silent. Much to his surprise, her silver eyes softened. "Why are ye asking *me* to get her out of here? Why not ye?"

"Because my brother needs her for his plan to work. If she's not around, his plan should end right then and there. Hopefully, that will give me the leverage I need in convincing him to leave this all behind and to come with me to Valtivar." Kaius looked up at the door, glaring in determination, and tried to hide the trembling in his hands at his sides.

Adhnis let out a loud sigh, commanding his attention. "Okay, I'll try my best to convince her to leave with me. It won't be easy though. She might get angry that it's not ye there, and she may not trust me after everything she's been through." She shrugged her shoulders.

He smiled. "I know, but she's a strong one and will see reason." Kaius looked away and grabbed his chin. "Actually, I have an idea. Tell her this. On my eighth nameday, she managed to drag Vincent to the Servants Quarters to celebrate my day of birth. I was feeling lonely that day. I had been bullied for no reason that morning and was told Vincent would be too busy to visit. Alaia had the castle's chef bake her three cupcakes with a rare ingredient she always requested on special occasions. They were chocolate lavender cupcakes, and they were so delicious, Vincent was taken aback, and a small smile creased his face for the first time in a long while. It was really nice. At least, until King Cecilio found us and, well . . ."

"Scolded ye three like the stinkhorn that he is." She pursed her lips in annoyance.

Kaius let out a soft chortle. "I swear, what *is* a stinkhorn?"

"Trust me, ye don't want to know." She giggled.

He rolled his eyes and grinned. "Anyway, tell Alaia that, and she should trust you, and . . . tell her so long as her father reigns as King, my brother and I won't be safe here. Please, Adhnis."

She raised her hands in the air and looked away with tightly closed eyes. "Okay. Okay, ye don't have to twist my arm or anything. Just . . ." Adhnis opened her eyes and looked at him with curved brows. She lunged toward his cheek, embracing him. Kaius startled for a moment until he sighed happily and cupped her legs with his hand in an attempt to return the embrace. "Be careful, Kaius. We *will* meet again."

His heart flipped in his chest and his breath hitched in his throat. Although his eyes stung, he refused to cry and instead smiled in thanks. "Be safe, my friend."

Adhnis squeezed his cheek for a moment longer, then hopped off and flew high up the mountainside, toward some windows above the gates. Kaius returned his gaze to the stone gate and placed a hand on its cold surface, feeling the curves of the simple carvings. He looked up toward the top of the gate, at the massive monster. His eyes trembled nervously.

Kaius stepped back, took a deep breath, and pushed against the gate. A loud clunk sounded from deep within the stone, startling him back. The doors then opened. "Okay Vincent, if this is your doing, I want you to know that I'm here to talk, not fight." Kaius' eyes softened and a heaviness hung in his stomach. "I want to save you from making a huge mistake if I can. Please come home with me, wherever that home may be."

13

KAIUS

FIRE AND DEATH

L IT SCONCES HUNG ON THE WALLS, lighting up enough of the hallway to see round stone pillars spread far apart on either side of the massive entrance hall. The hall looked as though it could stretch on for miles.

As Kaius traveled deeper into the passage, the darkness seemed to spread, thickening and threatening to envelop everything in its path, save for that of the small pools of firelight. Was he nearing the end, or was the darkness coming to meet him? He couldn't really be certain either way, but hoped there would be no monsters waiting for him within.

"So, you've finally arrived, little brother." A monotone voice broke the silence and softly echoed through the hall.

Kaius stopped and eyed his surroundings, but could see nothing, save for darkness. "Vincent, please, wherever you are, come out. I just want to talk!" His plea was met with further silence. Kaius' stomach churned, his palms sweating within his gloves. "Okay then," he whispered to himself, "I'll go first."

Taking a deep breath, he continued, his voice more confident. "Vincent, I'm sorry for not believing you. I . . . I should've listened. Should've talked with you instead of fighting. You've always been there for me. I never should've doubted you. Let me be here for you now."

The air was stale and smelled of a faint unpleasant odor. His words were met with another long stretch of silence. A bead of sweat slid down Kaius' brow as a torrent of worry and doubt swelled to life in his heart. "Vincent, I—"

"What changed?"

Kaius' lips tightened into a thin, pursed line and lightly quivered. "I've been having flashes of memories. I also learned a lot from a fairy of Eylowen Forest. These last few days have been . . . enlightening. Vincent, I-I'm so sorry."

A few moments passed before soft laughter sounded from the darkness. Kaius scanned the hall, searching for his brother, but the echo masked his location.

"Brother, please. I've . . . been to our home. I found the hanging horse outside." Kaius' chest tightened. "I found your journal. I've read all of your entries. End this madness, I beg of you!"

"Oh? You've read my journal, have you?" Vincent asked flatly.

After a long, breathless moment, a flash of white light exploded around Kaius. He shielded his eyes as best he could with his arms. His vision cleared and shock set in. Kaius was no longer surrounded by the darkened halls of the mausoleum, but instead outside, staring at a massive stone city.

Overhead the sky shone brightly in a sea of blue, save for a few clouds peppered here and there. Colorful confetti rained from above as bright streams of fabric crisscrossed between buildings.

People passed by in robes of various hues. Children with hair of bright white and eyes of violet ran about holding beautiful spinning pinwheels.

"Beautiful, isn't it. A city of mages, wizards, and sorcerers. The outside world had many names for what we were . . . what you and I are. This was our home. The city itself was a testament to our people's understanding of magic, built into its very foundation. That's how it came to be so grand, a diamond in a sea of quartz."

A sudden series of thunderclaps boomed in the sky behind Kaius. He turned in worry, but calmed as he noticed the people smiling, excitedly pointing and heading toward the sounds.

Crowds of people started forming in the square nearby. Those who passed him by and made contact with him phased right through, as though his body were no longer corporeal. He stared on for a moment, bewildered, and then followed. There he saw a small group of wizards conjuring various animals through the use of their arcane magics. Phoenix, jackalope, gryphowl, strix, chamrosh, so many creatures appeared. Most of which Kaius had only read about in books.

"Our magic was considered . . . different to that of the many types known to these lands. The fae folk work with spirits and nature for their magic. The Valtivarians *need* their runes for even the simplest of spells. Tourbiyonvans, those from the rose country far to the West, mark their bodies with tattoos to channel their elemental magic. We, on the other hand, have something unique within us. Something said to be gifted to us by our gods. We can conjure the four elements as many others do, but we can also conjure illusions and portals. It's been said that some of our highest order could even briefly stop time. The cosmic arcane energy within us made us powerful. It also made people *fear* us."

In an instant, the sun fell from the sky and the moon rose high. Fewer people filled the streets now, some holding their sleepy little ones in their arms.

As Kaius took in the stillness of the night and the soft, soothing buzz of cicadas, he spotted a small dot of light peeking over the city. It quickly grew larger and brighter by the second as it rose into the sky. Another suddenly popped into view. Two. Then eight. Twenty. Too many to count.

By the time he realized what was happening, screams sounded, and blasts rang out. Massive boulders covered in flaming pitch barreled through walls and homes with explosive force. The fire and fury washed over the city like flame to tinder.

"NO!" Kaius jumped back at the ready as his hand flew to his sword, in the moment forgetting he could do nothing to stop this tragedy and was powerless to protect the poor souls being slaughtered in front of him.

A boulder blasted through the home beside him, flashed across the street, and disappeared into the adjacent home, leaving a trail of flame and debris barring his way. Flaming arrows tore through the city.

Arrow after arrow soared through the darkness finding their mark, piercing head, chest, back, and arms, leaving their targets alight in flame. Arrows also struck buildings, bounced off stonewalls, and ignited banners and the hanging crisscross fabrics above.

Children sat crying beside fallen parents and loved ones while those lucky enough to have survived the volley thus far tried to fend off the barrage with their magic. The arrows never ceased, an endless rain of iron and fire, leaving the people no time to counter, no time to mount a defense. Loud screeches tore through the sky. He looked up and saw a ball of fire coming right toward him.

He screamed in panic and rolled out of the way. The large fireball crashed into the building behind him. Wails and howls filled the air as buildings burned.

"Vi-Vincent, please!"

"The Ligeras were behind the attack on us. Our home! OUR PEOPLE! They snuck in under cover of darkness, wiped us out in a single. Damn. Night. They killed our parents, Kaius!"

The surroundings changed once again. He was now inside a burning home. Kaius looked to his left and right, trying to find his bearings in all the chaos. A child cried loudly behind him. He spun around and saw a tiny, blond boy sitting in the corner, hugging his knees and calling out for his parents.

"RUN! You have to run. Take your brother and get out of here, it's too late for us!"

Kaius abruptly spun again, his breath catching in his throat. A man laid dead at the doorway with arrows marking his head and back, the fire was spreading across his clothes. Far to his left, an older boy with blond hair and tears in his wide, horror-filled eyes held the hand of a woman with snowy white hair.

"NO! No, I can get you out of here. I just need my magic and I can lift the boulder. Just tell me what to do!"

Kaius' eyes traveled down the woman's body half buried beneath a boulder. "My dear Vincent, my precious boy. There's no time for that, not now, but you and Kaius can still make it out. Leave—" She coughed, blood spurting from her lips. It flowed down her chin as tears poured down her cheeks. "Take Kaius and go!" Her teeth gritted as she clutched Vincent's hands, then pushed him back.

Her hand stayed raised as a faint smile grew on her face. "It's alright, Vincent. It's all—" She coughed, and a few drops of blood landed on Vincent's cheek. Then the color in her swirling violet eyes faded and her head dropped to the floor, her breath weak. "Going to be . . . alright . . ." The words came soft, limply from her lips, before her body went completely still.

Kaius stood there staring at the woman. He slowly looked at his older brother, in this moment so young, staring at their mother with mouth agape and unable to move. A sudden nearby crash caused Kaius to jolt. Vincent reacted quickly, hopping up from the floor, and rushed to his younger brother.

Unable to bear anymore, Kaius fell to his knees. He buried his tear-filled face in his hands and cried out, "Please. PLEASE Vincent, stop, just stop! I can't take anymore. I can't—" His stomach churned, and his heart ached.

Hearing the pitter-patter of little Vincent's footfalls across the wooden floor, Kaius looked up and saw his brother grab the younger version of himself. The vision then quickly dispersed and the real Vincent emerged.

He thrusted his hand toward Kaius. Jolting and shutting his eyes, he braced for whatever Vincent intended to do. To his surprise, he felt nothing, save for the stray hair strands brushing against his face.

"Kaius . . . your hair. Are you awakening?"

He slowly opened his eyes and was taken aback by Vincent's wide-eyed stare. His brother then raised his other hand to Kaius' face, pushing the strands back.

"Even your eyes are half violet. H-How? When did this happen?" Vincent asked, cupping Kaius' cheeks and inspecting him still.

"I-I . . ." Kaius raised his hands to meet his brother's, removing them from his face, and stared somberly at Vincent's hands now in his. "The fairy Queen of Eylowen Forest, Throstnie, she helped . . . open the way for me. The events of our past sealed it away, though it surged within me, trying desperately to come forth." He raised his gaze to meet his brother's, his violet eyes relaxing, but still lightly trembling.

"So, it was trauma that kept your magic at bay."

Kaius nodded. "Yeah, I . . ." He held Vincent's hand tightly and glanced to his right arm just above the wrist. "Vincent, I'm going to remove the oath placed over you by King Cecilio."

"No." Vincent stated firmly, taking Kaius by surprise.

"But if you just—"

"No!" Vincent slid his hand from Kaius' grip and cupped his younger brother's cheeks once more with a trembling smile. "Kaius, this magic is too strong. You're still coming into your powers. I-I know of another way to free us. It'll be—"

Kaius took a deep breath, quickly grabbed hold of Vincent's right arm, and closed his eyes to concentrate. He summoned forth the power within himself. A surge of warmth swelled within his chest.

"Kaius stop!"

Just as he felt Vincent's free hand clasp onto his shoulder, Kaius fell. He immediately opened his eyes and found himself surrounded by a familiar darkness.

"Okay, what if—" He turned around and spotted a small golden sphere glowing in the close distance.

Without a moment's hesitation, he ran to it. His footsteps echoed louder and louder as he drew closer to the sphere. Reaching the orb, he stopped and stared at it for a moment. "I wonder if this is it."

He raised his hands, cupped together beneath the thing, and brought them mere inches from its surface. Just as he was about to make contact, a cacophonous voice sounded around him from all directions.

Kaius . . . stop . . .

The voice echoed and reverberated throughout the void, just barely audible, but sounded vaguely like Vincent. Its tone, while masked in a thick layer of unnatural sounds, rang clear with panic. Undeterred, Kaius' resolve strengthened.

"I swear Vincent, I'm going to help you."

Kaius cupped the golden sphere. It suddenly exploded and out flowed countless runic knotted chains soaring all around him. He took a deep breath to relax his nerves and racing heart as his surroundings changed to that of night. The ground rippled as that of the sea brushed by a calm wind, oily, and mirroring the star filled sky above.

The air around him hummed and prickled his skin. Kaius looked up and saw a naked figure curled in on itself within a glowing sphere. He squinted, trying to focus his eyes to peer through the glow. The figure, though somewhat obscured, had a striking resemblance to his older brother and seemed to be sleeping peacefully.

Kaius' breath hitched in his throat. "Vincent." He raised his hands up toward the sphere, just able to touch it. Kaius took a long, deep breath and closed his eyes. "Break the chains that bind him. Loose the collar that quiets him. Cut the strings that guide him. Burn the chart that finds him. Free your child from darkness and raise him into the Mother's light."

As the last word left his lips, a fire ignited within his chest. Kaius groaned and grinded his teeth as the sweltering blaze surged through his entire being. He let out a scream, arching his back, his hands unable to pry free of the sphere.

Kaius just barely peered through wincing eyes. The wind and chains around him began to whirl. Faster and faster everything spun. His brother's prison radiated a blinding white light, slowly enveloping everything in sight.

Kaius jolted violently, his eyes opened, and he released an exhausted breath, as though he had been held underwater nearly to the point of drowning. He released Vincent and collapsed forward to the ground, his breath heaving, and rested his forehead on the backs of his hands.

Kaius' vision faded in and out. He winced as he noted more of his hair had turned white. Kaius stared at a long strand of hair in front of his face, watching the white envelope the blond.

Vincent's breath hitched. "You . . . You broke it? You actually broke it?" Kaius looked wearily up to his older brother, his violet eyes wide. Vincent's gaze then turned to Kaius. "So few of our people can break oaths and curses, Kaius, and yet you did it like it was nothing."

Kaius struggled to keep his head up. "I-I know, as I said, Adhnis and I read your books."

"Adhnis?"

"Sh-She's . . . the little Fairy Princess I've been traveling with." Kaius pushed himself up, fully extending his arms, and stared at the stone ground. "I . . . I wanted to try, okay. It was a long shot. I get it, but I just . . . couldn't leave you in such a prison." He reached out for Vincent's arm, clenching onto his sleeve tightly. "You're free now." Kaius looked up with raised brows, desperation ebbing its way into his heart. "You're free. Do you hear me, Vincent, you're free now!"

Vincent's eyes narrowed a little. "Kaius, what're you getting at?"

Kaius grabbed hold of his older brother's other arm, latching onto Vincent. "Drop this quest of vengeance and come away with me to Valtivar. It's where you've wanted to go anyway, right? No more royals. No more murder. None of it! Let's leave this place behind and never look back, please!"

Thoughts of the acts detailed in Vincent's journal forced upon him by King Cecilio raced through Kaius' mind. Practicing his magic on innocent animals and prisoners, honing his skills through one horrific act after another. Murdering nobles and commoners who voiced opposition to the King. The King even forced Vincent to use his body as a tool when need be. Spy and assassin.

No deed was thought too depraved, as long as it served Cecilio's ends. The thought made Kaius sick to his stomach as bile slowly snaked its way into his throat.

Vincent looked at Kaius quietly for a moment, his eyes soft. "Kaius, I can't just leave. There's still more to do." He cupped Kaius' cheeks and touched his forehead to his little brother's. A trembling smile creased his snow-white face. "Don't worry, everything will be fine. You'll see, with Mykronvan—"

"NO!" Kaius swiped his brother's hands away and clutched onto his arms, shaking him and pleading. "Don't you hear me? You don't *need* to do this! Just come away with me. We'll take your portal, maybe live somewhere by a beach. I know you love to listen to the waves crashing against the shore. Please, I can't bear to see you in pain anymore. I'm here to help. I don't know what I'll do if I lose you too!" Hot streaks of tears poured from Kaius' eyes as he dropped his head, his breath heavy, but slow. "I-I know I've been a terrible brother, ignorant to your woes, but . . . but I'm here now, and I won't let you destroy yourself, even if it's to protect me."

The hall fell quiet. Kaius trembled in anguish, struggling to hold himself upright. He looked into his older brother's wide eyes, searching for a way to make him see sense.

The wind was suddenly knocked out of him as he was sent flying backward several feet. Kaius hit the ground hard and rolled a short distance, stopping on his belly and groaning in pain.

"Where did you get that sword, Kaius? Tell me!" Vincent snarled at him.

Kaius struggled to open his eyes and slid his arms forward. As he tried to push himself up, the weight was too much to bear. He coughed and dropped his forehead onto his freezing gauntlets. "I—The fairies gave me the sword to fend off the monsters *you* summoned. It's . . . the only reason I've survived this long—"

"That sword is the means to locking Mykronvan away in Velkran forever! I've been searching for that damn sword for months, and you're telling me the fairies had it this whole time?"

Kaius winced and looked at the sword at his side. Had Throstnie known that when she gave him the sword? He shook his head as he fought to rise again.

"Who cares." Kaius, managing to get to his knees, raised his hand and stared at his palm. He then looked at his brother with brows furrowing. "We're leaving this place Vincent, whether you like it or not."

Kaius thrusted his arm forward, summoning a gust of wind, and unleashed the gale in Vincent's direction. Vincent, unamused, swiped it away with a simple flick of his wrist. Kaius' heart dropped into his stomach as his brother simply stood there, his head tilted lightly to the side and face as still as stone.

"Oh Kaius, do you want me to show you the true potential of our magic?" Vincent's expression darkened. "Fine then, let me show you how it's done!"

14

ADHNIS

THE FAIRY AND THE DAMSEL

TORCHLIGHTS FLICKERED IN THE DARK, decrepit halls of the
mausoleum. Adhnis kept her light as dim as possible to elude
anything potentially lurking in the shadows.

Flying through the winding halls, she passed several offshoot
pathways shrouded in darkness and followed the torches seemingly
leading her through the maze. Eventually, she came to a fairly well-lit
hall and found a somewhat worn-out door with a faint glow shining
from within.

"I wonder if the Princess is in there." Adhnis whispered to herself.

She flew up to the small, rectangular, barred opening of the door
and quietly peeked inside. A large black sphere floated in the center

of a sizable cell. A shroud of mist swirled within the orb. At its center, she could faintly make out the form of a young woman in a pink dress.

"That must be her!" Adhnis gasped, then jolted as she realized she had spoken her words aloud. She looked to her left and right, making sure she hadn't given away her presence.

Her stomach churned and a shiver crawled up her spine. The silence of the hall unsettled her. She couldn't put into words what it was about the place that unnerved her so. There was nothing here, after all. No dark beasts. No Kaius' brother. Not even a single guard. This was too . . . quiet.

Adhnis' hands rested flat on the wooden door, trembling ever so slightly. The feeling of something dark and powerful hiding within the mountains had troubled her since entering the ruined halls. She couldn't shake the feeling that there was something here, something horrible, but what could it be?

She looked up to the young woman and shook the thought away. "First things first, I have to free her for Kaius, then I can worry."

Adhnis quickly, but carefully, flew between the bars and up to the magical barrier caging the young woman. She inspected it for a moment, her body shuddering as a cold feeling crawled beneath her skin. She clutched at her chest, nervous and wondering how she could safely extricate the young woman.

She reached out a hand and slid a finger through the surface of the misty sphere. Black tendrils shot out, wriggling and crawling up her umber skin, causing her to jolt back and pull herself free.

Staring at the orb with more than a little concern, she hesitated. Doubt began to ebb its way into her thoughts. Her brows then furrowed. No. She promised Kaius that she would get the Princess out of here, and that was exactly what Adhnis intended to do.

Adhnis took several deep, concentrated breaths, her eyes tightly shut, and constructed a bright barrier of light to shield herself from the dark magic. "Here goes nothing!" She dove in headfirst, body outstretched as though she were an arrow, and pierced deep into the dark ball.

The mist within stirred at the intrusion, growing into a chaotic torrent, and pushed her in all directions. It assailed her almost as if it had a mind of its own, trying to force her out.

Resolved in her course of action, she pushed on toward the young woman at its center. Coming within arm's length of the human, Adhnis grabbed tightly to the fabric of the young woman's corset. The winds howled and grew even more violent. The force of the gust nearly caused her grip to falter, but Adhnis' determination was unscathed.

She grabbed onto the young woman as tightly as she could, closing her eyes, and reached deep within herself. "Remember what mother said!" Adhnis screamed at herself. "Bring the moon, light the path—NGH! Reveal the sun, warm the hearts! Unwanted darkness begone—AGH! Don't let fear in, don't let it hurt you! You are the light, now ILLUMINATE!"

Adhnis' light ignited as though she were the sun itself. Beams of her radiant light broke through the sphere's surface. In a blinding flash, the dark thing dispersed. Both Adhnis and the young woman fell hard to the ground, moaning in pain and exhaustion.

The young woman, coming to, rubbed her forehead gently. Her eyes struggled to open. Sliding an elbow back, she pushed herself to sit up.

Seeing the human move, Adhnis grabbed onto the young woman's corset as tightly as she could. However, weakened from using her magic, Adhnis could only muster enough strength to hold on for a brief moment before falling to the young woman's pink lap.

"Oh my, are you alright?"

Scooped up and brought close to the human's face, Adhnis' eyes widened in surprise. The young woman was a rare beauty. Her soft copper skin and leafy green eyes glowed faintly in the firelight. Adhnis' cheeks burned as if the sun was hitting her face.

"You're a . . . fairy, right? Did you break me from my prison?"

With labored breath, Adhnis nodded in affirmation. "Ye're . . . Princess Alaia Ligera, right?"

"I am, and you are?" Alaia tilted her head lightly. A few wavy strands of brown hair slid off her shoulder.

"Adhnis, erm . . . Princess of Eylowen Forest."

Alaia winced. "You're from Bosque Encantado." Her brows curved upward.

"Aye, I am. Listen, I promised Kaius—"

"Kaius? How do you know Kaius?" Alaia suddenly stood to her feet while Adhnis was struggling to keep her balance.

"Hey, calm down! I'm getting to that." Adhnis adjusted herself, sliding to her knees, and placed her fisted hands on her thighs.

"Sorry, please go on."

"Kaius asked me to get ye out of here while he confronts Vincent."

Alaia's stare softened, her shoulders lowering. "Excuse me if I'm a bit apprehensive, but how do I know this isn't a trick?"

Adhnis let out a few heavy breaths, her body tired from using so much magic. "That's okay, Kaius told me to tell ye something to gain yer trust. A memory."

"And what memory is that?" Alaia looked at her curiously.

"On one of Kaius' early namedays, ye had a chef make him and Vincent a lavender chocolate cupcake? Sounded delicious too. I hope ye can let me try it someday." Adhnis smiled weakly at the human Princess.

"So . . . Kaius is currently with Vincent?"

Adhnis nodded in affirmation. "Aye."

Alaia's mouth parted, looking at Adhnis with worry growing in her eyes. "Maldita!"[1] Alaia exclaimed, her gaze falling to the floor. "I know what Vincent is planning."

"Ye-Ye do?" Adhnis' heart raced.

"I may have been asleep in that dark sphere, but I was aware of what transpired around me. I listened while he vented his . . . frustrations."

Adhnis could feel the Princess's hands tremble beneath her.

"I understand him. I don't agree, but I understand." Alaia relaxed

1   Spanish for *Dammit!*

her shoulders and her eyes met Adhnis' again, now brimming with conviction. "I need to speak with them. I need to set things right."

"Wait, but Kaius—"

"I need to speak with him too." Alaia smiled as her eyes shined. "Kaius is going to leave for Valtivar, isn't he? He thinks they will be safe there, out of Padre's[2] reach? I'm sure he's learned of what Padre has done to Vincent, so it makes sense he wouldn't feel safe in these lands anymore. Am I right?"

Adhnis startled, unsure of how to respond, her mouth hanging agape.

"I thought so. I . . . learned something of Padre's past, and the two *need* to hear it. Please understand. It's my responsibility to do this."

Adhnis' lips quivered, her emotions conflicted. She looked at the Princess' conviction clear on her face and let out a loud groan. "NGH! Come on! Why can't ye humans just make things simple for once. Damn, just give me a moment."

Alaia flashed the little fairy an apologetic smirk while Adhnis placed her tiny hands on the Princess' palms. She closed her eyes and called forth gems, similar to the one on Kaius' gauntlet, to give the Princess a way to defend herself.

With a quick flash of light, Alaia's palms were covered in many small, clear blue gems forming a flower pattern that spread from her palms to the tips of her fingers. "There, that should do it."

"Tan bonita.[3] What are these stones?"

---

2   Spanish for *Father's*.
3   Spanish for *So pretty*.

"The gems allow me to channel my magic. It's to protect us both." Adhnis replied, standing herself upright. "Okay Princess, if ye're sure about this."

"I am." Alaia nodded.

"Okay, then let's find a way to get ye out of this cell."

Alaia nodded again and headed to the cell door. "There's no need, watch." She walked over to the door, grabbed the rusty iron handle with one hand, and pulled. The iron hinges creaked as the door swung open.

"Wait, first there are no guards, now ye tell me the door was not locked. Why not?" Adhnis looked to the human Princess, searching for answers.

"Vincent didn't think there was a need for extra precautions. With the hordes of monsters in and around the city and the magical barrier I was trapped inside, he was secure in the thought nobody would succeed in a rescue." Alaia peeked her head out of the cell alongside Adhnis.

"Okay Princess, the coast is clear, but we need to be careful. There's something not right about this place. I'm going to place myself within these gems." Adhnis smiled warmly and gestured to Alaia's hands. "If ye run into trouble, just raise yer hands and I'll do the rest. Got it?"

"Will you be alright? You look so exhausted." Alaia tilted her head and gazed at the fairy with worry clear on her face.

"Aye, don't worry. The space within these gems is ... well, different, to put it plainly. I'll be rejuvenated, my magical well unlimited so long as I'm in there, though my abilities will be fewer."

"Alright, I'll do as you say." Alaia smiled with relief and gave Adhnis a quick nod.

Adhnis briefly looked away and closed her eyes. As she took a deep breath, a gentle warmth swelled within her chest, filling her and spreading to the top of her skin. She felt the pull of the gems and her body moved forward. Thrusted suddenly downward, she entered a barrier that felt like colliding through brittle ice and freezing waters. Adhnis floated weightlessly for a moment while her body numbed and skin prickled with gooseflesh. She opened her eyes and found herself in a cosmic blue void, as though the night sky had exploded in an array of rainbow auroras and stars in all directions.

"Okay then, spirits of the eternal light, may I make use of yer energy?" She stretched her hands out to the void. The stars glowed and sparkled around her. Adhnis took a quick breath as lightning surged into her body, the charge crawled beneath her skin. While the sensation was off-putting, she was grateful for the power at her disposal.

Adhnis released a long breath of relief. "There, now we should be good to go."

"*Alright, which way should I go?*" Alaia's voice echoed through the magical void.

"Just follow the torchlights, they led me here and should take us where we need to go." Adhnis replied.

"By any chance, are you able to see while in there?"

A vision appeared in the cosmic sky, blurry at first, but becoming clear. Alaia's face looked at her, head tilted with an inquisitive expression.

Adhnis smiled. "Aye, whatever the crystals see, I can too. So ye'll need to face them toward any enemies so I can protect us."

Alaia nodded in understanding and followed the fairy's instructions, cautiously making her way forward with hands out for Adhnis to see. As Alaia neared the end of the first hall, a large creature, dark and muscular, appeared from around the corner and caused the Princess to shriek.

She quickly raised both hands toward the monster, the vision becoming much clearer for Adhnis. It roared at them, but the Princess held her ground.

A soft white glow brimmed to life on Adhnis' raised palms. The void reacted and glowed brightly in various shades of blue and purple. Adhnis then released the attack, a blast of magic hurtled from the gems on Alaia's palms and crashed into the creature, obliterating it where it stood.

"There, nothing to it." Adhnis exclaimed with a large smile.

"Oh wow, thank you Adhnis. That was . . . terrifying." Alaia said with a tremble in her voice.

"Don't worry about it. Now come on, let's find the entrance." Adhnis replied.

Alaia agreed and ran as swiftly as she was able in her extravagant gown more suited for a ballroom than combat.

Alaia continued forward, the path expanding the further they went. A few monsters barred their way here and there, but it was easy enough for Adhnis to make short work of the shadow beasts. As they made their way along the path, a sweltering protest rose in her chest. What was going on here? Where before there had been no beasts, now they thrived. There was something wrong here and Adhnis didn't like it.

The hall suddenly shook, the violent tremor sending dust raining down from the ceiling. Alaia stopped and hugged a wall to keep her balance. She let out several tired breaths as the quaking calmed. *"What was that?"*

"I wonder if Kaius was forced to use his magic against his brother?"

"Magic? Kaius can't use magic." Alaia raised her palms to her face, arched brows and wide eyes stared in concern and confusion.

"He couldn't before, no, but like his brother, he was born with latent magic inside him. My mother aided him in unlocking it before coming here." Adhnis answered, crossing her arms in equal worry.

"I . . . I had no idea he could—" The place shook again, this time weaker than before.

"Come on, best we not dawdle Princess."

"Please, call me Alaia." She responded with a small frown.

A small smile creased Adhnis' lips inside the gems. "Kaius was right about us it seems. I don't like to be called Princess either." The two chuckled softly, the tension of their situation somewhat relieved.

Continuing, they eventually came to a doorway leading into a massive hall. Entering, Alaia grabbed handfuls of the skirt of her dress and hurried to a nearby stone railing. She peeked over to get her bearings. *"I think this is the main hall. We might be on the second floor. It's too dark to know for sure."*

"Can I see?"

Alaia looked into the gems and nodded, then raised her palms outstretched for Adhnis. "The place looks really big. Granted, I'm tiny so most things look massive to me." Alaia chortled at the remark, but immediately stifled herself with an apology. "Okay then, let's find the stairs and—"

An explosive boom erupted from somewhere below them. An armored man hurtled into view, crashed into a round torchlit pillar, and fell to the floor. Both Adhnis and Alaia startled in shock, gasping loudly. The knight's white and blond hair lay loose over his face, his body still on the ground.

"KAIUS!"

KAIUS

PLEAS AND PROMISES

KAIUS CRASHED HARD INTO A ROUND STONE PILLAR. The air escaped his lungs as he fell to the cold floor. The weight of his body was burdensome as the hall spun wildly around him. His eyelids were heavy with exhaustion.

"KAIUS!"

He heard the dual panicked shouts of his name ringing out from somewhere above. Kaius knew those voices. Struggling to push himself up through the pain and haze clouding his thoughts, he turned his head to his right, to where he imagined the voices had come from. His vision blurred in and out of focus as he scanned the second floor, but saw no one.

Footsteps then sounded before him, jolting him back to the present danger before him and he redoubled his efforts to stand in vain.

Kaius looked up to meet his brother before him. He only saw Vincent for a moment before his brother seized him by a large chunk of his now mostly white hair and yanked hard, forcing Kaius to his knees.

"Tell me little brother, who are you *really* here for? Me, or the damn Princess!" With a wave of his hand, Vincent magically lifted Kaius off his feet and into the air. He paused briefly then tossed Kaius several paces away where he crashed again to the ground.

Kaius let out a strained fit of coughs, resting weakly on his side. He struggled to open his eyes, his vision obscured by tears. "I-I came for you both . . . Vincent. I came for you both." He whispered dryly.

"Hmph, is that so? Tell me, Kaius, what was it that made you finally hear my words? Was it when I took your *precious* Alaia from you? Did King Cecilio threaten you, finally showing his vile colors?"

Vincent's words bit deep into Kaius' heart. Tears freely streaked down his cheeks. He turned his head away, eyes firmly shut and felt the cold, rough stone against his forehead. "I-I'm sorry, Vincent. I'm so sorry."

"Apologies will change nothing, Kaius."

The coldness in Vincent's tone caused Kaius to wince. He really did hurt him. Kaius didn't mean to abandon his older brother. He just . . . He just—

"Vincent stop!"

Kaius jolted and turned, seeing a pink dress slide into view. Alaia stood before him, her arms outstretched, shielding him from his brother.

Vincent stared at the Princess with a look of disinterest. Looking her up and down, he broke the silence. "I see, like Kaius, you received aid from a fairy. Interesting, considering your family's history with magical beings."

"Abuelo[1] may have been a monster, but I'm nothing like him *or* my padre!"[2]

Both brothers startled at the mention of the King, staring at her with eyes wide. Kaius tried to push himself up, but only managed to lean on his elbows. He reached out for the Princess, grabbing the fabric of her dress and gently tried to pull her toward him. However, she didn't budge.

"Alaia—" Kaius started, but his words caught as Vincent began to approach them both.

She startled slightly and flinched as he raised a hand to her. Kaius feared an attack, knowing he was in no position to guard her. Vincent instead grabbed her chin, forcing her to meet his gaze.

"And how long have you known, little Princess?" Vincent's eyes creased accusingly, glaring at her.

Kaius couldn't see Alaia's face, but her body trembled with fear. "The . . . The morning of my sixteenth name day. So, only a few days."

A glint of light caught in her tears as they fell from her face. Her hands

---

1   Spanish for *Grandfather.*
2   Spanish for *Father.*

raised to clutch Vincent's wrist.

"You're the granddaughter of a genocidal madman *and* the daughter of an abusive manipulator. Why should I believe you? Is this meek display of sadness meant to sway me?"

Alaia firmly squeezed Vincent's wrist. "Please Vincent, you've known me since we were children. When have I *ever* shown to be like my padre or my abuelo? I've been nothing but kind to you both. You of all people should know I am *nothing* like them. I have never wanted for your death. I would never use you and your brother, for magical purposes or otherwise. Please Vincent, give me a chance. Give me the chance to set you *both* free."

Vincent's eyebrows twitched. He took a small step back. His hands flashed in a violet glow and Alaia raised into the air.

Hearing her pained groans, Kaius pleaded with his brother, "Vincent do—" Before Kaius could finish his sentence, his throat tightened and he was hoisted into the air as well. Looking at Vincent, Kaius saw the disdain and anger in his brother's glare. The look sent a shiver up Kaius' spine.

Vincent stared at them silently for a short time until his eyes drifted to Alaia. "Do you really think your father would just let us go? If you truly believe that, you're dumber than you are beautiful, Princess. Take a look at my brother. Go ahead, my bind can't stop you from doing that."

Kaius glanced as best he could to Alaia, seeing her struggling to turn to him.

"Do you see his hair, Princess?" Vincent asked flatly. "It's changing, and soon, he'll be able to do magic as easily as I. What in Helgad Inferis makes you think your father would let *either* of us go now? Your grandfather's fear of us was so great that he wiped my people off this world. Your father wishes to use people like Kaius and myself for power. *No* place is safe for us, so long as your father lives."

Kaius watched Alaia, her eyes slowly shining and steadily flowing with tears. "I-I . . . I know what my padre has planned, and I know the real reason your city fell!"

The hold over Kaius and Alaia suddenly released and the two fell to the ground, panting and coughing. Kaius glanced up at his older brother, who stared at Alaia in bewilderment.

Kaius turned to Alaia and placed a hand on her back to check her well-being. She shook her head, eyes tightly closed and facing down to the floor, rubbing her neck with her hands.

"Speak." Vincent commanded as his hands lowered to his side.

Alaia slowly opened her eyes, her gaze locked to the floor. "It was Valtivar." She whispered hoarsely.

Kaius remained still though his eyes were wide with shock. "Come again?"

She glanced at him and turned her head. "The reason . . . my people were able to sneak up on Kunnagar in the dead of night was because of Valtivar. Their seidr magic concealed my abuelo's army. All because—" She looked up at Vincent with pause, her brows curved and mouth opened.

"Go on." Vincent said through gritted teeth. Kaius turned to his brother, his hands trembling at his side.

Alaia closed her eyes and looked away. "The late King of Valtivar was furious with Kunnagar for refusing to acknowledge his rule during the country's unification. Since he couldn't have them, he refused to suffer their existence and instilled the seed of fear in my abuelo's ear, leading to Kunnagar's downfall."

Vincent winced. "What do you mean *late* king?"

"King Sigurd's sons usurped him a few years ago. Padre's idea of using magical beings for his own benefit came from Sigurd. In fact, Padre was furious with Abuelo for the loss of such potent . . . slaves, he called them. One night, while all were asleep, Padre suffocated Abuelo with a pillow, letting everyone *believe* he died in his sleep."

Kaius' heart skipped a beat. He let out a trembling breath. The truth of the King, and the Ligeras as a whole, came crashing down on him. Though he learned from Adhnis that it had been the Ligeras who felled Kunnagar, hearing it from Alaia's own lips was another thing entirely. Knowing that even Valtivar, his home country, was behind it made him feel a hollow ache in his chest.

Was there nowhere he and his older brother could go to be safe?

"There's . . . more." Alaia said hesitantly.

"What more pain would you possibly instill on my brother and myself?" Vincent replied coldly.

Alaia looked up to meet Vincent, a blazing fire behind her green eyes. The look startled Kaius. "The truth Vincent, you both deserve to know. Some of your brethren survive even now in Valtivar."

"What!?" Vincent lunged at her, his hands wrapping around her neck. He raised her to the tips of her toes and drew his face near hers. "What trick are you playing at?"

Kaius jumped with all his strength at his brother, trying to release Vincent's grip. "Vincent, please calm down! She can't explain if you're choking her."

Vincent turned his ire on his brother, snarling. "There's nothing to explain, this is all a—"

"AGH—Kunnagarians survived—fled to Valtivar!" Alaia exclaimed with struggle.

Vincent's eyes widened, disbelief clear on his face as Kaius noticed his older brother's grip loosen around Alaia's throat. With a deep draw of breath she continued, "When my padre found out, even though it was after King Sigurd had passed, he accused them of harboring that which belongs to him. He truly believes Valtivar will start a war for domination. He's growing desperate. Padre's plan—"

Kaius successfully freed Alaia from Vincent's grasp and pushed him away. Alaia keeled over, coughing violently while Kaius rubbed her back.

An uneasy feeling gnawed at the back of his mind. What could King Cecilio be planning? Kaius helped her to her feet and flashed her a pleading look. "Alaia, can you continue? Please?"

She met his gaze and nodded. "His plan . . . it involves you, Kaius. You and Vincent. He needs your magic to awaken, then plans to use you both to make the first move against Valtivar. Padre would have the two of you take down the fairies' barrier around Bosque Encantado and use *all* of you to his own ends. That's why . . ." Alaia went silent, looking as though she was afraid to continue. Kaius' heart pounded nervously against his ribs.

"Well, what is it?" Vincent exclaimed impatiently.

"Help me usurp my padre." Her brows furrowed over her eyes. Kaius was unsure if the look was that of determination or concern.

The hall fell silent. Both Vincent and Kaius stared wide eyed at Alaia.

"You want me to what?" Vincent asked softly, the shock clear in his voice.

"Hold it! I can't stay quiet any longer."

Kaius jolted as the crystals on Alaia's hands suddenly flashed and out burst Adhnis. Her arms crossed over her chest and silver eyes glared at Alaia. "Yer Father wants to use them for his own gain, now ye wish to do the same?"

"No of course not! I'm asking for aid. I can't do this alone." She looked up at Vincent, clutching her hands over her chest. "Vincent, I know you have no reason to trust me, but *please* believe me when I say I care for you both. I would see you both freed from my padre's hold. My people fear his iron hold on Rosado. All of Pacífica feels threatened by his rule. No one trusts him. Most only appease him so as to not catch his ire. Madre[3] has a plan. If we play our cards right, we can imprison him. Should we succeed, he won't be able to hurt you. Either

3   Spanish for *Mother*.

of you. Ever again!" Tears fell from her tightly closed eyes.

Kaius stared at her for a moment as a realization began to dawn on him. "We can do it." He whispered to himself just loud enough to gain the others' attention.

"Kaius, were ye able to—"

He quickly turned to his brother, interrupting Adhnis and staring at Vincent, unwavering. "We can stop him. We can overthrow King Cecilio! I removed the oath. He can't control you. All we have to do is play the part and he will drop his guard. We can deal with him for good!"

Vincent took a step back, looking at him not with concern, but with confusion and eyes trembling under pinched brows. "Kaius, I-I made a deal—"

"WELL DROP THE DEAL! You don't need Mykronvan's so-called aid."

"Kaius, calm yerself." Adhnis quickly flew before Kaius, making him take a breath. Alaia grasped his arms and had him take a step back. His hands now trembled at his side.

The choice was obvious. Wasn't it? They had to aid Alaia and stop King Cecilio for good. No being exiled to the demon realm of Velkran could be trusted, no matter how tempting an offer they made. Kaius glanced up at Vincent, eyes trembling. But what consequences would they face if Vincent suddenly rejected Mykronvan?

It didn't matter. They had to do this themselves.

"Vincent," Adhnis called, breaking Kaius from his thoughts. He looked to Adhnis now floating before Vincent's face, staring him down with furrowed brows. "Can ye really say, without a doubt, whatever deal ye made with Mykronvan won't involve hurting yer brother further?"

Vincent winced. "He-He wouldn't. He promised!"

"Mykronvan was banished to the Shadow Realm for a reason. He's just looking for a way out, and ye're it!"

Vincent swiped at Adhnis. She avoided him with a flip backwards and dove behind Kaius who quickly shielded her from his brother. "You know she speaks truth, Vincent. Please, trust us to make this right. There's no need to rely on such a malevolent being."

Alaia stepped forward with her hands clasped on her stomach. "Please Vincent, you don't have to trust me, but what about my madre? She often spoke up against Padre in your defense, even . . . cared for you. Can't you trust in her?"

Both Kaius and Alaia stared at Vincent in silence for a long while. With a large gulp, Vincent glanced at Alaia. "Can you . . . promise me that what you and your mother have planned . . . it will work? What if Kaius is forced to take Cecilio's oath before we take him down?"

"Then you can break it, as I did for you." Kaius reached out for Vincent's hand and grabbed it tight. "Vincent, I *swear* to you, we will win this. Please, don't go down *this* road. Take the path we're offering."

Feeling Vincent's hand begin to tremble in his, Kaius squeezed gently for comfort. Vincent then released a long breath. "It seems in all my anger, I've done nothing but hurt you, didn't I, Kaius?"

Kaius' breath hitched and he quickly shook his head with tears threatening to pour forth. "No, I—" He paused, not sure what to say. The two brothers looked at each other wordlessly. After a moment, Vincent's hand steadied and his fingers wrapped around Kaius' hands.

Kaius' heart swelled with joy. Wanting nothing more than to embrace his older brother, though he knew now was not the time. Their newfound alliance was tentative at best and there was still the matter of Mykronvan to be dealt with.

"Alright . . . we'll try it your way, but know this, Alaia, if anything befalls Kaius—"

"I'll be your shield. I promise. If Kaius convincingly serves my padre as he always has, without question, no harm will come to him. Padre believes he's got Kaius wrapped around his fingers. However," Alaia's frown deepened, "there's a chance you'll—"

"I'll receive a whipping or some other punishment likely already prepared by that bastard. I just don't want Kaius to experience anything like that *if* we go back." Vincent's eyes turned to slits, flashing Alaia a biting glare.

She winced and hesitantly nodded. "I-I understand. Come on, let's just—AGH!" Alaia let out a piercing shriek.

Before Kaius and Vincent had a chance to react, the three of them were bound by the wrists and lifted high in the air. Kaius looked down, his feet dangling helplessly below him.

"Shit! What is—" He looked behind him and found shadow monsters where before there were none. While sharing the same flesh as those he had battled since his journey began, their appearance was vastly different, almost human-like.

They stood tall and slender. Four glowing orange eyes peered from their heads topped by two arched horns, their skin as black as shadows. Kaius' heart leapt into his throat, and he quickly looked up to his hands to find a way to free himself. The dark tentacles wrapped around his wrists, grew, and morphed into a sphere on either hand, enveloping them down to his forearms. He turned to Alaia and Vincent, finding them trapped in the same binding.

A cacophonous, otherworldly cackle echoed through the hall, causing a chill to crawl up Kaius' spine. He stopped struggling and searched the surrounding chamber, but saw nothing, save for the five shadow monsters.

"Kaius!"

Kaius turned his attention ahead and spotted Adhnis flying hurriedly toward him. Just as she reached him, she was instantly encased in a dark sphere. She let out a muffled, angry shriek as the creature imprisoning her flung her far to the other side of the hall. Her light was just barely visible in the darkness.

"ADHNIS!" Kaius fought to yank his hands free, but only managed to tire himself as he swung to and fro. "Dammit, let me go!"

ENOUGH!

The same unnerving feeling from a moment ago fell over him

again. Kaius' stomach churned as he looked around, fear growing in his gut. Alaia hung beside him, her breath heavy and also looking for the origin of the voice. Vincent, however, held his wide-eyed gaze to a spot to his right.

Following his older brother's gaze, Kaius was taken aback as he spotted a massive door in the short distance, larger than the one at the entrance of the mausoleum. Similar stone carvings were etched into the face of the doors, but with one difference: a notable sword-shaped indentation in the dead center of its surface.

"Vincent, where does that lead?" Kaius asked, his voice shaking.

"I think you know *exactly* where it leads, little brother." Vincent glanced at Kaius, a spark of worry clear in his expression, then turned back to the doors.

Kaius' chest tightened, his mind swimming in a sea of dread. "The door to Velkran . . ."

COMMENCE WITH THE OPENING!

The monsters holding Vincent and Alaia began walking toward the doors. The two fought as hard as they could to free themselves, kicking and screaming, but try as they might, it was of no use.

Kaius cursed with a snarl. What could he do? What—

He winced as a realization dawned on him. Scolding himself, he looked up at his imprisoned hands. Magic. That was the key. He forced himself to immediately think of light. Its bright white glow. A sweltering heat exploded in the center of his chest and rushed up his arms.

He watched his hands, staring intently at the dark spheres, expecting the light to break forth any moment now. Moment after moment, nothing happened.

The surge of heat inevitably faded inside him.

His mouth fell open and eyes quaked in confusion. "No way, what is this? My magic isn't working! Vincent—"

"I know. I'm trying, but nothing's working!"

Just as Vincent and Alaia came before the massive doors, the cackling laughter returned, drawing their attention to the stone surface.

I WAS HOPING TO FIND A USE FOR THESE CREATURES! SO LONG AS YOU ARE BOUND, YOU WILL REMAIN POWERLESS! NOW, PLACE THEIR HANDS ON THE DOORS!

"I REJECT YOUR OFFER!"

The shadow beasts lowered their captives and stopped as Vincent and Alaia's feet touched the floor. Kaius stared on with bated breath as his arms grew numb.

"I reject your offer, Mykronvan!" Vincent bellowed again, almost desperately. "I don't want it. I've found another way to save my brother." He declared as he glared at the stone doors before him.

For a short time, there was no answer, only silence. Then a soft, echoing chuckle broke the quiet and slowly built to a booming fit of laughter. Kaius' throat dried, his mind a whirl of fear and concern.

MY APOLOGIES, DID I GIVE YOU THE IMPRESSION YOU HAD A

CHOICE? COMMENCE!

"NO!" The three screamed out as the lanky monsters forced an arm from both Vincent and Alaia to the door, toward two carved handprints.

Kaius watched helplessly as the two pulled and fought with all their might to no avail. As their hands drew close to the prints, the spheres quickly opened. The bright blue gems on Alaia's hand fell to the floor. Both their hands were pulled toward the prints as if by an invisible force.

A clunk sounded from within as their hands touched the prints, the two still trying to pull themselves free. After a moment, a bright light appeared around the edge of their hands. The light slowly started to change, new colors appearing one by one until their hands were bathed in rainbow light.

A strange silverish sheen enveloped the face of the stone, pulsating inward toward their hands. Faster and faster the sheen slid across its surface. The pulsating quickened and grew in strength until, with one last pulse, it ejected their hands from the indentations.

The world about them started to quake. Small bouts of debris and dust rained down from the ceiling. As Alaia was freed from the door, she rose high in the air and shrieked. She was then quickly swung back past Kaius. "ALAIA!"

She hit the ground hard and rolled for several feet, stopping on her belly. She let out a few hard gasps for air, but couldn't seem to pick herself up. Kaius tried to yank his hands free again, however, it was still no use.

"Dammit! Ju-Just hang on, I'll—" The loud grinding of stone gears sounded within the walls, interrupting him. An opening slowly began to form from the doorway.

Kaius could barely make out a strange misty void beyond the stone. Bright glowing orange eyes flashed open within, followed by a chilling laugh.

Vincent turned to Kaius, violet eyes wide with horror as a single tear rolled down his cheek. "Kaius, I'm so sorry." As the last word left his lips, a massive swirl of dark mist surrounded and consumed him.

"NO VINCENT!" Kaius cried out, his heart feeling like it was being twisted from the inside.

A bright light quickly emanated from the sword at his side. A powerful surge of heat exploded throughout his body. His white hair faintly glowed as it gently fluttered against his skin. He closed his eyes tightly, took a deep breath, and let out a powerful roar.

Pulses of light exploded out of him, one for every beat of his heart. As his roar quieted, he fell to the floor. Once his feet touched the ground, he collapsed to his knees, just barely catching himself before falling flat on his face.

Kaius' breath was heavy, and the world around him spun, his

vision was somewhat blurry. The last remnants of his blond hair were now gone, his strands fully engulfed in white.

He grazed his fingers through the loose strands in front of his face, feeling as soft as a cat's fur. Kaius groaned and tried to push himself up off the ground.

"Oh my, that was a close one."

A deep, velvety voice emanated from where his brother had stood, startling Kaius. He slowly looked up and saw a figure resembling Vincent.

It was draped in his violet robes. His white hair was unchanged. Even his facial features remained the same, but his fair skin was now turned to an ominous dark gray hue, like that of the surrounding stone. Vincent's once violet eyes were now replaced by black scleras and glowing orange irises that burned brightly at their center.

The figure smirked as he tilted his head to the side. "I must say, your brother's magical potency is astounding when compared to my previous host."

A pang pierced Kaius' chest. His heart ached and throat tightened. Tears flowed down his cheeks. "Vincent . . . What have you done with him?"

KAIUS

A BET WAS MADE

"**D**ONE WITH HIM?" Mykronvan spread his arms wide, an eerie grin creasing his lips. He touched a hand to the center of his chest. "I've done nothing, young mortal. He's right here, right where I need hi—NGH!" His body jolted, fingers twitched, and face contorted as though struck by a sudden surge of pain.

Kaius rose to his feet, quickly scanned his surroundings, and grabbed hold of the magical sword at his side. The shadowy humanoid monsters were nowhere in sight. Alaia laid unconscious at his back and Adhnis was nowhere to be seen, likely also out cold somewhere in the surrounding darkness.

He hoped the little fairy and the Princess were okay. If anything had happened to them—

"Dammit, this one's proving more resistant than I expected, and after everything I promised him. Ungrateful runt."

Hearing this, Kaius turned his attention back to Mykronvan, glaring angrily and baring his teeth. "Tsk! He rejected your ill-intentioned promise, Mykronvan, or did you forget that!"

Mykronvan blinked in bemusement and met Kaius' gaze. "Mykronvan?" Grabbing his chin, he continued, "Is that the name I gave your brother? In all honesty, I completely forgot."

Kaius stared wide eyed at the being inhabiting his brother. "You . . . You don't even remember your name? How could you forget what you told him?"

"Well, connections between Velkran and this realm can often become lost for days, years, and even centuries. The construct you mortals call time works differently there. It isn't a straight line. Conversations often span millenia, spoken out of order as the past becomes present and future becomes a distant memory. One tends to get lost in the drift you see." He placed a hand on his neck, stretching as though not yet acclimated to the body.

Kaius' jaw clenched, his grip tightening on the sword's hilt. "I don't care. If my brother is still in there, give him back. Give Vincent back to me!" He drew the gold and silver blade from its sheath and pointed it at the sorcerer.

The being flinched and raised a hand to Kaius, then smirked.

"Now now young mortal, let's not be too hasty. You wouldn't want to hurt Vincent's body would you? Besides, after all the pain you've caused him already, it'd be a shame for him to watch as I use his own hands to kill his baby brother." His orange gaze hardened. "Don't stand in my way. I've made a bet with Mother, and I don't plan to lose."

"A bet?" Kaius exclaimed, confused. "That's between you and your mother. Leave us out of it. Get out of my brother's body, now!" He stood firm, readying himself to fight.

The sorcerer watched, raised an eyebrow, and simply smirked. "She's your Mother too, after all."

"My mother is dead. What are you getting at?" Kaius snarled through gritted teeth.

"Not your *human* mother, boy. She goes by many names in this realm, but I believe the people of these lands, lacking imagination, call Her the Mother."

A shiver crawled its way up Kaius' spine, staring silent and wide eyed at the sorcerer. "Wait, what *are* you getting at? Who are you?"

The sorcerer shrugged in disinterest. "Centuries go by and tales are spun in many ways. Mykronvan was my host before Vincent. I must say, he was a *much* weaker sorcerer than your brother." He chuckled to himself. "Unfortunately, that weakness made it easy for your ancestors to banish me to that forsaken realm." The sorcerer gestured behind him with an outstretched thumb. Just as he did, a raspy howl sounded from deep within. Kaius looked to the open portal, and his body trembled.

He then refocused his gaze back to the sorcerer. "You're deflecting."

"No, stop interrupting. I'm getting to the point. Like *the* Mother, I too go by many names. I'm sure you've seen my signs, but the name given is Cretan."

Kaius' heart leaped in his chest, the name familiar. The nettle. "Cretan, the-the God of Chaos?"

"Hm? You're missing a title. I'm of both Chaos AND Rebirth. Honestly, are tales of me really so morbid?" His smirk turned to a disappointed frown. He then took a step toward the small set of stairs leading down to where Kaius stood.

Kaius jolted and slid a foot back, raising his sword to Cretan. "Stay where you are! I-I mean it, I'm warning you."

"No, I think not. As a matter of fact, I think it's safe to presume you don't even know how to use that sword. Which is perfect for me, really. Best to deal with you while you're helpless." Cretan raised a hand toward Kaius, a dark mist swirled from his forearm to his wrist and fingers.

Kaius startled and dug deep within himself, calling forth the light in the hope that it would be enough to stop the God. "Oh yeah?" He exclaimed, trying to hide the fear swelling within him. Quickly pulling the sword back, he readied an attack. "We'll see about that!" Kaius swung his sword before him in a horizontal arc, summoning a large blade of light, sending it flying toward Cretan.

A loud boom sounded, followed by an explosion of white smoke from where the God stood. Kaius' breath stilled. His hands trembled around the hilt of his sword. Had the attack worked?

As the white smoke began to dissipate, there stood Cretan, hand still raised, and ever so lightly shaking. The hand was no longer gray, instead now just as fair as Kaius' own and a glimmer of hope sparked within him.

"Vincent!" Kaius called out.

As the hand lowered, his hopes were dashed. Vincent's face, his skin, was still gray and those glowering orange eyes stared back at him. He was still Cretan, but how?

"That. Actually. Hurt." Cretan shook his hand as the gray hue returned, shrouding it once more.

The hall suddenly quaked, causing Kaius to stumble to the side, and he looked around. The quake was followed by a deep howling growl emanating from the dark void.

Cretan, seemingly unamused, glanced behind him with a disinterested stare. "If you want to do something then come out here yourself."

The howl sounded once more, again, shaking the hall as debris fell from overhead, and cracks made their way up the pillars.

"Fine. If you're so scared of the sword then be quiet and let me deal with it MYSELF!" Cretan's hand ignited in a bright violet glow as lightning screeched across his knuckles and finger tips. He quickly returned his gaze to Kaius and raised his hand. Cretan's hand thrust forward, sending a blade of violet magic hurtling toward him.

"Shit!" Kaius ducked down just in time to dodge the attack. The violet blade crashed into the ground behind him and Alaia.

He quickly glanced at her and realized the danger of his current position. If just one of those blasts hit her . . . Kaius cursed to himself. He needed to move. Raising his sword and slashing through the air, he sent another blade of light flying toward Cretan. To his surprise, the God swiped his hand upward, conjuring a blade of his own.

The two forces crashed into each other, exploding in a swirl of white and black smoke. Kaius panted heavily, feeling the toll of his magic with every cast, and slowly slid his way to the left. He didn't know how long he could keep this up, but he needed to make sure that Cretan didn't notice Alaia. Hearing her groan softly, he mistakenly glanced her way.

"You should be paying attention, boy!"

Kaius jolted and looked in Cretan's direction, seeing a bright violet blade coming at him faster than the attacks before. Kaius' body moved on instinct, raising the golden and silver blade in front of him to block the attack. The dark magic crashed into the sword. The force pushed Kaius back and he landed hard against a large pillar.

He groaned through gritted teeth, his jaw muscles sore as he pushed with all his might to hold back the dark blade. Kaius managed to straighten his arms and swiped the sword downward, sending the dark blade crashing to the ground beside him with a loud boom.

Not receiving even a moment's reprieve, Kaius spotted another dark blade flying straight toward him. He ducked down, his back slid against the stone, and the blade crashed into the pillar. A web of cracks spread across the pillar's surface as small pieces of rock sprinkled over Kaius.

Dust and smoke filled the air around him. Taking this moment of obscurity, he hid behind the pillar. With heavy breath and eyes tightly closed, he leaned his head back to rest against the stone, feeling utterly drained.

Footsteps echoed the hall. Kaius' heart raced fast against his chest. Just then, Queen Throstnie's words rang through his mind: *Originally the sword was protected by yer people, Kaius.*

His eyes flashed open and looked down to the sword in his hand. "That's right, this sword is *from* here."

"Not bad little mortal, but this is taking longer than I would like and—Oh my, and who is this lovely creature here?"

Kaius winced and peeked around the pillar to find Cretan slowly walking toward Alaia. She pushed herself up with all her might and tried to crawl away.

"NO!" Kaius screamed out.

He reached deep within himself, summoning forth light from the sword once more and swung the blade toward Cretan. Almost as though anticipating the attack, Cretan summoned a pillar of violet light to shield him from it.

Kaius' knees suddenly buckled. He attempted to catch himself on the stone pillar as the world around him darkened. He commanded his body to hang on. Violently shaking his head, he tried to recall everything he learned about the sword: *The Kunnagarians struggled to defeat the creatures until someone from on high gifted them that weapon. They used it to seal the beasts away.*

His brows curved inward. Sent from on high? Could this sword be from Bregadine? The realm of the Gods? No. That couldn't have been possible.

Memories of the past three days soared through his mind, to the day Vincent set his plan into motion. To when his magic awakened. Losing Vincent to the darkness. Kaius then opened his eyes and looked at the sword one last time, remembering his brother's words: *That sword is the means to locking Mykronvan away in Velkran forever!*

A shriek broke Kaius from his thoughts. He looked up to see Cretan's hand clutching Alaia's brown wavy hair, her face contorting as she gripped the sleeve of his robe. Cretan's opposite hand, enveloped by a deep violet light, was pointed toward Alaia like a blade.

Kaius' stomach dropped as though full of lead. His mouth was dry, and he stared wide eyed at Alaia, unsure of what to do.

"Come out of your hiding spot, little boy." Cretan chided with a smirk.

Kaius tightened his grip on his sword. His brows furrowed and eyes glared unflinchingly at Cretan as he forced himself to step out into the open.

"A few steps forward please. Can't have you hiding away again." Cretan pulled Alaia's hair tight, causing her to shriek through gritted teeth.

Kaius reached out. "Stop! Don't hurt her, please." His heart wrenched as he took several steps forward toward them.

Cretan chuckled as a smirk creased his face. "That's a good boy. I promised your brother no harm would come to you, but he said nothing about this one. Now, place the sword on the floor and leave this place."

"What!? You expect me to leave her with you?" Kaius exclaimed.

"I'll release her *after* you leave. You'll be needed outside soon enough. Someone has to greet that King of yours." Cretan shrugged and continued, his voice changed, now soft, but sharp. "Take vengeance on all of Rosado. Wipe it from the map if you have to, I don't care. They will pay for taking my home and my brother from me."

A shudder ran through Kaius' body. That was Vincent's voice. Kaius' eyes and lips trembled. Throat tightening, his gaze slowly moved to the sword clutched in his hand. "We found a way though." He whispered to himself. "We found a way to stop King Cecilio. He didn't need you!"

"I don't care. I've been trapped in Velkran for long enough. I was careless last time, and I won't make that mistake again. I will show them all the world *I* have envisioned. It will be better than this mess you lot call home now. You mortals are so riddled with flaws it's . . . infuriating." Cretan's brows furrowed over his eyes, shrouding them in shadow, save for the fierce orange glow of his irises.

Kaius turned his head away slightly with eyebrows raised. "What do you mean? You're the God of Chaos. How could you make a better world than the Mother of Light and Life?"

"As I told you, I am the God of Chaos AND Rebirth. For any and all destruction caused to the mortal worlds, *I* am the one that remakes it, but they never listen to my suggestions. Never let me make things as I see fit." Cretan shook his head in aggravation. "All those terrible emotions. Jealousy. Anguish. Obsession. Hatred. The suffering caused by these things infuriates me to no end. The only reason I was drawn to Vincent in the first place was due to the pain inflicted upon him by this girl's father. Why wouldn't I help him?"

Kaius' heart panged and swelled once again, trying to hide his worry. "Don't try to convince me you actually care about the likes of me and my older brother, whom you just took from me if you don't remember."

"Of course I care!" Cretan exclaimed passionately, causing Kaius to jump. "You remember. You saw what *her* family did to yours. Why would you even care what happens to her?"

Cretan pulled Alaia's head back. Tears poured from her green slitted eyes and down her copper cheeks. She groaned in pain through bared teeth. She then closed her trembling lips, eyes locked on Kaius, and her mouth began to move.

I'm sorry.

Kaius gently gasped, but controlled his emotions, his body relaxing as he watched her. "Because, Alaia is nothing like her father or grandfather. She's something different. Better."

"Hmph." Cretan glared at Kaius, though his gaze seemed

somewhat softer than before. "You know, once this world is remade in my image, it'll be free of hardship. No murder. No greed. Those tedious emotions will be gone. There will be true peace. She wouldn't have to live with such a belittling, mocking, abusive father. You could even live with your family made whole, Vincent included. Wouldn't that be a nice world to live in?" Cretan's brows arched high over his eyes, an almost empathetic glint in them.

Kaius' heart thumped hard in his chest. He glanced at Alaia, then back to Cretan. "Would I still know Alaia in this new life? And Adhnis?"

The corners of Cretan's lips twitched. "Maybe. Do as I say. Collect the fairy. Leave the sword and this place. Alaia will follow soon enough."

Kaius stared at Cretan, his heart and mind at odds. He looked to Alaia, her eyes wide and meeting his. She shook her head and looked down to the sword in his hand.

A world where Kaius' brother and he could live happily with their parents. Their people. Alaia would have a better relationship with her father. Was this such a bad thing after all? Kaius' brows scrunched together, unsure of what he should do.

"This world will be remade into a place of pure bliss I assure you, but first, the denizens of Velkran must destroy it. Chaos and Rebirth after all."

"What?" Kaius looked back to Cretan, eyes wide with horror. "You didn't say anything about the demons OR destroying the world!

What about no harm coming to me?"

The world around Kaius quaked fiercely, unbalancing his stance. A roaring howl sounded again from within the dark void, echoing through the hall. His grip on the sword tightened in an attempt to steady his trembling hands.

"No harm will come from *me*. I didn't say anything about *them*." Cretan's smirk turned sinister. "In order to remake the world, this one first needs to go. You know what, I'll take this one's life now. You'll have a chance to see her again in the next one."

Cretan pulled his bladed violet arm back, readying to strike Alaia down. Kaius' heart leaped into his throat. His body tensed as his heart screamed for him to move. He had to stop him. Taking a deep breath, he bellowed, "STOP!"

In an instant, a flash of deep violet enveloped the world around Kaius. His body felt heavy and could barely move, as if he was dropped into a tub of molasses. Kaius struggled to breathe, each breath coming in slow and shallow.

"A-Wh-Uh!" Kaius tried to speak, but he could barely manage a vowel.

Cretan and Alaia both stood as still as a statue. *What was going on?* He asked in his mind.

Kaius glanced down at his sword and felt something swirl inside his chest. He struggled, but managed to raise his free hand and rested it against his breastplate. A faint energy radiated from beneath the armor and warmed his palm. *Is this . . . Am I doing this?* He wondered, perplexed by what was happening.

Kaius winced as something Vincent told him came to mind: *We can conjure the four elements as many others do, but we can also conjure illusions and portals. It's been said that some of our highest order could even briefly stop time.*

Kaius stared at the ground before him. *I'm . . . stopping time? Shit!* He thought, utterly stunned.

Kaius raised his gaze back to Cretan, feeling the flow of time fighting to return to normal. *What to do? What to do? What CAN I do?* He raised a hand and stared blankly at his palm, his mind racing for answers. Then a realization dawned upon him. *The sword! It was created to combat the darkness. The sword is the key!*

Kaius looked at his sword and fought with all his might to aim it toward Cretan. *I'm trusting you not to hurt my brother.* He said inwardly to the blade as he fought to raise his arm even higher, the weapon growing more and more difficult to wield by every beat of his heart.

Ngh! Come on! Teeth gritting, he fought to focus the blade toward Cretan's chest, struggling to aim it true. The sword veered toward the shoulder of the arm holding Alaia and tried as he might, it took all his focus to keep it from drifting further.

Tsk! Kaius sneered with disappointment. This would have to do. *Okay then magical sword, whatever you did to the monstrous bird, I need you to do it again. Please!*

The sword burst to life with a bright golden glow. A chilling sensation flowed from the blade into his hand, up his arm, and spread like wildfire throughout his body. Kaius released a trembling breath and concentrated his focus on Cretan's shoulder. The light of the sword grew and grew, so bright it could rival that of the sun, but the beam didn't come.

Did he have to release the flow of time? How was he—

Before Kaius could finish his thought, the deep violet hue shrouding the world disappeared and a magnificent beam of light flew from his blade.

Everything happened so fast, Kaius nearly stumbled to the ground, but regained his footing at the last moment. He then heard a scream. Turning in its direction, he found Cretan cradling his left shoulder.

Alaia quickly stood. Wasting no time, she shoved the God to the ground and turned to hide behind a pillar.

"Alaia!" Kaius quickly called out.

"Kaius!"

Kaius jolted, hearing a familiar voice cry out. He turned to the right to see Adhnis approaching, struggling to stay afloat, and cradling her stomach with one arm.

"Adhnis, you're okay!" Kaius exclaimed with a relieved smile.

She dropped to the ground. "Aye, but we aren't done." Adhnis took a deep breath and raised her arms outstretched high to either side. "Gaoth, we need yer gale, please!" Before Kaius realized what was happening, she thrust her arms forward and a hurricane force wind filled the hall, knocking him back.

Taking him by surprise, he dropped to one knee and slammed his free hand to the ground, wrapping the tips of his fingers over the side of a protruded cobblestone. "Adhnis—NGH! What are you doing!?"

"Distracting him! The power of the sword still flows in ye right? Use it to save yer brother, hurry! I-I don't have much strength left in me!" Adhnis fell to her knees, her breath heavy, but arms held steadily forward.

Kaius tried to turn to see Cretan, however the wind threatened to knock him on his side. Careful not to loosen his grip, he slowly turned himself, keeping his body low to the ground. His knees slid one by one into position, carefully taking his time to steady his balance.

As he turned, his white hair shifted and fluttered in front of his face. His cape suddenly caught in the wind and flipped over his shoulder, shrouding his vision.

"DAMMIT!" He pushed the cape back with his sword arm as best he could, managing to get it back over his shoulder. As he looked up and found Cretan in the same spot he had been before Adhnis conjured the gale, faring no better than himself.

Their eyes locked on one another, glaring and bracing against the wind. As the strength of the gale began to dwindle, Kaius stood himself upright and lifted the sword, once more pointing the blade toward Cretan.

"This sword was made by the gods of Bregadine, right? I'll use what they made to lock you back in Velkran where you belong."

As the wind dissipated completely, the corner of Cretan's lips stretched into a condescending smirk and laughed. "Oh yes, by all means lock me up, but to do that, you'll need to push *this* body into Velkran."

Kaius was taken aback. The whole body? But that would mean—

"Kaius!"

Startled, he turned his head and spotted Alaia hanging onto the pillar she had hid behind. "Trust in la Madre's[1] light."

Kaius' heart skipped a beat. He looked down at the sword, recalling Vincent's hand when struck by the sword's light. The Mother's light. The light. *Her* light. That was it. He returned his focus to Cretan and closed his eyes.

Thinking of the Mother's sword in his hands, Kaius asked for the power to help him save his older brother. To push Cretan from Vincent's body. To take him back into Her embrace, to Bregadine, or Velkran, he didn't care which. All that mattered was getting the dangerous being out of his realm.

The power of the sword surged through him, sending a chill through his entire being. It was a sensation unlike any other, as if a presence was with him, guiding his hand. His blood froze and muscles tingled. His eyes flashed wide open, and his body ignited, surrounded by a bright golden glow.

"*Cretan!*" Kaius' body tensed, his mouth was moving, though the words were not his own. "*It's time you returned home. Now come!*"

Cretan scoffed. "You think I'm just going to give up with my goals within arm's reach? I don't think so!"

1   Spanish for *The Mother's*.

As the last word left his lips, the sword flashed as bright as the sun itself and a beam of light barreled from its very tip, heading straight for Cretan. He straightened himself, taking a defensive stance, and raised his hand as he had when summoning blades of darkness to combat the light.

His body suddenly tensed and jerked unnaturally, as though seized by an invisible force. "NGH! NO—"

Cretan let out an ear-piercing scream as the light struck him in the dead center of his chest.

Once the light pierced clean through, it ripped a figure shrouded in pure darkness from Vincent's body. As the beam of light dissipated, the shadowy figure floated lifelessly in the air a moment longer before fracturing and fading completely.

Kaius let out a trembling breath as he stared at the body left standing before him. The skin was fair again, but the eyes were closed and still. The figure groaned, swayed, and fell forward, landing hard on the stone floor.

"Vincent!" Kaius ran to his older brother and knelt before him. Then found that he was unable to release the sword from his grip and looked to his hand. Why couldn't he—

"Kaius . . ."

Kaius immediately turned to his brother, now struggling to raise himself up off the ground. Kaius still felt a presence deep within himself. Foreign, yet strangely warm and nurturing. "Vincent, are you okay?"

Vincent raised a hand to Kaius' shoulder, his breath heavy. "N-No time, the door . . . you have to close . . . the doors . . ." His hand slipped from Kaius' shoulder, back to the ground to keep himself from falling.

Kaius looked up to the open doors leading into Velkran as the world quaked. A terrible howl sounded once again and glowing orange eyes started appearing in the dark void. The sword then hummed, feeling almost as if it were telling him to hurry. A sharp shiver crawled its way up his spine.

"Oh shit!" Kaius quickly stood to his feet and bolted toward the doors. He glanced at both sides, wondering how he could possibly close the massive stone opening.

A strong pulse then emanated from deep inside him, spreading to the very tips of his fingers. Looking at one of his palms, he somehow understood what he needed to do. "I see. Okay then."

Stepping back, Kaius raised his free palm toward the open doors, the golden light around him glowing brightly once more. The creatures within the void roared and shrieked in terror as they retreated back further into the darkness.

Kaius felt an unusual sensation, almost as if something were emerging from somewhere deep inside him. He glanced up and startled, seeing two large, ethereal bright golden hands place themselves flat against the doors, pushing them closed with ease.

The creatures within howled furiously. Shadowy figures shifted about in the darkness, seemingly unable to move forward. The stone gears within the walls began to grind once again. As the doors closed with a loud clunk, Kaius took a few steps back and raised his sword high in the air.

Finally able to free his hand from the hilt, the weapon floated into the air above him and suddenly hurtled toward the doors, embedding itself in the indentation with a loud clang. The sword's light flashed and spread across the doors' surface, bathing the stone in a radiant light.

After a moment, the blinding light covering its surface faded away. Kaius' glow was gone as well, and his body grew heavy. The world began to darken and the sensation of falling overtook him.

"Kaius!"

He felt someone's arms wrap around him, halting his fall with a groan and guiding him to rest in their soft embrace.

"Kaius? Kaius, please say something. Open your eyes!"

Kaius struggled, but just barely managed to open his eyes. He smiled, eyes locking with Alaia's. She held him against her sweetly.

Speaking was difficult, however he managed a few words. "Alaia . . . did we . . . do it? Did we win?"

Her green eyes shined in the firelight and her lips stretched into a large smile. "Yes. Yes, we did. Your brother's safe and so is Adhnis. We're all safe, all because of you. I—" She hesitated, cheeks flushing a deep red, and tears welled in her eyes.

"A-Alaia?" His eyelids were heavy, but he fought to stay awake. Her startled expression filled him with concern.

She cupped his cheek with a hand, tears now flowing down her face. "Kaius, I can't keep silent anymore." Taking a deep breath, she said with conviction, "I love you. There, I said it, Padre be damned. I love you."

His eyes widened with surprise and his heart fluttered. "Y-You do?"

She quickly nodded. "Yes, and . . . I really want to kiss you." Alaia chuckled, her cheeks almost glowing red.

His sight blurred, but a smile crept across his face. "I love you . . . too, but I'm so . . . so tired."

"Then rest. I'll take care of you and Vincent. And Adhnis too. I promise. I'll take care of all of you." She said, squeezing his hand with reassurance.

"Thank you . . ." With that, he gave into exhaustion. The world blackened, and he fell fast asleep.

17

ALAIA

I WON'T BE LIKE YOU

LAIA RUSHED OUT THE DOORS OF THE MAUSOLEUM. The mountains towered behind her, and the skies were coated in darkness. Panting heavily, she regathered large handfuls of the skirt of her dress and scanned her surroundings.

"It's so dark, I can barely see a thing." She looked to Adhnis, resting on her shoulder with a wavy strand of Alaia's brown hair in hand. She noticed the fairy's light was weaker than when they first met and began to worry. "How are you feeling?"

Adhnis let out a huff of breath. "Tired. It's taking everything I have left to keep myself awake." She leaned over and fell against Alaia's neck, her grip slipping down the hair strands.

Alaia took a deep breath and exhaled softly, trying to quell her growing concerns. Hearing a groan echo from the mountainous hall, she startled and looked back. After a moment, Vincent came hobbling forward, entering Adhnis' faint light. His face was contorted, clearly struggling to carry an unconscious Kaius on his back, even with him removed of all his armor.

She stared at them for a moment longer before approaching Vincent, raising her hands to offer help. He immediately shot a glare her way, causing her to stop in her tracks. "I don't need your help." Though his tone was no less fiery than what she had become accustomed to over her time as his captive, his words seemed to have somehow lost their bite.

Her eyes softened and her hands lowered to her sides. "Do you plan to carry him all the way back then? That would be a struggle, even for one trained for the rigors of knighthood like Kaius, let alone one who's spent most of his time with his nose to books."

"If I mu—" Vincent walked past Alaia, but stumbled as he came to the steps leading to the courtyard and fell to one knee. He huffed heavily. His arms trembled. However, his grip on Kaius' legs held fast and kept him close.

Alaia knelt beside him and gently grasped his shoulder. "Vincent, you need to rest. Take it slow. Like Adhnis said, she could only do so much to heal your body. I know how you feel, but . . . please, try to take it easy, for Kaius' sake."

She watched him pleadingly. He looked to the ground, his lips curling in, and his chin quivered. After a moment, Vincent acquiesced. He released Kaius' legs softly to the ground, grabbed his brother's arms, and sat himself down. Leaning forward, he carefully slid Kaius down to a seated position. Kaius' back slowly rose and fell, resting peacefully against his older brother.

Vincent glanced at Alaia, his expression somber. "I really hope . . . you know what you're doing. I will never forgive you if something happens to Kaius."

Alaia's heart quickened, but she steadied her gaze. Just as her lips parted to respond, the clopping of a horse's hooves sounded nearby, followed by a soft whinny. Alaia turned and spotted a black and white mare shaking her head, her mane flapping against its neck.

Relieved, she released a sigh and squeezed Vincent's shoulder. "A horse!"

"A horse?" Adhnis perked up a little. "Oh right, Kaius' mount. Honestly, I thought the skittish thing would be long gone by now." Adhnis said, her voice just above a whisper, and shrugged against Alaia's neck.

"Good thing it stayed. This creature will make the trip much easier." Alaia stood up and made her way to meet the horse as it approached. She took it by the chin with a serene smile and stroked the mount's long face.

Alaia's mind raced with thoughts of her padre's[1] plan for Vincent and Kaius and the things he had done to secure his hold on the throne. Her family's hands were drenched in the blood of innocents, and she

1   Spanish for *Father's.*

hoped to prevent further bloodshed if at all possible.

"The plan my madre[2] and I have put together will work. It has to. We . . . We've taken all the necessary steps and made many allies who would see my padre overthrown. I don't know why he thinks I am anything like him or why he assumes I will accept what he's done, but I will not. I'm . . ." Alaia released the horse and turned to look at Vincent, trying to convey her conviction. "Créame,[3] Vincent, my padre's reign will end, one way or the other. That, I promise you."

Vincent's violet eyes trembled, the cold wind gently brushing his white hair against his fair face. He cradled Kaius' arms, and his gaze lingered on the cobblestone floor. "King Cecilio is here."

Alaia's heart leaped into her throat. She walked to the side of the horse to look out into the darkness. There on the path ahead, leading through the city, a number of firelit torches were headed their way.

Adhnis sighed. "Your father is one impatient stinkhorn. Are ye ready, Alaia?"

She could feel Adhnis' gaze resting on her. A glare fell over Alaia's face as she watched the fires steadily grow as they drew closer. "Sí,[4] it's now or never." Alaia responded contemptuously. She then scooped Adhnis up in her hands and held the fairy close to her face. "Adhnis, can you fly to Vincent? I want you to stay by him, to keep them both safe should the need arise."

"Are ye sure?" Adhnis responded, seemingly taken aback.

---

2   Spanish for *Mother.*
3   Spanish for *Believe me.*
4   Spanish for *Yes.*

Alaia nodded. "Please. Just keep them safe for me."

The fairy let out a long sigh. "Okay, but once we near Eylowen Forest, I . . . I have to return home."

"I understand. Go." Alaia turned and stretched her hand out toward Vincent, watching as Adhnis hopped off to fly toward the Bravehearts. Vincent caught her and placed the fairy on his right shoulder, Kaius was still resting on his left. Alaia then turned to face the numerous rows of firelight now beginning to form figures in the darkness.

One of the figures approached on an elegantly armored horse of crimson and gold. A golden crown rested atop the short wavy brown hair on his head. Alaia's padre, King Cecilio, stopped before her. "Alaia, estás bien?"[5]

Alaia quickly looked away, her anger and disappointment swelling in her chest. After a moment of silence, her padre slid down from his horse. At the sound of his grieves clanking on the cobblestones, her stomach churned and pulse quickened. Stay strong, she told herself. She needed to have courage. Alaia could face him. She would face him, for them. Alaia returned to meet her padre with heavily furrowed brows shadowing her green eyes, smelling the faint scent of pine and bluebells typical of her padre.

Stopping just before her, King Cecilio opened his mouth, but paused as he glanced past her to the brothers on the steps, his green eyes widening. "Kaius, his hair—"

"You will not hurt them."

5   Spanish for *Alaia, are you alright?*

Padre's brow lightly twitched. He returned to her and folded his arms behind his back. "Them? Is there a reason you show *mercy* to your kidnapper?" His strain on the word mercy caught her attention, as though the concept was foreign to him.

She bawled her hands into fists and took a deep breath. "If you lay blame on anyone, lay it on yourself. His actions were the consequences of your intention to place Kaius in harm's way—"

"I told Edurne this, and it seems I must tell you as well. I will do whatever it takes to safeguard *my* kingdom and *our* family's hold on the throne. Many vipers whisper in our halls." His eyes narrowed into slits. "Do you wish to see your madre's head on a pike?"

Her body trembled at the suggestion, trying to hold her courage, her conviction, as best she could. Swallowing down her fear, she continued, "Have you considered that there might not be such talk if you truly cared for your subjects?"

"Hmph. You think the people wouldn't rise up if I was a *kind* king? Then you are still a naive child."

A pang pierced her heart at the insult.

"Be I caring or tyrannical, it matters not. The people are fickle and will turn on you at a moment's notice should they see their *interests* no longer lie with you. Tráeme a los curanderos para los chicos."[6] Padre ordered, his tone cold and eyes calculating as a pleased smirk creased his face.

A shiver traveled fast down her spine. Anger began to overtake her fear. She wanted to yell at him, release her outrage, but knew

6   Spanish for *Fetch me the healers for the boys.*

better. He wouldn't listen. Padre never listened to anyone. His way was the only way, or so he thought.

Her padre stood silently, looming over her for a moment while awaiting the healers' arrival. Four people in white robes drew close and hopped down from a wagon. They bowed to the King and swiftly made their way toward Vincent in silence.

"Are you just going to sit there glaring at me *boy*, or do you want to be useful and do something for your brother? I was foolish enough to not use the magic of command on you before due to your brother's presence, I'll not make that mistake again. Vincent—"

Alaia's eyes jolted open and she quickly spread her arms out wide. "NO!" Her padre glanced down at her, silently taking in an irritated breath. "Kaius and I got through to him. There's no need—"

"Yes, that's nice dear." Padre raised a hand and pushed Alaia aside as she stared wide eyed at him, her blood boiling again. Walking past her, he continued toward Vincent and Kaius. Vincent's grip on his brother tightened, though his expression was still, save for the anger in his violet eyes.

Her padre leaned down to him, their faces close. "What you pulled. Will not. Go. Unpunished. Try something like that again, and Kaius *will* share your punishment. Do you understand me."

Alaia watched Vincent anxiously, his breath caught in his throat and his eyes glossed lightly. His lips then stretched into a thin, quivering line, and he looked to the ground in defeat.

Padre straightened upright. "I thought so." With a nudge of his head, the healers bowed and approached the brothers. Two of them lifted Kaius and carefully carried him to the wagon. The other two gently took Vincent by the arms and guided him along behind his brother.

Adhnis looked to Alaia as she and Vincent passed by. She raised a hand to her heart and bowed her head, silently mouthing a few words.

Everything will be okay.

Alaia subtly nodded in thanks to the little fairy and watched them enter the wagon. They were both draped in wool blankets. Kaius lay flat on the floor of the wagon. Vincent sat at his head, looking at his little brother. Only la Madre knew what he was thinking as he swiped a few errant white strands of hair clear of Kaius' face. Once everyone was situated, the wagon's driver snapped the horses' reins. Alaia watched as they faded in the distance. Worry swelled in her heart.

Her padre turned to Alaia once more. She met him with a distrustful glare. "Now that I have my two sorcerers, it should be easy to deal with the fairies and defend our borders from Valtivar. Our plan is coming together, despite this insufferable hiccup."

"Your plan, not mine. I'll not help you enslave anyone." Alaia's brows furrowed hard over her eyes. She knew her padre to be cold, but hoped her glare caused him some measure of discomfort.

"You will understand in time that what I do *is* for the benefit of this family *and* this kingdom. One way or the other." Padre passed her by without another word, his face stoic.

"Why do you think I'm anything like you?" She growled through gritted teeth, her frustration breaking through.

He turned to her with an aggravated, yet weary look in his green eyes. "I'm going to tell you something I should've told you long ago, Alaia. The crown weighs heavier than you think."

Alaia was unnerved by his dismissive tone and watched, stunned as he turned from her and walked to his horse. Her hands closed tightly into fists, her knuckles turning pale. Anger for her padre, her entire family, threatened to consume her. She wouldn't let this stand.

"I'm nothing like you."

KAIUS

USURPING THE KING

"**K**AIUS, YOUR ROBE IS CROOKED."

"It is?" Kaius exclaimed.

He looked down to inspect his violet robe and found his shoulder cape hung longer to one side than the other. Fumbling with the fabric, he tried to straighten it as best he could. It proved difficult to hold the cloth firmly due to the tremble in his hands, frightened at what had been asked of him.

Vincent chuckled. "Here, let me."

"Y-Yeah, sure." Kaius let his hands fall to his sides.

As Vincent began straightening the garment, Kaius averted his gaze, finding it difficult to look his older brother in the eyes. His breath was uneasy and a bead of sweat rolled down his forehead, despite the light snow falling outside making the air colder.

"Kaius, I know you're nervous." Vincent said flatly. "You shouldn't be."

"Vincent, I . . . I'm not you." Kaius responded with a tremble in his voice.

Vincent's hands paused, his posture stiffened. Kaius took a deep breath. His eyes drifted downward. He felt apprehensive to continue, but knew he needed to get his thoughts out in the open. There had been enough silence between the two that had, in part, led to Vincent's revolt and their battle with Cretan just a month and a half ago. If things were going to be different, he needed to speak his mind.

"I've never killed anyone, okay." He exhaled a soft sigh. "I-I don't know how you're all expecting me to just—"

Vincent cupped Kaius' cheeks and tilted his little brother's face up to meet him. His violet eyes were stern, but what caught Kaius' surprise was the glint of fear hiding within. "Kaius, I . . . I know the Queen and Alaia are asking a lot, but this has to be done. Thanks to those two, much of Cecilio's power has been cut off. His hold over the throne is weak and he knows it, but that's made him dangerous. You've seen what he's done, seen him lash out. The fairies don't have much time!"

"But to kill all those people?" Kaius' voice pleaded with a crack.

Vincent wrapped his arms around Kaius' shoulders and pulled him close in an embrace. Kaius trembled against his older brother's chest, his mind awhirl with everything that had transpired since their return to Rosado.

King Cecilio made Kaius' magic oath quite the spectacle. It took place with all the members of his court bearing witness, and he punctuated the ceremony with an announcement of his plans to invade Bosque Encantado, and enslave the fairies. The evening sent a shudder down Kaius' spine, causing his blood to run cold. Luckily, King Cecilio's plan couldn't be set into motion until Kaius mastered his magic. Until then, he would have to wait to make his move. At Queen Edurne's instructions, Kaius played the part of the bumbling apprentice, hiding his progress to buy her and Alaia time for their plans to bear fruit. The two worked in secrecy, gathering their allies while severing the King's hold over Rosado and Pacífica as a whole.

The King, for everything he was, was no fool. He took notice of his dwindling support and went mad with rage. One after another, nobility and merchants suspected of treason began losing their heads. Little did he know, his lashing out had been anticipated. He had always underestimated the Queen, and that mistake made him blind to the trail he had followed to this very day, murdering his own supporters and in so doing, causing his hold on the throne to slip. The plan shook Kaius to his core upon first hearing of it from Alaia. Even if done for the right cause, Kaius didn't like the idea of blood being spilled, but understood there was no way to avoid that. Either the plan would continue and those supporting the King would lose their lives, or the fairies would fall into slavery, many on both sides likely dying in the process of taking the forest. So Kaius acquiesced.

"Kaius," Vincent called softly, "if it was I, or Alaia, bent over the execution block, would you stand back and watch, or would you fight to save us?"

Kaius' breath hitched in his throat and a few tears flowed from his violet eyes. Vincent took a small step back and cupped Kaius' cheeks again. "Know that if it ever came down to it, I would kill. Every. Last. Person. In that throne room if it meant keeping you safe. If securing your future happiness means killing for Alaia or Adhnis, I will pay that price too. I am the monster that Cecilio has made me."

Kaius stood in silence, staring at Vincent with shallow breath.

"It's a terrible thing, Kaius, I know. Perhaps when all is said and done, when you and I finally know peace, I can be something else. But first we must do what needs to be done."

With that, Vincent pulled his hand from Kaius' face and stepped away. Kaius stumbled a little, his knees feeling weak. Was it really necessary to kill? Why must it be? There just had to be another way. He couldn't do this. Kaius would be in their way. He just couldn't.

The door of their chamber suddenly swung open, startling Kaius. Both he and Vincent turned to see two guards standing in the doorway, out of breath and eyes wide. "The Queen sends for you both! Word is Lord Julián and his family have been arrested along with a few others of the Princess' supporters. If true, the coup must happen in the throne room. Now."

"Dammit! That's sooner than I was hoping." Vincent urgently

turned to Kaius, making him jump. He looked his younger brother up and down, then placed a hand on Kaius' shoulder. "Just follow my lead and keep Alaia safe no matter what. Everything will be alright, Kaius," Vincent promised softly.

Kaius found the sentiment relieving, even if only a little. He forced a nod, and Vincent did the same in return. The two then left their joined chamber and followed the guards escorting them to the throne room. To keep up appearances, they kept a steady pace, not so fast as to draw attention, but not too slow as to arrive too late.

As they neared the throne room, King Cecilio's voice could be heard booming from within. Kaius' palms moistened, and his chest tightened. His stomach hung heavy while bile clawed its way into his throat, but he kept his head high and gulped it back.

As the small group passed through the threshold of the throne room, Kaius was stunned to find the hall packed not only with nobility, but guards lining the walls.

The throne room had been restored to what it had been before Vincent's attack. All the banners that had been torn down and destroyed now hung from the ceiling, restored, save for those belonging to families branded traitors. The Ligeras' banner was now even grander than it had been before that day.

As Kaius scanned the hall, he recognized many of the guards. Those he didn't recognize, he assumed, served only King Cecilio. "That's not good." He whispered to himself.

"Kaius, you promise I broke the oath?" Vincent held his eyes ahead and his face still, but his voice was laced with concern.

"Yes," Kaius answered quickly, "that choking sensation that came over me when he used the voice of command doesn't happen anymore. I'm just . . . terrified of messing up."

Vincent subtly nodded. His posture was tall and still, so sure of himself. You couldn't guess without knowing that a couple of weeks ago he had received the last of his incremented lashes, a total of forty spread out over a month's time. Even though Vincent had been badly whipped and sentenced with repairing homes, strongholds, and the protective wall that surrounded and segregated the city, Vincent never faltered. It infuriated King Cecilio to no end and gave Kaius pride in his brother. Adhnis secretly came when she could to relieve Vincent of the pain, but no matter how much she and Kaius wished, the scars had to remain for appearance's sake.

Kaius startled from the thought as the King continued his frantic yelling with renewed vigor. Before he could continue forward, Vincent grabbed Kaius' arm and pulled him far to the right side of the throne room. They snaked their way through the crowd until they finally found themselves behind Queen Edurne and Alaia, standing quietly at the side of the hall rather than on the dais with King Cecilio.

Vincent leaned forward inconspicuously to the Queen's ear and whispered, "Whenever you're ready."

She softly gave him a nod without turning. He positioned himself behind her, arms crossed behind his back. Kaius stood behind Alaia.

Her shoulders trembled, and she held her hands in front of her.

Kaius looked up to King Cecilio standing on his dais in front of the thrones, flailing his hands about and yelling in sheer outrage.

"The fact that I've done so much for my kingdom, my country! This is how you lot repay me, by whispering in the shadows and plotting like the cowards you are! So be it. Let this be an example of what happens to those who move against me. Bring me the traitors!" King Cecilio bellowed with a gesture toward the door at the side of the room. Soon several guards emerged with a number of high-ranking Lords and Ladies in tow, roughly ten.

Alaia let out a light gasp. Lord Julián Vicario was held at the head of the procession. He was a distinguished man, roughly the same age as Queen Edurne and would soon be turning forty. He had control over Rosado's Ports, shipping schedules, trading, and just about everything to do with sailing. His position afforded him great sway over who the people followed and trusted.

Unfortunately, that meant what the guard had said earlier was true. Kaius held his fists close at his sides, trying to hide his shock. Alaia always said she counted herself lucky to have Julián as an ally. How had the King found him out?

Julián glanced up toward Alaia and the Queen, and lightly shook his head at them before being forced to a stop and dropped to his knees before King Cecilio. Alaia startled and was visibly flustered. She looked at her mother, whose expression fell sullen.

Queen Edurne took a deep breath and mumbled, "That stubborn fool."

"Does that mean the coup is off?" Kaius' brows curved upward in confusion as he fiddled with his hands.

Alaia gently shook her head. "No. It doesn't. He may have suggested waiting until just before the invasion of Bosque, but this changes things. His support is too great to lose. If we are going to do this, it has to be now." She glanced at her mother. "Madre?"[1]

Queen Edurne glared at her husband who's attention was swept up in the theatrics unfolding before them. "Not yet. Vincent, if Cecilio orders their execution, you must stop it, please. If we lose even one of them—"

"It shall be done." Vincent positioned himself between Queen Edurne and Alaia, leering out from just behind their heads. His hands dimly began to glow in a soft violet hue.

Kaius' heart quickened. He was still unsure if he could really kill if things came to that, but he also couldn't fail Alaia. She needed the aid of those arrested. Without them, the city would likely fall under civil war and tear itself apart. Were that to happen, there would be insurmountable death. This was the lesser evil. If they said it had to be done, then . . . it had to be done.

"So this is who has been leading the so-called rebellion against me, or maybe, you acted alone, Julián." King Cecilio's words were venomous, hate dripping from every syllable. He glared at Julián, and the man glared right back.

"I don't know what you mean, Ceci." Julián replied flatly, his expression still, causing fury to burn brightly on Cecilio's face.

1   Spanish for *Mother*.

King Cecilio's brow twitched. "Don't. Call. Me. That. TRAITOR! I am your King!"

Julián smirked. "Oh? Not fond of childhood nicknames anymore, my King? Did Papá[2] beat that out of you for befriending *riff-raff* like me?" He laughed. The King's face flushed in a deep crimson. "You're nothing but a weak—"

"ENOUGH! I'm tired of this game, raise swords, NOW!" The guards who escorted the prisoners in and now stood over them, unsheathed their swords. The crowd gasped. Many cried out in disbelief as the guards placed their sword points to each of the accused's necks. "Once we are finished here, know that your children and families will be next. Let this example serve as a last warning to all in attendance today. I will not abide treachery!

Alaia jolted. Before either Kaius or her mother could stop her, she stepped forward. "STOP!"

Everyone turned to her as she approached Julián. Both her father and Julián's eyes went wide with shock.

"I am the one you want." Alaia said confidently. "I severed your connections! I'm the one standing before you in opposition because it must be done. You've spread terror for far too long, Padre,[3] and it *needs* to end."

The room went deadly silent, save for King Cecilio's heavy, enraged breath. He took a few steps down his dais, staring at her for a long while. A sudden laugh escaped his lips. He was beside himself.

2   Spanish for *Father.*
3   Spanish for *Father.*

"You? Really now? You expect me to believe a sniveling little girl, preoccupied with flowers and dresses, who doted on a meek pathetic boy who's barely got an ounce of his older brother's power, is the one responsible for all of this?" He scoffed, dismissing her with a gesture of his hand. "No. I think not. It's more likely that since you are involved, you are a pawn of your madre. I bet she went behind my back, opening her legs for Julián, and promised him my crown. She too can't do anything on her own, incompetent as she is." The King shot a glare at his wife and sneered. "Am I wrong?"

Kaius looked at Queen Edurne. To his surprise, her expression was still and composed. She took a few steps forward to stand beside her daughter and answered, "Yes, and about so very many things."

At that moment, several of the guards pulled out pink ribbons and wrapped them around their wrists, showing their allegiance to Alaia as their ruler.

Exasperated, King Cecilio winced and looked at Alaia. Her green eyes stayed locked on her father. "Kaius, I'd like you to prove to my padre just how very wrong he is, if you would be so kind."

Kaius took a deep breath and glanced at Vincent, who nodded for him to continue. Kaius released a steady breath and summoned forth wind to come to his aid. Within moments, a torrent swirled and built in strength around him. He quickly pulled his arm back and thrust it forward, sending a gale past the prisoners and crashing into the unmarked guards, pushing them to the other side of the hall.

Swords fell to the floor with a clang as armored soldiers collided.

The people in attendance screamed and moved away from the dais. Kaius relaxed and looked at King Cecilio, the man's eyes dark and burning with murderous intent. His hands trembled and Kaius wondered if the man, in this moment, felt even a hint of the fear he had struck into countless others. He then stepped beside Alaia and stood tall with her, even though his stomach fluttered nervously.

Vincent then walked past him and with a snap of his fingers, burned the ropes binding Julián and the others, freeing them. Crossing his arms over his chest, he shot a defiant smirk at the King.

"But . . . how? The oath—"

"Broken." Alaia interrupted her father. "The Bravehearts are free of you. As for Kaius, you should have placed more faith in him. He is far stronger than you could ever know. Now," she locked her hands in front of her stomach, keeping her eyes focused on her father, "will you step down peacefully? I do NOT want this to end in bloodshed, Padre."

King Cecilio's breath was heavy, his teeth bared and snarling. "You should've thought of that when you set your schemes in motion! GUARDS!"

Every soldier on either side of the conflict unsheathed their swords. Those who had fallen struggled to their feet and stood at the ready. The innocent bystanders rushed toward the main doors and slammed into guards beginning to pour into the room. Tensions came to a climax and fighting inevitably broke out. In all the chaos it was hard to tell who had the larger numbers, Alaia or her father.

Kaius scanned the room, his muscles tense and fear building. He, Vincent, Alaia, and her mother were surrounded by allies and enemies alike. His body was heavy with anxiety. Alaia screamed out to her mother. Four guards rushed and encircled the four, protecting them as best they could. More and more soldiers packed into the hall. As swords crashed, Vincent's hands ignited with bright orange flames. He clapped them together high above his head, creating a dome shaped barrier of fire around them.

The heat swirled quickly about and pushed the would-be attackers back. With a flick of his wrists, Vincent pulled his hands free of the fire and thrust them forward, expanding the fire in an explosion in all directions. The flames washed over all nearby who were not marked by a ribbon. He and Kaius had enchanted the pink ribbons to be in unity with their magic, to keep them safe.

A gurgled scream sounded behind Kaius, startling him. He spun around to see a soldier at his side fall to the ground. Blood spilled from his neck, and a pool quickly formed around his head. The two soldiers who struck the man down stepped forward, raising their swords to fight Kaius.

"Make sure to capture that which is mine! I still have use for these traitors." King Cecilio bellowed the order, looking unnervingly composed given the situation.

Screams of anguish sounded all around.

"Surrender, beast!" The two soldiers yelled out, pointing their blades at him, and cautiously stepped forward.

Kaius felt like he could vomit, but choked the sensation back. He fought to steady his breathing and raised his hands toward them. "Listen, we-we don't have to fight. We don't! Please, just open your eyes. King Cecilio has to be stopped, or he'll just keep—"

"Trade him for you and your brother, who sicked those shadow beasts on us? No!" One of the two men interrupted.

A pang pierced Kaius' heart. He knew people would take time to forgive Vincent. Even if he continued working toward making amends, there was a chance the people would never truly forgive him, but to choose a monster like Cecilio, it just didn't make sense. Were he and his brother a detriment to Alaia's plan? The thought shook him.

"King Cecilio promised he could keep us safe from monsters like you two and those freaks in the forest. He will enslave all of you beasts. King Cecilio is our *true* savior!" With that, the two soldiers lunged at Kaius.

He needed to move, to fight back, but was too terrified. What if he killed them? Kaius would just prove them right, that he was a monster. His body was frozen at the thought.

"KAIUS!"

Kaius felt a sudden tug of his robe, pulling him back hard. Vincent soared past him. His hand was glowing brightly in violet light. A volley of arcane arrows fired from his hand toward one of the soldiers, sending the man flying back in an explosion of glittering amethyst. The other soldier, however, ran past the attack and swung his sword upward, slashing his blade across Vincent's face. He gave out a scream and fell back onto the floor, clutching his face.

Kaius couldn't breathe. He stared wide eyed at his older brother, and time slowed. Blood flowed down Vincent's face like a waterfall. Kaius' hands trembled terribly at his side. His brother was hurt because of him, because he was too scared to act. Kaius' body suddenly felt cold.

An electrifying surge swelled within his chest. He closed his eyes and exhaled, causing his body to ignite in a bright violet glow. Just as time began to flow again, he let out a powerful roar. Violet ethereal tendrils whipped through the room and swirled around him. He could scarcely hear anything save for a reverberating ringing cascading over him like waves on a beach. Opening his eyes, the light blasted outward, and everything went silent.

He fell to the floor with a heavy humph. Arms trembling, he struggled to support his weight. Kaius' heart pounded like a war drum in his chest. Sweat slid down his face. Raising his eyes to Vincent still huddled next to him, Kaius crawled to his brother.

He quickly ripped off his shoulder cape and carefully pulled Vincent's hands from his face. A line of red stretched from his right cheek, over the bridge of his nose, and ended just above his left brow. Kaius' heart wrenched at what his hesitancy had wrought. His older brother groaned in pain as tears flowed and mixed with blood.

Tears filled Kaius' eyes as he did what he could to bandage the wound. "I-I'm sorry, Vincent. I'm so sorry, I didn't—I wasn't—"

"Stop—" Vincent huffed out a breath, "apologizing." He then

released a weak laugh. "You did great. Don't believe me—" he swallowed, "just look around."

Kaius' brows raised high over his eyes, confused, and he looked up. Many soldiers had been knocked to the ground and lay there dazed. Even King Cecilio lay flat on his back, but was breathing. Those still on their feet were all marked with pink ribbons. Kaius blinked in stunned surprise.

People began pouring into the throne room, all carrying ropes and chains, and were being led by Lord Julián brushing the light snow off his clothes. Those who had sided with the King were abruptly bound and those unfortunately lost in the conflict were laid by the hall's entrance.

"Edurne, Alaia, are you alright?" Julián bellowed as he rushed toward them.

Kaius turned to Alaia and Queen Edurne who were knelt on the ground, out of breath, but safe, still surrounded by a number of their guards. The Queen nodded. "Yes, thank you, Julián."

Alaia's green eyes trembled. She was visibly shaken, but otherwise unscathed. She released her mother's hand and rushed over to Kaius and Vincent. She knelt down beside Vincent, pushing her extravagant fuchsia gown back, and carefully cradled his head. She turned to one of her guards nearby. "Send for a healer, quickly!"

He groaned through gritted teeth as she lifted his head and gently laid him to rest on her lap. His blood seeped through the cape and stained her dress.

"Adhnis will be here soon." Alaia looked to Kaius, her eyes meeting his. "I sent word to her this morning. She'll know just what to do to heal you. Don't despair, either of you. Your brother is going to be fine, Kaius." She said his name softly and showed him a warm, confident smile.

Kaius released a steady breath and held tight Vincent's hand. He then startled, hearing a commotion coming from the dais.

"Unhand me, I am your King!" King Cecilio's hands were tied behind his back, and two guards were dragging him down the steps. He fought back as well as he could, even headbutting one of the guards, however, he was swiftly struck in the gut and pushed to the floor by the other. He landed before Lord Julián and Queen Edurne. He glared angrily as he struggled to catch his breath. "How dare you do this, after everything I've done, this is—"

"Cecilio, do you even remember what you promised me?" Queen Edurne looked at her husband sternly, her face a mixture of pity and contempt.

King Cecilio's eyes narrowed. "What of it!"

The Queen released a soft, disappointed breath. "You promised you would never be like your papa, that you would make this kingdom safe for our little Alaia. Do you truly think that's what you were doing all these years? Look at what your tyranny has caused." She then stepped aside and gestured to the blood splattered floor and the growing pile of dead at the other end of the hall.

"This was your doing woman, not mine!" King Cecilio growled

and spat at her feet. "I have done everything I have, killed everyone I needed out of the way, to keep our family safe. Do not think to lecture me on virtue when you know nothing of what it is to rule. You've been little more than a prop at my side, enjoying the advantages of all I've accomplished."

"Tell me, were you the victor today, would you have me killed as you have so many others?" The Queen winced, as though disturbed by how he might reply. "Don't answer that. For the sake of all the years we've shared, I'd like to believe you aren't *that* far gone."

"I was naive for a long time." Alaia turned to face her father. Her eyes burned with anger, and she looked at him quietly for a long moment before speaking. "You were strict, but I always thought you were a good man. You had to be. You were my padre after all. Then I learned about our family, what Abuelo had done during his rule, and how he really died." She straightened her body, defiant and confident. "When I learned of just what kind of man you were, of what you had done and planned to do still, I was horrified. The people of this city, our guards, the nobility who stood by you, Kaius and Vincent, even myself and Madre, we were all just tools to you. Tools to be discarded when our use had run out. Don't claim to have committed such atrocities in our names. Everything you have done was to serve your own ambitions. You've ruled through fear for far too long. There must be a better way."

Kaius watched Alaia, stunned and unsure what to say.

He then glanced at King Cecilio. The man seethed with anger, and upon noticing Kaius' eyes on him, venomous words poured from his mouth. "Well, impudent boy, do you have a speech for me as well? Best say your peace while you still have a tongue!"

Vincent squeezed Kaius' hand, garnering his attention. "Kaius . . . you don't owe him, or anyone—" His eyes fluttered, struggling to keep himself awake, "an explanation. You did what you thought was right . . . that's all that matters."

Alaia grabbed Kaius' other hand, smiled softly, and nodded in agreement.

Kaius then took a deep breath and turned his eyes back to Cecilio. "I believe I've done enough for you already. You don't deserve another word."

"Hmph, coward." Cecilio grumbled.

Kaius' hands shook in aggravation, but he didn't bother responding. He knew there was no point. His words wouldn't change a thing.

"Escort my husband to a cell," Queen Edurne said flatly. "He should be made comfortable, but I want multiple guards stationed to watch him at all times. They will need to be vetted as my husband will likely try to sway them to his cause. Should he open his mouth, have him gagged. It is imperative he not be given an opportunity to escape." The guards pounded their chests in salute and promptly took the King away.

Kaius watched as they left and sighed with relief, returning to Alaia and Vincent. Vincent's face contorted, and his skin was pale.

"Vincent, just hang in there! Adhnis will be here soon, she has to be."

"Don't worry . . . I don't plan on dying anytime soon." Vincent said, his breath soft, but weak. "Kaius, I'm proud of you."

Epilogue

KAIUS SAT ON A STONE BENCH IN ONE OF THE GARDENS of the Rosado castle while the sun was high overhead. He flipped through the pages of one of the number of spell books now afforded to him, fidgeting lightly as he was yet to grow accustomed to the violet robes gifted to him by Vincent.

He came across a page filled with familiar writing within. Kaius brushed his fingers over the dried ink, following the curves of the elegant quill strokes of his older brother, and chuckled at the added crude commentary likely penned in annoyance.

It had now just been over four months since Vincent went against Cecilio, kidnapping Alaia and almost dooming them to the whims of a deity seeking desperately to remake the world. The events of those few days still haunted him.

Kaius took a deep breath and exhaled steadily, trying to relieve his troubles. His mind then turned to Alaia's rebellion against her father. His fingers twitched on his brother's book, and he quickly closed it shut. He rested his arms over it and stared at the grass beneath his boots.

Kaius' shoulders trembled. Many had given their lives that day. His breath quickened. The moment Vincent's face was forever scarred was embedded in his mind. Were it not for Adhnis' arrival, Vincent likely wouldn't have survived the night.

The nearing crunch of grass pulled him from the dark thoughts. Just as he looked up, he was tackled by a young woman wearing a dress of lavender. As Kaius lost his balance, the two fell to the ground with a heavy thud, and an uncharacteristic yelp escaped Kaius' lips upon landing.

The young woman lifted herself up with a large smile beaming on her face. Her brown, braided hair cascaded down her side, shielding them from the sun's rays. "Kaius, there you are. I've been looking everywhere for you. I hope . . . Your face, what's wrong?" Alaia tilted her head curiously.

"Oh . . . nothing really. You're just crushing my crotch is all."

"By la Madre, lo siento mucho Kaius!"[1] She quickly slid off him, remaining close, and watched as he gasped in relief.

He slid his elbows back and pushed himself to sit up. Pausing, he

1   Spanish for *By the Mother, I'm so sorry.*

noticed her still kneeling between his legs, inspecting his lower half.

"Oh my, this could be serious indeed. Perhaps we should call for the healers? That could take too long. Maybe I should take a look, just to be safe." As she playfully began adjusting his robes, he jolted and immediately pushed her hands away.

"Alaia, what are you doing!?" Kaius' cheeks burned immensely. He tried to hide his embarrassment, but was unsuccessful.

Alaia let out a giggle followed by a burst of laughter. "Dios mío Kaius,[2] I'm only joking. You should see your face." She gently nudged Kaius' shoulder.

He let out a soft chuckle, though his heart raced in his chest. She reached out and softly wrapped her fingers around his chin. Before he could react, Alaia pressed her lips against his.

Kaius' eyes lingered on her for a moment longer before giving in to the taste of her lips, the scent of lantanas and Valencia roses filling his nostrils. He raised a hand and weaved his fingers through the soft strands of her hair.

Amongst all the terrible events of the past four months, there was some good to be found. Waking up after the battle with Cretan, finding himself on the road to Rosado, Alaia and Vincent there beside him. Adhnis had unfortunately already left them for her home in Eylowen Forest. Alaia wrapped a hand around his, looking at Kaius peacefully. Since then, the two had grown closer with each passing day.

She had always been more confident and passionate than he, unafraid to show her emotions with those she cared for. Kaius, on the

2   Spanish for *My goodness Kaius.*

other hand, was more reserved and shy with his feelings. In the time before usurping her father's throne, she had to be careful so as not to draw attention to herself or cause hardship upon Kaius. She secretly left him gifts, small things from treats to poetry left on his pillow. The sentiment always made him blush.

As she released him from the embrace, he leaned toward her, wanting more. She slid two fingers over his lips and looked at him tenderly. Letting out a defeated sigh, he met her gaze with a smile. "It would seem you have me on strings when you kiss me."

Alaia's hand jolted away from him, her posture noticeably rigid. "Please, don't ever say that, Kaius. I would never use you and I will never treat you that way." Her eyes softened. "I'm with you because I love you."

"Y-Yes. I'm sorry, it was a poor choice of words. I wish I was better at . . . being romantic." He wrapped his hand around hers and pressed his lips to her knuckles, kissing her gently.

She tilted her head and lightly blushed. "I'd say you're doing a fine job of that, Kaius." His name left her lips softly as she leaned in and kissed his cheek. She then slid away, laying on the grass beside him, and invited him to do the same.

Raising his arms high in the air, stretching, he gently fell back to the grass. The two relished their time together in silence, watching the clouds roll overhead through the bright blue sky. The recently bloomed leaves on the trees rustled in the soft spring breeze.

Kaius took a deep breath and exhaled steadily. "So . . . how did the visit with your father go?" He noticed her jaw tighten as she looked away.

"It went . . . it was as it usually is. We met. We talked . . . for a moment it was almost pleasant. It wasn't long before he began complaining that his already lavish cell isn't lavish enough. We argued. I stormed away as he began lecturing that my method of . . . well, technically Madre's[3] method of ruling, will get us *killed*. I won't even be wearing the crown until my twenty-first nameday."

Just as he was about to respond, Alaia turned her head back to him.

"Anyway, Kaius, you do remember about today's meeting, don't you?"

His brows furrowed, his eyes looking back to the sky. "Yeah, to be honest . . . I'm nervous."

"Oh good, I'm glad I'm not the only one." The two laughed warmly for a moment before quieting and lying in silence a bit longer. Alaia turned her head toward Kaius, causing him to look at her in return. "Do you think our meeting with the Valtivarian King and the leader of the remaining Kunnagarians will go well?"

Kaius stared at her for a moment, taking a nervous gulp before answering. "This meeting has to go well. Vincent and I only knew of one way of living for so long, believing in a lie. He and I need to know if they can be trusted."

"Do you . . . plan to leave with them?" Alaia asked softly.

His chest tightened. "Would you wait for me if I did?"

3   Spanish for *Mother's*.

Alaia's breath hitched in her throat, seemingly taken off guard. Her face then softened, and a smile grew there. "For you, of course. You best not keep me waiting too long though." Her small smile turned into a playful smirk, causing Kaius to giggle.

"Anyway," she rolled over on her side and placed a hand on his chest, "Adhnis should be here soon. Where did she want us to meet her?"

"Vincent's and my chamber." Kaius slid his hand over hers with a smile. "What do you think we should do before—"

"Kaius? Kaius, where are you?" A voice rang out in the distance. "Adhnis has just—Oh!" Vincent's cheeks glowed brightly pink, failing to keep a stoic expression on his face. "Am I . . . interrupting?"

Kaius propped himself up on his elbows, looking at his brother. A shudder of guilt ran up his spine at the sight of Vincent's scar stretching across his face.

"Hi Kaius. Hi Alaia!" Adhnis waved at them from atop Vincent's palm, startling Kaius from his thoughts.

Alaia giggled as she sat herself up. "Not at all, and hola[4] Adhnis. By any chance, could you give us just a moment?"

"Sure, but don't take too long. I received word from your mother, the Valtivarians have reached the city gates."

"Already? Alright, just wait for us at the entryway then. We'll be there shortly."

Vincent bowed his head then turned away as Adhnis yelled out, "Don't keep us waiting ye two!"

4   Spanish for *Hello.*

Alaia and Kaius laughed. He jumped as she swung herself around to him. She quickly leaned in and pressed her painted lips to his again, kissing Kaius deeply. As their lips parted, she looked at him softly. "Listen to me. No matter what happens, whether you and Vincent choose to stay or choose to go, know that you will *always* have a home here. Warm and welcoming, free of shackles. Of that you can be certain. Promise me you won't forget that, or me, for that matter." She locked her fingers in his, her green eyes trembling lightly.

A confident smile grew on his face, and his eyes glimmered with hope as he tightened his hold on her hand. "Always."

Acknowledgements

Oh wow! First off, thank you so much for reading RaF. Seriously, thank you, it really means a lot to me that you read the story to the end. Secondly, please don't forget to leave a review. Reviews help small time authors like myself to be seen by other readers. So when you have the chance, please leave a review for RaF, I would be very appreciative if you did.

Alright, now I do want to address something about RaF, and that is yes, I went back and re-edited the manuscript. If I wanted to create the audiobook, the internal character dialogue would have proved an issue so I scaled that back. Now that it's fixed, I can begin work on the audiobook. Here's to hoping I can get it to you by Summer or Fall of 2023.

Oh, one more thing, I can't just end this acknowledgement without thanking my Alpha Reader, my husband Marcus, and my amazing Beta Readers: Grace, Briana, Jamie, Lexie, Rowan, Tanni, and Alex. You were all super great and helpful in getting RaF to where it is. I also want to thank the wonderfully amazing cover artist Nicole Deal and my editor Jennifer Jarrett. When I first got this cover back, my jaw just dropped. It was beautiful and amazing and I loved your take on Kaius and Adhnis, Nicole. You're just the best. Also thank you so much

Jennifer for going through my manuscript and helping me fix it lol. I'm nothing without you and I'm happy you were there to make RaF the best it could be.

The story of RaF has come a long way since it was a video game idea from me and my husband, but because we didn't have the means to make that a reality, the project was shelved for a very long time. That is, until my husband encouraged me to look at it again to turn it into a novel instead. I'm so happy that he did and I'm ecstatic at how the characters and the story came out, and I hope you liked it too. RaF is just one of many stories I have, and I hope you look into my other books. Again, thank you so much for reading, stay tuned for more stories to come.

~A.J. Torres

ABOUT THE AUTHOR

Adlin(A.J.) Kennedy Torres is a writer who likes to dabble as an anime artist for fun. She enjoys Fantasy and Science Fiction stories. Adlin particularly loves to write Fantasy and easily gets immersed in books like The Goddess of Nothing at All and Aletheia. She's loved Fantasy stories ever since she was a kid picking up The Lord of the Rings and Eragon for the first time.

Nowadays you can find Adlin in the hot and horribly humid sunshine state of Florida, hanging out, playing video games with her husband, and chasing her son around the house with two needy dogs and a very chill cat.

Instagram and Twitter: @A_J_Torres0

.

www.ingramcontent.com/pod-product-compliance
Lightning Source LLC
Chambersburg PA
CBHW030322200626
46816CB00006BA/1896